# Forever
# Wild

# Forever Wild

*A Novel by*
*Tony Holtzman*

CLOUD
SPLITTER
PRESS

BOOK THREE OF ADIRONDACK TRILOGY

Second edition, 2017, *Third Printing 2019*

Cover design by Eva Cohen
Cover photo by Tony Holtzman

For wholesale orders, visit North Country Books at
www.northcountrybooks.com

For information on Tony Holtzman's *Adirondack Trilogy*
visit www.cloudsplitterpress.com

For individual orders contact your local bookstore or
www.amazon.com

ISBN 978-0-9984893-2-2

*To*

*The Year-Round Residents of the*
*Adirondack Park*

# Acknowledgments

I will not repeat the sources and people I acknowledged in Books One and Two of this Trilogy unless they contributed in a major way to this final volume. Legislation plays a key role in *Forever Wild*, and two books were highly instructive in describing and interpreting the process: Alfred L. Donaldson's *A History of the Adirondacks, II* (Reissued by Purple Mountain) and Philip G. Terrie's *Contested Terrain* (Syracuse). Lawrence P. Gooley's *Oliver's War* (Bloated Toe Publishing, 2007) is a true account of the local resistance to the Great Camp owners' effort to privatize land. Stephanie Barrett, Senior Librarian, Reference Services, New York State Library, Albany, patiently tracked down the New York State private parks acts, which enabled the Great Camp owners to privatize.

Once again, my daughter Deborah did an extraordinary edit and made substantive suggestions. Steven C. Holtzman, my son the lawyer, critiqued the trial in Part III to make sure I wasn't egregiously off base in presenting legal issues. Steven's son Alex, my grandson, provided useful information on rifles that he had learned from completing a school assignment and then going beyond. Maryhelen Snyder, a well-known poet and friend since college, generously read and critiqued *Forever Wild* as she had the previous two novels.

Thanks again to Ron Donaghe who did the final edit and offered many useful suggestions.

Finally, people in the Adirondacks who have read and in some cases reviewed the previous two novels, gave me the encouragement to continue. They include Neal Burdick, Dorothy and Jay Federman, Ed Kanze, Suzanne Orlando, Nathalie Thill, and Fran Yardley. The late Dr. Virginia Weeks, a wise and sympathetic year-round resident of the Park, offered untold suggestions and encouragement since the project's inception.

# *Preface*

———•———

In the prefaces to books One and Two of this trilogy I indicated that some of the characters and all of the places were real, although the topography may not have been exactly as described. That continues to be the case in *Forever Wild*. For example, the view from Little Panther Mountain in 1890 may have been as I describe it, but it certainly isn't the view today. I continue to take liberties with times and places. Although real, neither Beth Joseph Cemetery in Tupper Lake, nor the Jewish congregation of that name, existed in the eighteen eighties. I am not a builder; the vocabulary used in describing construction is accurate to the best of my knowledge, but I may have made mistakes. Some will argue with my descriptions of Adirondack Guideboats.

In the Preface to Book Two of the Trilogy, *The Railroad*, I indicated that the railroad from Long Lake to Tupper Lake, along the Raquette River, was fictitious. So was the railroad from North Creek to Long Lake, but the last attempt to circumvent the "forever wild" amendment to the New York Constitution was to build a railroad from North Creek to Long Lake. Part of the proposed route lay over State lands that would be protected when the Amendment went into effect just days after the unsuccessful effort.

Dates that I have adhered to faithfully are those when laws and the "forever wild" amendment to New York State's constitution were passed. Keeping to those dates is part of the reason that I had to speed up other aspects of the story. In reality, the anger about the Great Camps' usurping public land did not reach fever pitch until the early nineteen hundreds when Orrando P. Dexter, a wealthy landowner, was assassinated and when Oliver Lamora waged a years-long unsuccessful battle against William Rockefeller's attempt to expropriate his land. In my story, the anger manifests a couple of decades earlier. The term "Great Camp" was not used until the twentieth century.

Although events that occurred in the previous two books are referred to in this third book, *Forever Wild* stands on its own, and reading the first two is not a prerequisite for comprehending it. The first two can be profitably read afterward because they shed light on other aspects of conflict in the Adirondacks.

What makes the Adirondacks such a fascinating topic for novels is not only its beauty but its history of conflict—conflict between farmers, workers, and small businesses on the one hand and the landed gentry or the lumber and railroad magnates on the other, with the government of the State of New York usually on the side of the vested interests. The tension continues to this day with the Adirondack Park Agency, legally responsible for land use within the Park, besieged by conflicting interests.

Billionaire owners of thousand-acre Great Camps are relics of the past. Today we have wealthy summer residents many of whom own valuable shorefront property. Their lots are not big enough to hurt year-round residents by excluding them from hunting and fishing, but a few of them have hurt the community in other ways. I find it appalling that a few have changed, and exhort others to change, their legal residence from the districts in which they live most of the year to the townships in the Park so they can vote to lower school and property taxes. This may save them a few dollars, but it gravely affects the wellbeing of the year-round residents, including children.

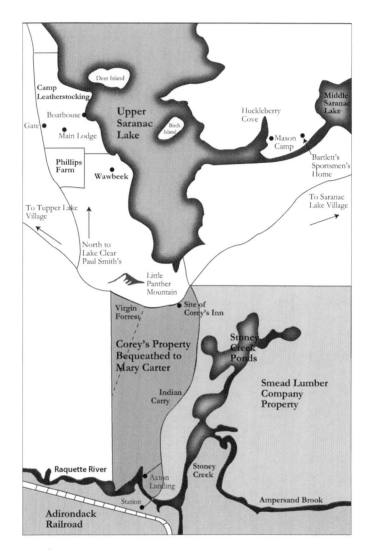

Southern Upper Saranac Lake and Environs

# PART I

# 1
# Forever Wild

*The lands now or hereafter constituting the forest pre-
serve shall be forever kept as wild forest lands. They shall
not be sold, nor shall they be leased or taken by any cor-
poration, public or private.*

—Bill introduced into the
1885 New York State Legislature

WHEN it seemed possible the "forever wild" bill
would pass, the Lumberman's Association called its
lobbyist, Lloyd Massing, back from Albany to attend a Board
meeting at its Glens Falls office. The freezing February rain
from which the Board members escaped did not help their
mood as they shed their overcoats and trudged into the
gas-lit Board Room. They were irate that the Assemblyman from Franklin County, Cyrus Carter, had spoken in
favor of the bill. He was repeatedly labeled a turncoat. Lloyd
reminded them that Carter had gained his living by lumber-
jacking for many years but that he might vote to protect the
forests. He had, after all, voted for proclaiming lands owned
by the State as forever wild and given a fiery speech in the
1883 Assembly in support of it.

After Lloyd left, Charles Smead, heir-apparent of the
Smead Lumber Company, reminded his fellow board members that after the 1883 Assembly session Massing and his
family visited the Adirondacks at Carter's invitation. "My

sources tell me that Massing was very upset about the fire that killed that old innkeeper." He paused, recollecting, "Corey, William Corey was his name. Carter's done a bit of reverse lobbying if you ask me. I'm not sure I trust Lloyd's loyalty any longer." He took a cigar from the humidor on the table, clipped and lit it, and took a few puffs to let his last remark sink in.

The Chairman of the Board spoke. "Surely, Charles, you know his father, George Massing, owns the biggest sawmill here." He helped himself to a cigar. "What do you propose doing about your lack of trust?"

"I think we should put him on probation. If this damn 'forever wild' bill passes I think we'll have Massing to blame. He was able to beat back the effort in 1883, but Carter and his ilk are marshaling Assemblymen who supported us then to oppose us now. Massing doesn't have the drive he had before Carter invited him to the Adirondacks. He lost several days' work when he returned and rumors were that he'd been drinking."

There was grumbling around the table. "Lloyd acquitted himself quite well this afternoon, Charles," the Chairman said, "and I'd hate to incur his father's wrath, gentlemen. But if you agree with Charles, then I'll agree to probation and hope he improves before George Massing blows a gasket." The Board voted for probation without dissent.

The Chairman sent Lloyd a message that he wanted to see him the next Monday morning before he returned to Albany. The Chairman told him the Board was unhappy with his performance. "I suppose we have to write off Carter, but if more Assemblymen defect, you'll be in big trouble. Stay away from Carter, Lloyd. Don't forget your mission." He never used the word, 'probation.'

Lloyd was shaken. He stopped at the bar outside the train station and ordered his first whiskey in several weeks. On the train, he thought about how Cyrus Carter had complicated his life. If only he hadn't accepted Carter's invitation to visit the Adirondacks. Carter had shaken his belief that the lumber companies would hurt no one. The folly of this belief, made evident by the death and destruction he witnessed, had lost him esteem in the eyes of his wife and maybe his son.

When he arrived in Albany he bought a bottle of rye whiskey and went straight to his hotel room. He poured himself half a tumbler.

Lloyd felt trapped. He could see no alternative to lobbying for the Lumberman's Association. He hated Carter for removing the scales from his eyes. He hated Carter for not letting him rescue Corey, even if it might have cost him his life. He hated Carter for exposing his ineptitude as a fisherman and hiker to his wife and children.

———•———

Cyrus Carter saw Massing ahead of him as he walked out of the Assembly chamber a few months later, as the session approached its end and crucial votes were coming up. He quickened his pace and tapped Lloyd on the shoulder, surprised that Lloyd's suit was not as neat as it used to be. Massing turned, squinted down at Cyrus. Still compactly built after years of logging, but now with his hair almost completely white, though his beard was gray, Cyrus was five and a half feet tall compared to Lloyd's six feet. After a moment of searching his memory to match the image, he smiled and laid his hand on Cyrus's back. "Cyrus, my old camping buddy, how are you?"

As Massing's alcohol-laden breath reached him, Cyrus had to catch himself from stepping back and turning away. He doubted Massing would understand, let alone remember, what he was about to say. Nevertheless, he proceeded. "I'm good, Lloyd. I hope you are too."

"Couldn't be better." He slapped Cyrus on the back. "What can I do for you, old buddy?"

"I've co-sponsored two bills, Lloyd. One is for a ten-hour day; the other is for obliging employers to pay into a fund to compensate workers for injuries on the job. I don't expect your Association to support them, but I hope they won't oppose them. In the long run these measures will be in the companies' best interest."

Lloyd peered at Cyrus's lips after he finished speaking, trying to filter out the background noise in order to comprehend what Cyrus had said. Before his message had gotten through, Lloyd again slapped Cyrus on the back. "Thanks, Cyrus. I'll pass the word along. You've been loyal to us, haven't you?"

Cyrus smiled. He doubted that Massing remembered where Cyrus stood. He stepped backward, out of Lloyd's reach. "Depends on how you look at things, Lloyd. Anyway, thanks for hearing me out."

As he walked out to the cool air on the portico, Lloyd's mind cleared. His hands trembled. In the mountains, Carter had almost persuaded him that such laws would lead to more productive workers. He knew the Association would be vehemently opposed to them. He was in no position to argue. He felt as if Cyrus was tightening a noose around his neck. To stop his hands from shaking he walked a few blocks to his favorite bar, though it was early afternoon. In Albany, away from his wife, children, and parents, Massing was slipping again. He had become resentful of Alice and susceptible to advances of women, often buying them drinks. From the time the Lumberman's Board recalled him to Glens Falls until now, his intoxicated behavior had become a topic of gossip among lobbyists and legislators, soon reaching the Board itself—confirming Charles Smead's suspicions—and Lloyd's father.

When the "forever wild" bill passed late in the session, Lloyd was barely conscious of it.

———•———

The day after the Assembly adjourned, Massing went to the Albany office of the Lumberman's Association to collect his paycheck. The office manager handed him a sealed envelope and said "Good Luck."

Massing stared at him uncomprehendingly. "Thanks," he said. On his way to the Capitol, he stopped at his bank. He could not pay for all his drinking on his expense account and was low in cash. He tore the envelope open and pulled the check out. Out of the corner of his eye he saw a slip of paper flutter to the floor. He reached under the glass-top table that held pens and various forms and retrieved the slip. He endorsed the check and read the slip as he stood on the teller's line.

MEMORANDUM

To: Lloyd Massing

    From: The Lumberman's Association

    Date: May 15, 1885

    RE: Termination

We regret to inform you that your services are no longer needed. The enclosed check will be your last compensation from the Association.

When past sessions ended, Massing had continued to work for the Association, shuttling between Albany and Glens Falls. Typically, he had about a week's work to finish in Albany, writing reports, visiting legislative staff, and the like. Slowly it dawned on him that the memo released him from any obligation to remain. He reached the teller's window, slid the check under the bars and got his cash. He counted it, folded it neatly, and put it in his pocket. He walked outside into the spring air. The trees were just beginning to blossom. He spied an early robin strutting along the sidewalk. Then his second thought came, a variation on the first: *I'm free! Thank god! If they're not going to pay me, I'll be damned if I'll finish my work.* He took a little skip, something he had learned in his theatrical training, but had not done since. *This calls for a celebration,* he said to himself. He walked back a block to his favorite bar. The bartender greeted him. "Good morning, Mr. Massing. You're looking cheerful this morning. Hope you haven't been drinking elsewhere."

"No, no, Sam! I've just gotten good news." Massing looked around at the empty stools and tables. "Doubles all around, Sam. The drinks are on me!" he joked.

Aware that this was payday for many of his customers, Sam ventured, "Gotten a raise, have you, Mr. Massing?" He set the double whiskey in front of Massing.

"No, quite the opposite. I've been fired!" He raised his glass to Sam and swallowed its contents quickly.

Behind the bar, Sam arranged the glasses he had just washed. He looked up at Massing curiously, decided not to say anything, and started drying the glasses. Massing caught Sam's inquisitive glance as the scorching whiskey slid down his throat. The flame from the whiskey spread over his body.

"I hate my job, Sam." He plunked his empty glass down and Sam refilled it.

"Then I guess you've got another one?"

"I hadn't thought about that," Massing replied. The euphoria from his first reactions and the drink dissipated momentarily. "My father wrote me a couple of weeks ago, warned if I didn't stop drinking, I was headed for trouble. He got me this damned job, but I'll be damned if he'll get me another." He finished the glass in one swallow and buried his head in his arms on the bar. *What will I say to my father, to Alice, to the children? What will they say to me?*

"You want another?"

Lloyd raised his head. "Another job? No, not for the moment. I want to celebrate the loss of this one. Refill it, Sam." Again he buried his head. *Celebrate? Alone, totally alone, how can I celebrate?* His ticket to go back to Glens Falls was in his pocket, and he could go today instead of next week. Sam plunked the refill in front of him. "One more for the road," Massing slurred. He tossed it down, reached in his pocket, peeled off ten dollars from his neatly folded money, and slapped it on the bar. Without waiting for change, he stumbled out.

Staggering into the train station an hour before the train left for Glens Falls, Massing went into the bar and passed the time with two more double shots. The conductor had to help him board the train. He quickly fell asleep, slumping down into the purple velveteen cushioned seat. At Glens Falls, the same conductor had to rouse him and assist him along the aisle and down the steep steps at the end of the car. Outside the station, a light spring rain was falling, enough to muddy the earth, making the streets slippery.

Lloyd Massing never made it home. His body was found in the rock-strewn Hudson River a few yards below the bridge between the train station and his home.

———•———

Cyrus left Albany on the same train as Lloyd, eager to see his wife Mary who he knew would be pleased by the passage of the "forever wild" bill. She had come to the Adirondacks as a fledgling schoolteacher and fallen in love with Jean, a young logger who was killed breaking a logjam the day after he had gotten Mary pregnant. Cyrus—his leg broken in the same logjam—married Mary when her son, John, was a year old. Mary loved the woods even before logging took its toll and she could not countenance the destruction of the forests or the lumberjacks. Mary was responsible for Cyrus's realization that the supply of trees was not inexhaustible and needed protection. He and Assemblymen from the City had won over a few other legislators from the Adirondack and Catskill counties, persuading them to defy the Lumberman's Association effort to kill the bill, which also authorized the governor to appoint a three-member Forest Commission to oversee compliance with the forever wild provision. Mary would be disappointed that a bill that would let the State buy back private forests, making them forever wild by addition to the forest preserve, had not gotten out of committee.

Cyrus was less eager to face his son, Tommy, who would take little comfort that the labor bills he had gotten his father to introduce were favorably reported out of committee, greatly surprising and annoying the Lumberman's Association. When he was eighteen, Tommy helped lumberjacks for the Adirondack Railroad win an hourly wage, instead of being paid by the number of logs they cut, and a ten-hour day.   Shortly afterward, he was forced to jump from a trestle he had helped build to avoid being killed by a runaway caboose.  He was left paraplegic and mute and turned his anger into writing on behalf of the working man, agitating for workman's compensation laws and a ten-hour day. Lobbyists had managed to get Cyrus's labor bills beaten on the Assembly floor, although Lloyd Massing was of little help. Cyrus could see the legislature ridiculed in one of Tommy's articles for *The Nation*.

Cyrus had boarded the train to Ausable Forks just before it pulled out of the Albany station. He took his seat several cars in back of the one occupied by Lloyd Massing. He did not notice Massing leave the train at Glens Falls.

# 2

# Alice

*Glens Falls, New York*
*May 29, 1885*

Dear Mary,

I doubt that you or Cyrus knows that Lloyd
is dead. The Lumberman's Association fired
him on the last day of the session. The Chairman
told his father that his drinking interfered with
his doing his job. Either he jumped or fell off the
bridge near his father's mill on his way home from
the train station. The children were upset enough
to hear that they would never see their father
again, but when his parents came to our home and
ordered me to pack their things so the children
could live with them, I became hysterical, all to
no avail. Lloyd's mother screamed that his death
was my fault. Can you imagine? They have not
even allowed me to see Donald and Elizabeth.

Lloyd's father owns our house, so although
women now have the right to inherit their
husbands' property, I have no claim on it. He
has allowed me to remain in the house until he
sells it, but without the children I shudder every

*time I enter. So far I have been unable to find a job. I suspect Lloyd's parents have a hand in that. They want me far away from the children. I do not want to give them that satisfaction, but I don't see how I can survive in this poisonous atmosphere.*

*I do not want to return to Westport. My mother died the year after Lloyd and I were married, and my father has more sympathy for the Massings than for me. He is hardly aware of Donald and Elizabeth's existence.*

*I draw little comfort from knowing that what happened to me happens to countless other women: abuse, desertion, and severance of children, with no recourse to the courts. How will we ever gain equality?*

*Your friend,*
*Alice Massing*

Mary had started reading Alice's letter standing near the wooden kitchen table painted white. Horrified, she took a seat in one of the spindly kitchen chairs. When she finished reading, she laid the letter on the table and tended to the wood-burning stove. Cyrus came in a few minutes later. Rinsing her hands in the sink basin, then wiping them on her apron, she pointed to the letter. "Read this," she said.

Cyrus quickly sat down as he began to read. He slumped in the chair. "I am partly responsible."

Mary walked in back of him and gently put her arms around his shoulders. "No, you're not. Somehow you knew he could be persuaded that lobbying for the lumber companies was wrong. You had no way of knowing that he would deal with his conscience by taking to drink."

Cyrus did not reply immediately. "Poor Alice. I wish there was some way I could help get her children back, but as a woman she's not likely to get far in the courts. Besides, if I tried to start a legal proceeding on humane grounds, Lloyd's father would hire the best lawyers in Glens Falls to contest it. We wouldn't have a chance."

"We can help in other ways," Mary said. "Alice can move up here. Until she gets a job she could live with us. If you don't mind, we can fix up your study for her. It probably wouldn't be long; I hear Dr. Trudeau is hiring people to help take care of patients in his new sanitarium. In the meantime, she would be a big help caring for Tommy. What do you think?"

The possibility of having Alice under his roof stirred mixed feelings in Cyrus. It was not the temporary loss of his study; since he had been admitted to the bar and then been elected to the Assembly, he didn't use it much. It was having the attractive Alice—he remembered her talking earnestly as he rowed her across Lower Ausable Lake in the moonlight—under the same roof. Temptation might be more than he could stand, not that he loved Mary any the less. That Alice might not be interested in him never entered his mind.

"We'll have to pay her way," Mary continued, "and arrange to pick her up at Ausable Forks."

Cyrus didn't respond.

"Of course, our little village doesn't have the bustle of Glens Falls," Mary said. "She might not like it here." Mary wondered if Cyrus was listening. "But maybe she'd prefer to get away from there as along as she can't have her children. What do you think, Cyrus?"

Cyrus shook off his reverie. "Yes, you're right. Why don't you write her today? If she's interested I'll post a money order, and then I'll clean out my study."

———•———

Cyrus met Alice as she descended from the train at Ausable Forks in early July. He hardly recognized her. Small but lissome the last time he saw her, now she seemed frail and gaunt. The sparkle that had animated her brown eyes when they crossed Lower Ausable Lake two years earlier was gone, and streaks of gray permeated her flat auburn hair. She managed a smile as Cyrus greeted her, hugging him tightly for a moment before he took her two suitcases from the porter and led her to his carriage.

They said little as the carriage clattered over the path. Cyrus broke the silence as they traveled along a broad, rocky stream, telling Alice it was a branch of the Ausable River flowing swiftly out of the high peaks. In front of them the mountains began to rise and soon Whiteface emerged on their right, its flanks streaked with bare scars of avalanches. They passed through the tiny village of Lake Placid and finally arrived at the Carters' house in Saranac Lake in the evening. Mary ran out to greet Alice, giving her a warm hug. Cyrus unhitched the horses and put the carriage in a shed he had built at the back of the house. He fed the horses and brought the baggage into the house. In the meantime, Mary took Alice on a tour of their home, showing her Cyrus's study. She had moved the desk to the parlor, bought a bed that she had fitted with a brightly colored quilt, and placed a rug woven by one of her suffragist friends on the floor in front of the bed. The bookshelves were lined with Cyrus's law books.

"Oh, Mary!" Alice hugged her again. "You don't know what a palace this is. I'm so grateful to Cyrus for letting me use his study. I'll move out as soon as I find a job."

"Don't even think about moving out. Even finding a job can wait. There's plenty for you to do around here. Moving Tommy is more than I can handle." From her previous visit, Alice knew that Tommy could not use his legs. She wondered whether he had regained his ability to talk, but was afraid she might upset Mary by asking if he had not. "Cyrus is away so much," Mary continued, "—he'll be in Albany the entire winter—he can't help even though he wants to. And I'll be teaching in September. Lisa hopes to find a job, too. When she marries Peter O'Rourke junior, she'll be gone altogether. You can help in the kitchen, too, and when spring comes, I'll need help in the garden." So excited to show her kindness to Alice and to encourage her to stay, she spoke breathlessly. "As soon as we settle my Uncle's estate, I'll sell his property and have enough money to build on to this house. Then it will really be a palace. We'll give Cyrus back his study and give you a room of your own. You'll join our local suffrage movement, too."

With tears in her eyes, again Alice hugged Mary. "I can't believe my good fortune. Of course, I'll pay for my lodging when I get a job."

"We'll see about that when the time comes." Mary led Alice back to the front hall where Cyrus had left Alice's two bags. Mary picked them up and led Alice to her room.

For many days after Alice arrived, she hardly ate at all. Listlessly, she accompanied the family on outings in which Tommy was either tied flat on the back of Cyrus's wagon or propped rigidly between his parents in the front seat of their carriage. They picnicked on the south shore of Upper Saranac Lake, or a little ways up the Indian Carry on the banks of the Stoney Creek Ponds. Once, they went in the opposite direction to John Brown's farm and the site of his grave. Gradually, Alice's appetite returned, she participated more in the family's conversation, and insisted on helping with chores.

With Cyrus, Mary, and Lisa around over the summer Tommy had little need of Alice's help. Seldom did he address a note to her and she felt uncomfortable initiating conversation with him. Alice had watched how Lisa and Mary lifted him, and by the time they returned to school in September she was strong enough to help Tommy out of bed and into his wheelchair. At first she was embarrassed to put her arms around him and have him do the same to her in order to get leverage, but he didn't seem to mind at all.

Cyrus usually went to the law office he shared with Lawrence Venable and after breakfast Tommy wheeled himself to the parlor to read or write. So after she did the dishes and straightened up, Alice would take long walks by herself. In October, Tommy scrawled a note to her: *If I could join you on your walk this morning, I'd be very pleased.* This soon became part of their daily routine, if the weather allowed it. On balmy days she wheeled him down to Moody Pond and then along the path around it. Pushing him back up to the house was hard work but she enjoyed it. These trips expanded Tommy's world. Alice would have liked to talk, but she did not think it right to discuss what was most on her mind, getting her children back. It would be a soliloquy, not a conversation.

One day she heard a quivering wail from the pond. Without thinking, she said, "What a strange sound that duck makes." She paused, trying to recollect. "I think I've heard it before."

Tommy kept a pad of paper and a pencil on his lap and quickly wrote, "*It's a loon,*" and held it up for her.

"Oh, I heard them when your father rowed me across the Ausable Lakes. That sound must be why people think they're crazy." Standing in back of him, she saw Tommy nod and then he wrote another note. *They also dive.* She looked across the pond again. The loon was gone but soon popped up about fifty yards from where she last saw it. This exchange gave Alice the idea that she could ask Tommy about flora and fauna. He could easily write his answers in a few words. As they passed leafy hardwoods and lacy or needled evergreens, Alice asked him to name them, which he obligingly did in writing. After a few days of this, he wrote her a note before leaving the house one morning: *Today, I will quiz you.* As they walked he pointed to various trees, plants, or an occasional bird. Much more often than not Alice answered correctly, which Tommy acknowledged by clapping his hands. When they returned, he passed her a one- word note: *Bravo!* Alice leaned forward, took his pad and pencil, and substituted an *a* for the *o* at the end of the word. Tommy looked at her for explanation.

"If you're complimenting a woman, it's 'Brava.'" She had learned that from Lloyd who had learned it in his theater days.

With the fresh air and vigorous activity, Alice regained weight, her cheeks filled out, her color improved, and in conversation around the dinner table, Cyrus occasionally saw sparkle in her eyes. The strands of gray became less evident as her hair took on luster. Tuberculosis was not the only disorder cured by the north woods, he thought. Having her so close had not evoked the uneasiness he had worried about. It was a pleasure to watch her interact with Tommy, whose temperament improved not long after Alice arrived. They each had their own grief but together their sorrows canceled out.

Stocky like his father, but clean-shaven (Alice heated the water for his shave and brought him the equipment) and with a more engaging smile, Tommy appealed to Alice. One day while she was washing the breakfast dishes, she found herself calculating his age in relation to what Lloyd's would have been and what Donald's was. Tommy's was mid-way between. The care that she would have lavished on both of them went into caring for Tommy, easing the pain of Lloyd's death and the children's kidnapping, as she came to call it.

Tommy began showing her his writing and asking for her suggestions. When this first happened she wrote out her comments. One day, he passed her a note: *Why don't you speak your comments. It will save time and I won't be any more offended by what you say than what you write.*

Alice blushed. *It just wasn't to protect Tommy's f*eelings, she first thought, *but simply because reciprocating by writing seemed more natural.* On second thought, she had admitted, *writing is less threatening than speaking it, and I don't want to appear threatening.* Nevertheless, she promised out loud, "I will."

*Good,* he wrote. *I like your voice.* Alice blushed again.

Their walks ended with the first snows. In anticipation, Tommy had ordered books to keep him engrossed over the dreary winter. He read the local paper, *The Adirondack Daily Enterprise*, from front to back every day and when some story caught his ire, he quickly wrote a letter to the editor. Almost all of his letters were published, but they never got a rejoinder and, when he proposed changes, nothing ever happened.

As the days shortened, Alice spent even more time thinking about her children. One day, she was out shoveling snow off the path leading up to the Carter house when Cyrus came home earlier than usual. "That's not necessary for you to do, at least not by yourself." He started to take the shovel but she resisted.

"I have little else to do. I can't take Tommy out when snow covers the paths and roads. Besides, anything I do helps take my mind off Donald and Elizabeth."

Cyrus gently took the shovel from Alice and propped it in the mound of snow her shoveling had built along the walk. He took her hands, now considerably harder than when he had held them helping her out of the boat between the Lower and Upper Ausable Lakes. "I understand. Have you written Lloyd's parents?"

"As often as I can afford the postage. Never a reply. I doubt they open my letters." Plaintively, she looked at him. "What will become of Donald and Elizabeth, Cyrus? They'll forget me by the time they're fully grown. I want them back."

"The Massings practically own Glens Falls. I don't think legal action will get you anywhere, and you'll have to put up with accusations of being a poor wife and a worse mother."

Alice released her hands from Cyrus's and reached for the shovel. Tears streamed down her cheeks. "What really troubles me is that Donald and Elizabeth will think I've for-gotten about them, that I'm as bad as the Massings say I am. I wish I could get some word to them."

"I can make inquiries to find out where the children go to school. Perhaps we can find a way to deliver a letter or at least have someone—maybe even me—tell them where their mother is, and that she loves them very much. I'm not sure it would be a good idea to tell them that their grandpar-ents have intercepted your letters. It might put the children adrift." Alice started to clear off the ramp that Tommy used to go outside. She brightened at Cyrus's suggestion.

"That would be wonderful, Cyrus, if you could!"

"As for what will become of them," Cyrus continued. "When Donald and Elizabeth reach majority, they will be able to decide."

"As long as they know I still love them, they'll do what's right, I know that." She put her shovel down and hugged Cyrus. "Thank you, Cyrus. I am so grateful for everything you and Mary have done for me."

"It may take a while to get word to them."

"I understand. Just knowing you will arrange something makes me feel better."

———•———

The New Year, 1886, came. Alice had spent many days drafting letters to Donald and Elizabeth. Cyrus took the final versions when he left for the Assembly session in Albany, promising to get to Glens Falls to see what he could find out and, hopefully, deliver them.

On weekdays, Alice was usually up first, stoking the fire in the kitchen stove and helping Mary and Lisa with breakfast. Now twenty years old, Lisa had a job assisting with the younger children while Mary taught the older ones. Mary and Lisa had already left for school by the time Tommy announced his awakening by tapping the floor with a pole he kept near the head of his bed. Alice would open the door to his room, smile, ask how he slept—to which he usually replied with a nondescript shrug. She would help him on to a bed pan and then, leaving the door open, go to the kitchen where she filled a large basin with hot water. She carried it with both hands to Tommy's bedside. Mary had taught Alice how to help wash him. At first, this embarrassed Alice, but Tommy did not seem to mind. Having learned to do this, Alice had no problem helping Tommy dress. The most difficult part of the morning operation was getting Tommy out of bed and into his wheelchair. Alice helped him swing his useless legs on to the floor. Slipping her arms under his and around his chest, she managed to pull him to a standing position and then seat him solidly in the wheelchair. Tommy wheeled himself into the kitchen while Alice ladled out porridge that had been simmering on the stove.

One bitterly cold morning in February, with snow piled partway up the windows, Alice responded in her usual way when Tommy tapped. She helped wash and clothe him and lifted him to a standing position before seating him in his wheelchair. As she did, her foot slipped and the wheelchair rolled away with a clatter. Alice kept her arms around Tommy, and Tommy instantly wrapped his arms around Alice, hoping to steady them, but the momentum of her slip brought them down, Alice on top of Tommy. Their faces were less than an inch apart. Tommy did not let go but moved his hand to the back of Alice's head and pressed her towards him, kissing her lips. Despite the cold, his lips were warm and Alice let hers linger, closing her eyes for a moment. She felt her heart pounding. Tommy showed no sign of letting go. Extricating her arms, she moved her lips away and, propped on her elbows, she looked down at Tommy who smiled beatifically. "Was that an accident?" Alice asked in neutral tones. Tommy did not move. She pushed herself on to her hands and knees and got up. Raising Tommy to a sitting position on the floor and handing him his pad and pencil from his night table, she repeated her question softly.

*The fall or the kiss?*

Alice was flustered. She smoothed her dress. "I meant the kiss."

Tommy reached up to take her hand but she moved away. He had no choice but to write: *I've wanted to kiss you for some time. I love you!*

The answer frightened Alice. She had become fond of Tommy. Adrift after Lloyd's death and her children's abduction, Alice once again felt useful caring for him, but there was more, as she now realized. Bright, clever, and winsome, Tommy was good company. He was better than she at submerging his suffering—or so Alice thought—as he listened to and communicated with others. Being with him distracted Alice from her own anguish. Their asymmetrical way of communicating required particular concentration. Alice's affection for Tommy had simmered on the edge of her consciousness. The kiss brought it bubbling to the surface, scalding her feelings, leaving her to wonder where she—or they—went from here.

Alice pretended nothing had happened. She retrieved the wheelchair. Making sure of her footing, she placed her arms around Tommy and got him into the wheelchair. She went to the kitchen where she ladled out his porridge. Putting on her galoshes and wrapping her shawl tightly around her shoulders, she went out to retrieve *The Enterprise* from the front yard. She set the paper in front of Tommy on the kitchen table and went about her tasks, ignoring him as much as she could. When he finished eating, she cleared the table and washed the dishes. He, in the meantime, wheeled himself into the parlor where he started to write. Silently, she went to the coat rack in the hall, put her coat on and had her hand on the outside door knob when it occurred to her that this departure from her winter routine might alarm Tommy. She went to the entrance of the parlor and announced, "I'm going for a walk. I'll be back soon." Tommy glanced up, smiled, and bent over his work.

Enough of a path had been beaten down by pedestrians that walking was not difficult. The dry snow crepitated under Alice's brisk steps as she followed the trodden path without any destination in mind. She was trying to sort out the unexpected turn in her relationship with Tommy. Involuntarily, she put her mittened hand to her lips in a vain effort to recall the kiss, the first since she and Lloyd had made love before his last trip to Albany almost a year ago. Alice realized that she and Tommy could make love every weekday morning during the school year—although she was not sure how far Tommy could go—if she wanted him. She also knew the pleasure would wear off without further commitment. That she was nine years older was a minor consideration. Whether they were truly in love was more important. Tommy did not have much of a field to choose from while Alice had not, until that morning, even thought of having to choose.

As she headed aimlessly down Helen Street toward the village, she wondered about the practicality of marriage. Tommy's only source of income would be his writing; without enormous good fortune he would not earn enough to support them. If she were to continue to care for him, she wouldn't be able to work. Hiring someone else to help care for Tommy would require more than they could afford. Cyrus and Mary would surely help, but Alice was too independent to want their assistance perpetually.

Alice owed a lot to the Carters; caring for Tommy was one way of paying her debt. When she first moved in, Mary had mentioned helping care for Tommy as one of the "chores" Alice might do. Mary had correctly perceived that being useful was very important to Alice, as her usefulness as a wife and mother had been shattered by Lloyd's death and his parents' stealing her children. Mary might not be surprised that her son would develop a crush on Alice, but that Alice would reciprocate would surely astonish her.

As she crossed Broadway Alice was almost hit by a horse-drawn sleigh. Surprised she had walked so far, she reversed her direction, reviewing her options. She could confront Tommy openly about what he wanted. She could return to the house, still pretending nothing had happened, but face a recurrence or variation of the morning's interaction, which would simply postpone having to make a decision. She could tell Mary that she was ready to seek a job in the Village and then find a room elsewhere, but she wasn't sure she wanted to sever relations with Tommy or the other Carters. Her departure would leave the family in the lurch. Before Alice had arrived, Lisa was able to get Tommy washed and dressed in the morning, but now Lisa was working and would soon get married.

By the time she climbed back up to the Carter house she had resolved nothing. She stamped her feet outside the door and took her galoshes off as soon as she entered. Tommy was not at the kitchen table, where an envelope addressed to her was propped against the sugar bowl. Taking the envelope, she walked to the parlor where Tommy sat in his wheelchair, huddled in his coat and several blankets, reading by the cold sunlight that filtered through the south-facing window. She set the envelope down on the desk. "How foolish of me, I should have built a fire before I left." Tommy pointed to the envelope. Alice was torn between eagerness and fear of what he had written. "Yes, of course, I'll read it. Let me get a fire going first." He shook his head, no, but she was already cleaning the ashes from the previous night's fire. With the logs and kindling piled next to the hearth Alice adeptly built a fire and had a blaze going quickly. Tommy wheeled himself close to the fireplace, held his palms toward the heat, and soon shed his outer blanket. Alice picked the envelope off the desk. "If you don't mind, I'd prefer to read it in my room." She turned to the entrance before Tommy could respond.

She was sorry to leave the warmth of the parlor, but she did not want Tommy watching as she read. Sitting on the edge of her bed, she opened the envelope carefully.

*Dear Alice,*

*I know my advance this morning startled you, but for a brief moment, at least, you seemed to derive as much pleasure as I did. I could not, indeed would not, have asked for more.*

She felt her face flush.

*I have wondered for some time how I could show my affection for you. Our fall gave me an opportunity that was too good to miss.*

She could not help smiling faintly in agreement.

*Although I am supposed to have a facility with words, I could not bring myself to convey my feelings in writing—for fear of being rebuffed I suppose. Yet now that the first delicious moment has passed, I fear I am in a worse predicament, judging from your unexpected and rapid departure after breakfast.*

Alice put her left hand to her throat as she continued to hold the letter in her right.

*After you left, I tried to put myself in your shoes. (As I can't even put my feet in my own shoes, doing this is extraordinarily difficult.)*

Another smile, while at the same time, a tear trickled down her cheek.

*I expect you are wondering what to do next. You could tell me you do not care for me at all, or at least not in the romantic way my kiss signified. Then, I would do my best to tame my feelings and their expression. You could tell me that my feelings are reciprocated but you see no outlet for them and we should desist from overt expression. Then, we should discuss the matter further. You could leave. Then…I don't know.*

*Alice, darling, I do know it was misfortune that brought you to me—I mean your misfortune not mine—and that my overture while you are still griev-ing over the loss of your children (temporary I hope) and your late husband, was premature. To see your beauty and vigor restored and to believe that I contributed—*

*until this morning—has made me feel useful. You cannot*
*imagine how important that is to me. Please forgive me*
*for complicating your life, but I do love you.*
    *Thomas*


Alice laid the letter on her bed so her tears would not stain it. She dried her eyes and stared out the window. The room was plunged into gloom as a cloud passed over the sun. Composing herself as best she could, Alice returned to the parlor. She found Tommy as she had left him, seated before the fire. She sat on the low hearth, her back to the fire, looking up at him. She took his hands and looked intently into his eyes. Her face remained immobile, making it difficult for Tommy to interpret the gesture. "At times like this, I wish I couldn't talk either."

Tommy's pad and pencil were on his lap. *You can try writing this time; I won't mind.*

"No, I'll give it a try." She let go of his hands, got up, turned his wheelchair around, and took a seat on the cushioned chair so their faces were at the same level. "Tommy. I am fond of you and you have helped me over my grief. Until this morning, I didn't know whether I should treat you as a youngster—I am nine years older—or a man. Now you've made it clear how you want to be treated." Needing time to phrase her thoughts without giving offense, she got up, poked the logs closer together and added another to the fire. Her back to Tommy, she continued. "In time, Tommy, I might come to love you."

Unseen by Alice, Tommy raised his eyebrows, pleased there was still hope.

"But I'm not ready…" Her voice trailed off and she stared into the fire.

He wrote something, tapped her back with his pad, handing it to her when she turned. *Why aren't you ready?*

"You gave the reasons. Besides, I had not thought of the possibility."

*Do you think you could do better than me?*

Alice started to cry. "I don't know. I don't know."

*Where do we go from here?*

Alice pulled a handkerchief from her sleeve, blew her nose, and dried her eyes. She returned to the chair. "We must avoid the opportunity from arising." She paused. "I think I should get a job."

*Who will dress me and get me out of bed?*

Alice smiled. "You'll just have to get up earlier so Mary and Lisa can do it before they go off to the school."

*Will you still stay with us?*

"For the time being, I suppose so."

———•———

Tommy made no further advances in the next few weeks and did not send her any more love letters. On an unusually balmy day in March, after the snow on the roads had melted, Tommy asked: *Would you like to take a walk?*

Alice was pleased to do so even though the paths and roads were muddy, impeding progress with the wheel-chair. Near Moody Pond, their favorite destination the last autumn, Tommy scribbled a note: *I bet you can't tell the hardwoods at this time of the year.*

"I'll try." She had no trouble with the birches, even distinguishing white from yellow. In the fall he had showed her not only the differences in leaves but in the bark. After some hesitation as she tried to recall what Tommy had taught, she was able to identify mountain ashes by their smooth, gray-ish brown bark, red maples by their gray furrowed bark, and cherry trees by their smooth, reddish bark.

A few weeks later, Alice got a job with Dr. Edward Trudeau as a receptionist, appointment maker, and secretary. Trudeau had attracted international attention for his ability to cure tuberculosis, or at least arrest its progress. The sickest patients stayed in his sanitarium but many others rented specially designed rooms—"cure porches"—in private homes throughout the village. Keeping track of them was one of Alice's jobs.

*Dr. Trudeau is lucky to have gotten you,* Tommy wrote her. *You are a fast learner. I'll miss you.*

# 3

# Blackmail

SOON after the 1885 legislative session ended, the Chairman of the Board of the Lumberman's Association called an emergency meeting to consider how the Association could wreck the "forever wild" law. In June, when the meeting began in the Association's headquarters in Glens Falls, the sun was shining brightly, but when thunderclouds blotted out the sun, the Association's manager interrupted to light the Board Room's gas lamps. They cast a sickly yellow pall over the room and before long generated considerable heat and the faint odor of methane. The men were eager to finish their business.

The Board voted to give New York Governor David Hill a substantial gift for his reelection in 1886. Hill had succeeded Grover Cleveland who had been elected President of the United States in 1884. One of the Directors knew Hill and was charged with persuading him to appoint a lumber company executive as one of the three members of the Forest Commission, charged by law to administer the "forever wild" provisions. The Board also voted to discuss with the railroad companies how, together, they might reduce the appropriation to the Commission, thereby limiting its ability to buy back private forests to keep them forever wild. If they succeeded on both counts, they would manage to snatch victory from the hands of defeat.

Next, the Board turned its attention to Cyrus Carter, whom they considered prominent in getting the law passed. Charles Smead began the discussion. "In 1886, we've got to defeat Carter at all costs. If he wins we'll have a hard time hanging on to the other upstate Assemblymen. We've already had a few more defections." He stopped to pour a drink of water from the carafe at the center of the table. "And to add insult to injury, we've heard that Carter's wife is going to sue the Smead Lumber Company and the Adirondack Railroad for the forest fire that killed her uncle and destroyed most of his thousand acres of prime forest."

"Surely you're insured?" another lumber company representative asked.

Smead put his glass down. "Of course, but if Mary Carter succeeds with her suit—and I'm sure her husband is complicit—our premium will go up. Besides, we'd like to get that property even though only a small part of it will be harvestable in the near future. We don't want them giving it to the State to be kept forever wild."

The Chairman interrupted. "Let's not get off track. Our objective is to get rid of Cyrus Carter."

"If we could uncover something about Carter," another Board member commented, "some indiscretion on his part, we might be able to influence the vote." Several others nodded their assent.

"Carter used to work for us," Smead added. "As I recall, Ben Anderson hired him. I'll see if Ben can pin something on him."

"Wasn't Anderson's daughter married to Lloyd Massing? He might not be willing to cooperate." George Massing, Lloyd's father and owner of the Glens Falls mill, who had joined the Board, nodded.

A mill owner from Westport interjected. "I've heard that

Anderson's daughter is active with the suffragists." George nodded again. "When old Ben found out he was infuriated."

"Another reason we shouldn't have trusted Massing," Smead commented. "Carter's wife is a suffragist, too."

Another Board member reached for the humidor and took a cigar out. "These women are a strange breed. Some of them go beyond wanting the vote; you know, free love, that sort of thing."

George Massing spoke for the first time. "Lloyd's widow, I hear, has gone to live with the Carters in Saranac Lake. Neither she nor Cyrus Carter is any friend of the Massings." He did not say anything about his grandchildren.

The Chairman pushed his chair back, putting his hands on the edge of the table. "Well, if we agree that Carter is dangerous, we can proceed along several fronts. We can dig something up that would embarrass him if it got out—every man's got something in his closet—and we can discredit his wife. A lot of the men, like Ben Anderson, aren't happy about seeing the vote extended to women. If Carter defends his wife, he's likely to lose votes."

"If she practices free love we should be able to get something on her. Carter'll be cuckolded," the Westport mill owner reflected. "That'll cost him votes, too."

Charles Smead replied to the Chairman's proposition in a loud voice. "Of course Carter's dangerous," He looked around the table. No one disagreed. "I say we march on both fronts. I'll find out more about Carter. Maybe I'll turn up something on his wife at the same time."

They all got up at once as the meeting adjourned, relieved to go out into fresher air.

Ben Anderson seldom got mail so the personally addressed envelope surprised him. His eyes failing, he went to the east-facing window of his parlor, held the letter close to his face, and read it in the bright morning light.

Charles Smead, Jr.

Smead Lumber Company

Saranac Lake Village, New York

October 3, 1885

Dear Ben,

It's been three years since we last saw each other. Since then, we've moved the Company headquarters from Elizabethtown to Saranac Lake, near your old stamping ground at Axton Landing. Both there and later, when you worked at our old headquarters, you were one of our Company's most conscientious and loyal employees, for which my father and I are eternally grateful.

I will be passing through Westport on October 15 and would like to take you to lunch at the Hotel Westport and chat about old times. I've enclosed a return envelope for you to reply. I hope you can make it.

Respectfully,

Charles A. Smead, Jr.

President

"I wonder what he wants?" Ben asked himself. He quickly wrote Smead that he would be at the Hotel at noon of the appointed date, a Thursday. Smead had pasted a stamp on the envelope so Ben had only to give it to the mailman the next morning.

Charles had spent Wednesday night at the Hotel, having taken the stage from Saranac Lake by the same route Anderson and his daughter Alice had driven to and from Frank Miller's trial for the murder of Sean O'Rourke. That trial had been a turning point in Anderson's life. After the trial, Ben had gone to Smead's father, the President of the Company, and asked for a job in Essex County, closer to home; he did not want to risk arrest in Franklin County for instigating murder in conjunction with plotting the kidnapping of a fugitive slave. The senior Smead, since retired, offered him a desk job at the Elizabethtown headquarters, auditing the reports made by the jobbers in various camps, apparently not aware that Anderson's own dealings as a jobber had short-changed the Company. Ben's wife was quite obese and had suffered her first attack of dropsy soon after the trial. She died in 1876. About that time, Ben's eyesight had begun to fail. The Company gave him a retirement party in 1882. He was fifty years old.

Twelve year-old Alice Anderson had been stunned about her father's part in O'Rourke's murder and never looked up to him after the Miller trial. She left home for Glens Falls as soon as she finished high school. Her intelligence, poise, and beauty soon won her a job as a secretary, unusual for a woman. When she became engaged to her boss's son, she had asked her father to give her away. Afterward, he got wind of her suffragist activities and was ready to disown her. They had not seen each other since the wedding. The only time Alice wrote was to tell her father of the births of her two children.

---

With the morning bright, Charles arranged for a table overlooking Lake Champlain. By the time Ben arrived, clouds scudded across the sky, coalescing and turning the sparkling blue water a depressing gray. The water grew increasingly choppy. Ben entered the dining room and peered around. He could only recognize faces when they were very close. Charles, who was sipping a cocktail at his table, did not recognize Ben immediately. He was neither tall nor stocky when he worked for Smead, but now he was stooped and thinner, his plaid shirt hanging loosely over his sparse frame. Charles got up to greet him and steered him to the table.

Ben's meals at home were sparse. Holding the menu close to his face, he ordered with relish. When Ben's cocktail arrived, Charles raised his glass. "Here's to you, Ben, and the success you brought to our Company." They clinked. Charles swallowed the rest of his drink in one gulp and ordered a second. One was enough for Ben.

"Well, I suppose I've done my part," replied Ben. "It wasn't always easy, you know. When I was a jobber, it was hard to get jacks to work as hard as they could. Nowadays, when you're paying them by the hour and not by the trees cut, it must be even worse."

"If they don't match up to our expectations, they don't last," Charles replied. His second cocktail arrived. Taking a sip, he added, "Actually, Ben, I wanted to talk to you about your jobbing."

Ben's guard went up. *Was Smead going to raise the trial or my attempt to swindle the Company by selling hemlock bark to the tanneries and my other misdemeanors? Had the Company finally found out after all these years?* "I did the best I could, Mr. Smead." Not very tall even when Charles knew him as a jobber, Ben was bent now, withered and deferential, making it hard for Smead to imagine lumberjacks taking orders from this runt of a man.

"I know that, Ben." Their appetizers arrived and they ate silently for a few minutes. Charles pushed his plate away and continued. "Actually, Ben, I wondered if you recall Cyrus Carter, our Assemblyman from Franklin County, ever working for you."

"Oh yes, I remember Cyrus very well." Ben did not follow legislative matters and had no idea how Carter voted. He guessed that in a county like Franklin, where logging was still the major industry, the lumber companies had helped elect Cyrus, so he spoke well of Cyrus to Charles even though Cyrus had threatened to expose his swindling and had revealed his role in the plot to kidnap the fugitive slave, J.W. Loguen, at the Miller trial. (Ben felt no remorse for the attempt and still smarted at the way Carter had portrayed him at the trial.) "As a matter of fact," Ben continued in a positive tone, "During the War, I hired him back, bum leg and all. He could still out-walk and out-chop most other loggers."

Disappointed that Ben had nothing bad to say about Carter, Charles said distractedly, "Yes, I've noticed that Carter walks with a limp. Do you know how he got it?"

"Oh yes! That was a tragic accident."

Charles became more alert and beckoned Ben to continue.

"We had dumped all our logs into the Raquette at Axton Landing, containing them in a boom so they would reach

the mill all at once." He glanced up at the ceiling, calculating. "Must have been the spring of 1858. I ordered Cyrus
to take the boat and cut the boom to get the logs moving."

*That must have been dangerous*, Charles thought, but kept
silent and let Ben continue.

"Of course he couldn't do it alone; I assigned three other
men to go with him." He paused, trying to get the scene
into focus. "Come to think of it, Cyrus asked me to replace
one of the men, Sean O'Rourke, with Jean, the *Frenchie*; I
forget his last name. He was very young and inexperienced,
but strong and loyal to Cyrus."

Impatient with this level of detail, Charles urged, "Yes,
yes, go on."

"Well, the men in the boat broke the boom, but still
the logs didn't budge." The entrée arrived and Ben paused
to eat. After a few mouthfuls, he drank from his goblet of
claret. "About that time a terrible storm came up. Upstream,
lightning hit a heavy birch tree which fell on the jam and
loosened it up; the logs began to move."

Charles began to suspect that this story would not be
useful for discrediting Carter. Nevertheless, he always liked a
good story and did not interrupt.

"When the storm came up, Cyrus, who had been rowing, changed places with Jean, who had been standing on
the transom. A few minutes after the tree fell, the logs at the
beginning of the jam began to move swiftly. Jean pulled hard
on the oars to keep ahead of the logs. The sudden movement
knocked Cyrus out of the boat. He managed to stand on a
few of the logs but then fell into the water. The next thing
we saw was Jean jumping into the river—to rescue Cyrus
I guess. The logs were battering the boat. We saw the men

in the boat pull someone out of the water; we couldn't tell if it was Cyrus or Jean. We waited for the other one to get picked up, but he never was. When they got to shore, the boatmen told us that Jean had been hit by a fast-moving log and had gone under. Sean O'Rourke found his body far downstream a few days later." Ben resumed eating.

"What about Carter?"

"While he was hanging on to the side of the boat a log slammed into his leg, crushing it against the side of the boat. We took him to a doctor in Tupper Lake who set the leg."

The waiter came to clear away the plates and take their dessert orders. While they waited, Charles offered Ben a cigar, which he readily accepted. Both men lighted up, taking a few puffs until a cloud of smoke rose from the table. One thing puzzled Charles. "You said Jean was inexperienced. Had he ever broken a logjam before?"

Ben blew out a puff of smoke. "No. Axton was his first logging job. Before I sent the boat out, I asked for men who had experience in logjams. Sean O'Rourke volunteered, but not Jean."

"Then why did Carter want Jean in the boat?"

Gathering his thoughts, Ben puffed on his cigar. "Well, Cyrus and Jean came to the camp together." Ben thought back to that evening when they first walked into his office shack at Axton Landing; he remembered recognizing Cyrus as the man who had walked out at Fourth Lake, starting a minor insurrection. He doubted Smead wanted to hear about that. "Jean was strong, maybe a foot taller than Cyrus. They were already friends when they arrived at Axton Landing."

Charles wondered why Carter exposed his friend to

such danger. *He couldn't have known what was going to happen,* he reasoned, *but still, he knew the situation was dangerous.*

Anderson interrupted his thoughts. "There was no love lost between Jean and Sean O'Rourke."

Charles looked at Ben through the haze of smoke. "What do you mean?"

"They had a big fight the previous New Year's Eve over at Corey's; Jean and his *Frenchie* friends against the micks, Sean and his brothers. Sean came back to camp with a cut over his eye. As I learned from the men later, Jean got angry when Sean asked to dance with Jean's girl Mary. I don't know whether she was really Jean's girl at the time but she sure was later. She had a baby just about nine months after Jean died. John, she called him. She made no secret that Jean was his father. Said he had promised to marry her, but then he got killed." Ben paused to take another puff. "When John was a year old she married Cyrus."

Charles was incredulous. "You mean Jean's girl is now Mary Carter?" Ben nodded.

Pushing his chair away from the table, Charles stood up and pulled out his watch. Finally, he had something he might be able to use against Carter, but he wasn't sure exactly what. "Ben, if you'd care to have coffee, I'll arrange it, but I've got to get going or I'll miss the stage. It's been great seeing you again and I found your story very interesting. Too bad about Jean, though." Ben stood. He had not finished his dessert. Gently, Charles pushed Ben down. "Sorry to leave so quickly, the waiter will bring you coffee. I've taken care of everything. Hope to see you soon, Ben." Ben sat down to finish his pie. Charles stopped on his way out to hand the waiter some bills and pointed to Ben. He was out the door before the waiter brought Ben his coffee. Anderson mulled over their conversation as he drank. *What in hell was that all about? I can't believe he just came to shoot the breeze.* When he finished, he scratched his head and gingerly threaded his way past the tables. Emerging in the gray afternoon light he picked his way back home.

———•———

Charles had plenty of time to catch the stagecoach, but he was so excited—elated may be a better word—that he wanted to get outside and put all the pieces together. *Could it be that Cyrus Carter was in love with Mary and wanted to get Jean out of the way so he could marry her? But then why did Carter trade places with Jean in the boat, taking the dangerous position for himself? Carter couldn't have known Jean would leave the oars to try to save him.* Charles started to walk toward the livery, thinking back to the start of Ben's story. *Did Mary know it was Carter who had asked for Jean to come on board?* he wondered. If she didn't, then threatening to tell her could be used to blackmail her husband. If she did, Charles's visit to Westport would have been a waste of time. *We've got to find out if she knew.* On his way to the livery, Charles stopped at the telegraph office where he sent two messages, the first to the Chairman of the Board of the Lumberman's Association:

**HAVE GOT SOMETHING ON CYRUS CARTER STOP WILL REPORT TO YOU GLENS FALLS MONDAY 10 AM STOP CHARLES SMEAD**

He had no hesitation that his news would be of enough interest that the Chairman would postpone any previous engagement. Smead's second message was to Edward Green, agent for the Allied Insurance Group, who had requested to see Smead at the Company's Saranac Lake office on the same Monday to discuss "an urgent matter."

> DONT COME SARANAC LAKE MONDAY STOP
> INSTEAD COME LUMBERMANS ASSN OFFICE
> GLENS FALLS 10:30 AM STOP WILL MEET YOU
> THERE STOP CHARLES SMEAD

Charles met promptly with the Chairman at 10:00 A. M. the following Monday. Before Charles could begin, the Chairman remarked, "I haven't been idle, Charles. I've learned that Mary Carter has acquired a reputation through-out New York State for trying to get women the vote. She got her husband to support a bill giving women the vote and he even spoke in its favor. Women's suffrage is not of direct interest to us, Charles, but it reflects what's being called 'pro-gressive' politics. Our men in the Assembly voted against it." He poured a glass of water from the pitcher. "Now, Charles, why don't you tell me what you've got? Seems like our activities might be converging."

Smead related what he had learned from Ben Anderson. He had calmed down considerably since leaving Westport. He concluded, "Of course, if Mary knows that Carter asked to have Jean on the boat instead of O'Rourke, there's not much we can do with this story."

"I agree. But first, do you think this Anderson man is reliable? Did you tell him you wanted to get something on Carter?"

"No, of course not. He thought I wanted to hear good things about Carter. I almost stopped him in the middle of his story, thinking it was a waste of time. Only when he told me that Jean drowned and that Carter had wanted him in the boat did I realize we might have something."

"The question is," the Chairman said, "how are we going to find out if Mary knows? We also have to see if there's a way that her suffrage activity can embarrass Carter."

His male secretary interrupted to tell them that a Mr. Green had arrived on instructions from Mr. Smead.

"Oh, I'm sorry," said Charles, "I forgot to tell you I've invited Edward Green, the adjuster for our insurance company, who may be able to help us on the first count. He has something urgent to convey and was going to come up to Saranac Lake, but I thought it more convenient for all of us to meet here in Glens Falls." Green was shown in and joined the other two at one end of the conference table. The chairman offered Green a cigar, which he refused, and a glass of water, which he gratefully accepted.

In his thirties, Green had a clean-shaven face with baby-smooth cheeks, aquiline nose, deep-set black eyes, and glossy black hair brushed straight back. Over six feet tall, his stature and handsome facial features were striking and not easily forgotten.

"I think it would be best, Mr. Chairman, if Edward tells why he requested to see me today—I think it will interest the Association—before I explain why I asked him to meet us here."

"Very well," Green began, turning to the Chairman. "As you may know, Sir, in July 1883 a spark from an Adirondack Railroad locomotive started a forest fire that destroyed land belonging to William Corey near Axton Landing. It also took Mr. Corey's life. In his Will, Corey left his inn and all of the surrounding land to his niece, Mary Carter."

"Cyrus Carter's wife," Smead interjected.

"Charles and I were just talking about Mrs. Carter," the Chairman said. "I didn't know that she was heiress to her uncle's land."

"If the probate court accepts the will," Charles commented.

Green continued, "My Company insures both the Adirondack Railroad and the Smead Lumber Company against natural disaster and liability claims. The Railroad suffered relatively minor damage as a result of the fire, as did Smead, but Corey's property suffered extensive loss: everything north of the Raquette River that belonged to Corey, including his inn, was destroyed. I visited Mr. Smead last month to make a preliminary estimate of the damage to all the properties affected by the fire."

"There's no doubt you'll reimburse our loss, is there?" Charles asked. "You said it was minor."

"I don't think so. There are complications, however." Both men looked directly at Edward. "*The Nation*, a radical magazine, has just published an article by Thomas Carter, the Carters' son." He bent down, opened his brief case, and laid a copy of the magazine on the table, open to Carter's article. He had circled one passage, which he proceeded to read out loud:

> Neither Smead Lumber nor the Adirondack Railroad offered to compensate my mother, to whom Uncle William bequeathed the property, either for the property loss or for his death. The law as it now stands does not compel them to do either.

Edward continued. "Two weeks ago Mary Carter filed

a liability suit against the Railroad and Smead in the New York District Court for Franklin County."

"I'd heard she was planning to do that," Charles said.

"What does she claim?" The Chairman asked.

"The suit states that because of both the Railroad's and the Lumber Company's negligence, Corey was killed and his property destroyed.

"The Railroad's negligence perhaps, but not Smead's," Charles said indignantly.

"Come now, Charles," the Chairman said with some annoyance, "your company's shoddy practices—failing to clean up the toppings and dead branches left after logging—increased the chance of fire." He turned to Green. "How much does she want?"

"Twenty thousand dollars."

Charles whistled. "That's outrageous."

He paused, looking directly at Green. "Of course, our insurance will pay if it comes to that."

"Frankly, gentlemen, my company cannot afford to pay this claim. We would insist on a trial."

"What are the chances the Mrs. Carter will win?" the Chairman asked,

"It depends on who the judge is and if Mrs. Carter gets a jury trial," Green replied. "That's not the point though. With the growing hostility to the railroads and lumber companies across the country, you'll be in for a lot worse if the case comes to trial. It's sure to get national publicity."

"Regulation, you mean?" the Chairman asked.

"And strict enforcement of the 'forever wild' law, or laws more harmful," Charles added. "There's a move to set aside the whole of the Adirondacks, six million acres. God knows what restrictions the legislature will put on the region."

The Chairman started to doodle on a small pad with a Ticonderoga pencil. "Populism. I suppose it could spread from the south and west to here."

"It's not only the masses, Sir," Smead continued. "The Rockefellers and Vanderbilts have discovered the Adirondacks. They're planning to build great camps and want to preserve the woods for their private hunting and fishing. And the forests they don't buy could eventually be bought by the State to add them to the Forest Preserve." That's the end of our business.

"We were able to beat back a one million dollar appropriation that would have allowed the State to purchase additional forests," the Chairman chuckled. "All they got was fifteen thousand dollars for expenses of the Forest Commission!" He turned to Green. "Let's get back to the matter at hand. You have some suggestions, Mr. Green?"

"It's really up to you," Green started, "but if Smead and the Railroad made an offer to purchase the Corey property for, say, ten thousand dollars, the Carters might be satisfied and withdraw the suit. The Carters would avoid court costs and get themselves a pretty penny. You'd avoid the publicity of a trial, which could hurt even if you were to win."

"And it gets your insurance company off the hook, doesn't it?" the Chairman noted angrily.

"Not exactly. We'd still have to pay for the damages to the Railroad and Smead's property; I would guess something like five thousand dollars, but I'll have to return to Axton Landing to examine the damage to both your forest and the railroad in more detail. If the Carter suit goes forward, I'll also have to examine the Corey property. If Smead and Adirondack Railroad made an offer to which the Carters agree, my company would be spared the possibility of a much larger payout if the Carters' suit were successful. We might also contribute to a ten-thousand dollar settlement with the Carters." Green turned to the Chairman. "It might be in your Association's best interest to contribute to this settlement, too."

"Self-interest all around. Have you discussed this with the Adirondack Railroad?" asked the Chairman.

"I have an appointment with Mr. Durant on Thursday. If you are agreeable, we can arrange a joint meeting with your lawyers, draw up the proper documents, and make an offer to Mrs. Carter."

Charles turned the copy of *The Nation* that Green had laid on the table around to face him. "This story, the lawsuit, they are a real thorn in our side, and in the railroad's too."

Not sure he wanted his Association dragged into this matter, the Chairman interrupted. "We can't do anymore on the Carter lawsuit today; we'll have to discuss it with the full Board. Charles, Why don't you tell us how Mr. Green might be helpful in the other matter?"

Smead turned around to make sure the door to the Board Room was closed. "Before I continue, can I have your word, Mr. Green, that what I am going to say stays within the confines of this room until such time, if ever, that the three of us agree it can go beyond, and then only to a limited number of people?"

"You have my word, Mr. Smead."

"Before you got here, Edward, the Chairman and I were talking about ways to discredit the Carters. Cyrus Carter voted for the 'forever wild' bill in the Assembly. The Board of the Lumberman's Association has concluded they want to see him defeated in 1886."

"I'm not surprised," Green commented.

"I've just returned from Westport where I learned from the jobber who hired Carter as a lumberjack before the Civil War, that Carter commanded a boat in which Mary Carter's lover at the time, Jean, was one of the three-man crew. The boat's mission was to break a logjam—dangerous business."

"She had a lover while married to Carter?" Green asked.

"No. It was before she married him. In fact, Jean was the father of Mary's first son, born nine months after Jean was killed. But listen carefully, Edward. Carter insisted that this lover, Jean, come on board even though he had no experience with logjams. Minutes later, Jean went overboard. A log smashed into his head. His body was recovered downstream a few days later."

The men were silent for a moment. Then Green asked, "Surely Mary—what was her maiden name?" Both men shrugged—"Surely Mary knew about this before she married Carter?" Green thought for a moment. "If he didn't tell her it sounds like he's hiding something." He paused, "Like premeditated murder."

The Chairman intervened. "I don't think we can go that far. Charles failed to tell you that Jean had jumped into the water after Cyrus had fallen overboard, perhaps to rescue him, and that Cyrus's leg was badly broken before he could get back in the boat. What we don't know, Mr. Green, is whether Mary knows that Cyrus asked for Jean to be in the boat. If Mary doesn't know, threatening to tell her could be used to, uh, influence Cyrus."

Charles had been skimming Tommy's story in *The Nation*. "Look here, he pointed, the drowning is mentioned in this article:"

Another buried there was drowned trying to rescue my father, a worker for Smead, who was ordered to break a logjam under circumstances that were hazardous in the extreme.

Again silence. Edward could see where the Chairman and Smead were going and he was not happy about it. "I don't see how I can help you."

"You said you have to go up to Axton Landing." The Chairman turned to Charles, "That's near the Village of Saranac Lake, right?" Charles nodded. "You'll have to ask Mary Carter for permission to survey Corey's property, right?" Again Charles nodded.

"That would be one way of gaining access, yes Sir," Green admitted. "But I couldn't come out and say, 'By the way, Mrs. Carter, did you know your husband asked for your lover to be in his boat before he drowned'—what was it—twenty-five years ago?"

Charles and the Chairman were momentarily embarrassed. "Of course," the Chairman coughed, "you couldn't ask her immediately. If you were to sound her out on a possible settlement, you'd get to know her better, learn about her past history. You might have the opportunity."

"Supposing I could get to that point. She'd want to know how I knew."

"Tell her Ben Anderson told you," Charles answered.

He's the jobber who told me. If you'd feel better about it, I can arrange for you to hear the story directly from him."

"I don't think that will be necessary." Green stood. "Gentlemen, this has been a most interesting meeting. I came with a proposition for you and now you've proposed one to me. I need to think about it." He looked at the Chairman. "I'm sworn to secrecy. I suppose you'd rather I didn't discuss it with my Director."

The Chairman nodded. "And by the way," he added, "We hear Mary's an active suffragist. Regardless of our other proposal, perhaps you can confirm her position on women's right to vote and other rights as well." He smiled.

"That should be easy enough," Edward replied.

They shook hands all around. "Well," said the Chairman as he showed his guests out, "we've got almost a year before the campaign heats up."

## 4

# Gathering the Evidence

I N early spring, the Adirondack Railroad, the Smead Lumber Company, and the Allied Insurance Group had agreed
on an offer of ten thousand dollars if Mary would withdraw
her suit against them. Charles Smead grew impatient when the
winter snows melted and Edward Green had not appeared at
Saranac Lake. He was relieved when Green wrote him in April.

Allied Insurance Group

Albany, New York

April 14, 1886

Mr. Charles Smead

Smead Lumber Company

Saranac Lake, New York


Dear Mr. Smead:

Forgive my tardiness in keeping you informed of
my plans. Now that the Adirondack Railroad and your
company have agreed on an offer, to which the Allied
Insurance Group has generously agreed to contribute
$5,000, I am prepared to come north for two purposes.
First, to convey the offer to Mrs. Carter, and second,
to examine the damage caused by fire in 1883. If Mrs.
Carter does not withdraw her suit in response to the
offer, this will include a survey of the Corey property.

In any event, I will arrive in Saranac Lake on Friday, April 30. I will be in touch with you to arrange a visit to Axton Landing to survey the property in question. I will stay as long as necessary to resolve the matters we discussed last fall.

Sincerely,

Edward Green, Adjuster

Smead smiled as he read the last sentence, noting that Green had written 'matters', the plural. He hoped Green would be able to conduct his business at Saranac Lake while Cyrus was still in Albany.

———•———

When he arrived at Saranac Lake, Green made inquiries about lodging and was steered to Martin's Hotel, on the northeast shore of Lower Saranac Lake, about a mile from the town center. On his first morning, a mild and sunny Saturday, with barely a breeze to ripple the lake, he set off on foot to explore the Village and wander past the Carters' house high on Helen Street.

In full sun, a woman was digging up earth in a narrow swath along the side of the Carter house. Her back was to the street. "That should make a fine flower bed," Edward said.

The woman stood, turned to the voice, clapped the dirt off her hands and then wiped her brow with the back of her hand. "I hope so," she replied amiably. Fifteen feet separated them. With the sun in her eyes, the woman saw the man only in silhouette. He was tall but not excessively heavy. There was something familiar about him, but uncertain who he was, the woman ventured, "You're new in the village, are you not?"

"Yes, ma'am." Edward had the advantage of the sun. The woman was tall and attractive, the few lines on her brow and face hidden in the sunlight. Her light brown hair was tied back in a bun, the gray streaks hardly visible. A few strands had escaped and the woman made an effort to tuck them back. "I wish I could say I was moving here. Such beautiful surroundings and charming people, too."

"It's a little early to be a tourist," the woman ventured as if trying to solve a puzzle. "Besides the black flies will hatch soon; it won't be pleasant to be outside then."

"No, I'm here on business. As a matter of fact, perhaps you could help me."

"I'd be pleased to do so," she said, wiping her hands on her skirt as she stepped closer to the stranger.

"I'm looking for the Carter residence and Mrs. Mary Carter in particular."

By this time the woman had reached the border of her property and stood close to Edward shielding her eyes from the sun. She immediately realized who he reminded her of and closed her eyes for a second, either to clear the vision or recall Jean's features, and gasped. Edward asked, "Are you all right, ma'am?"

She recovered quickly and smiled. "I'm fine. Just that you reminded me of someone I once knew." She turned to her right, and he to his left, so the sun shone between them. "I'm Mary Carter."

"Oh! I knew the Carters lived on Helen Street, but I didn't know this was their—I mean your—home." He paused in embarrassment. "I expected an older woman."

"You're very kind, young man, but I'm probably old enough to be your mother."

"I doubt that. It would make you close to sixty. I can't believe you're that old."

She felt her face flush, as it had not in years. "You're right about that." She smiled and added, "But then you must be older than you look."

"Yes, I get kidded about my baby face."

Mary gave her hands another wipe and then offered her right to Green. Her hand was warm, her grip firm.

"Edward Green, Mrs. Carter. Very pleased to meet you." Mary looked toward the door of the house. "If you have some matter to discuss, perhaps we should go inside."

She led Edward into the house. Alice had gone for a walk with Tommy, and Lisa was visiting her fiancé Peter.

"Is Mr. Carter at home?"

"Cyrus, my husband, is still in Albany. He's the Assemblyman for Franklin County," she said proudly. "Is it me you wanted to see or Mr. Carter?"

"It's you, ma'am."

"Well, then, come in. Alice Massing has taken our son Tommy out for a walk. He's paraplegic, you know."

"I know." He reached into his jacket and produced a copy of *The Nation* with Tommy's article. "Uh, perhaps I should come back when they are at home." He scratched his forehead wondering about the impropriety of seeing a married woman alone in her home.

"Nonsense! Besides, you've got my curiosity aroused. I hope you're not selling pots or pans or anything like that." Again she paused, looking at the kettle on the stove. "Can I fix you some tea?"

"That would be lovely. Can I give you a hand?"

Mary had already added some kindling to the belly of

the stove, which was still glowing, and then a log. "No. That's all there is to it. The kettle has plenty of water in it still." She went to the cupboard and came back with a tea egg and a jar of loose tea. She pointed to a chair near the kitchen table. "Please sit down." Taking a pitcher from a shelf above the stove, Mary took two pinches of tea from the jar, placed them in the egg and set it in the pitcher. The water soon was steaming. While the tea steeped she went back to the cupboard, got two cups, and set them on the table. "I do have some milk," she said, looking at the icebox. "And of course sugar."

"Sugar will be fine."

Mary brought a small bowl of sugar and two teaspoons to the table and took a seat in the chair opposite Edward's.

Edward continued, "No, I'm not selling pots and pans. As a matter of fact, I have a 'buying' proposition to make." For the first time, Mary looked at him suspiciously. "Mrs. Carter, I don't want to mislead you. I represent the Allied Insurance Group."

"We can't afford insurance," she said as she poured the tea.

"I'm not selling insurance." Edward took a teaspoon of sugar, slid it into his tea, and then stirred methodically. "My Company insures both the Smead Lumber Company and the Adirondack Railroad. I understand that you are bringing suit against them for your uncle's death and the damage to your uncle's property…"

"'Destruction' is a better word," she interrupted.

"Very well, destruction." He took a sip of tea and glanced at *The Nation*, which he had laid on the table. "The companies want to avoid a trial, Mrs. Carter. They are confident they can win, but they want to avoid adverse publicity."

"They deserve the adverse publicity. Maybe that will get them to change their destructive policies." She picked up her cup. "My uncle's property was not insured." Her features hardened.

"Please understand my position, Mrs. Carter. I am not condoning the behavior of the companies we represent. I have a job to do."

Mary sipped her tea. The warm fluid calmed her. "What exactly is your job?"

"Well, first I have to examine the damage to the Smead property and the Adirondack Railroad's right of way."

"I can't help you with that."

"Second, I would like to examine the extent of damage, uhh, destruction, to your uncle's property."

"Why would you need to do that? It's not insured." She reflected for a moment. "Does that have something to do with the 'buying proposition' you mentioned?"

"As a matter of fact, it does. The Smead Lumber Company may be interested in buying your uncle's property. I would have to go over it, inspect it if you will, to see its worth."

Edward had drained his cup. Mary stood and poured him a second. "Not much for a lumber company. There's only one stand of old growth left on the northwestern part of the property. It will be years before the rest grows beyond scrub and saplings."

"I understand. Still, as I mentioned, Smead and the Railroad want to avoid litigation."

Mary was disappointed. She wanted to like Edward. With his resemblance, he might have some of Jean's favorable characteristics. She sat down opposite Edward and looked fully into his face. Their eyes met. Her voice was barely audible, but her intent was clear. "In other words, you want to bribe us to drop the case."

Edward did not look away as Mary expected him to do. "Not me, Mrs. Carter. The lumber company and the railroad."

She looked toward the door, wondering when Alice, Tommy, and Lisa would return.

"Do you know how much we've sued Smead and the Railroad for?"

"Twenty thousand dollars," Edward replied.

"Even with court costs and a reduction in the settlement we expect to win ten thousand dollars."

Edward smiled. "Smead, the Railroad, and my company would be willing to match that in return for your uncle's property. Besides, Mrs. Carter, you might not win. You're the litigant in this case. Neither the judge, nor the jury—which will be all male—might look favorably on a woman trying to gain the deceased's property. You can be sure Smead's attorney will belittle you."

Mary thought back to the last trial in which she was a witness. Frank Miller's prosecutor tried but did not succeed in belittling her. She was not a party to the suit in that case; in this trial she would be. Beginning to feel uncomfortable in Edward's presence, Mary stood. He finished his second cup and also stood. "You mean your clients will give me ten thousand dollars for uncle's property if I drop the suit?" Green nodded. "So nice of you to drop in, Mr. Green, your proposition doesn't thrill me, but I'll think about it." She offered her hand and shook his firmly, quickly letting go. "Where are you staying?"

"At Martin's Hotel on Lower Saranac Lake. I plan to stay the week. Longer if necessary."

"There's a lovely view from their back balcony. I imagine the sunset would be spectacular."

"I'll make a point of being there this evening," he replied. "If you would care to let me know what you decide, I'll let you know about the sunset."

"I know where to reach you if I have something to say. Good day, Mr. Green."

———•———

From the back porch of the Hotel the sunset was indeed spectacular. Inside, at the bar, Edward had ordered a double whiskey and then taken it outside. He sat in a sloping rustic chair—easy to slide into, hard to get out of—and gazed down the lake, dotted with islands, toward the glow of the sun behind the clouds, casting the lake and the islands in advancing shadow, colors changing from sparkling blue to black and back to blue as wind squalls danced around the lake. Off to the west the slope of the largest mountain—Ampersand he was told—had been gouged out by lumbering and fire in its lower reaches. When the sun shone on its upper slope, the conifers stood closely, dappled here and there with the lighter yellow-green of blossoming hardwoods. Edward sipped his drink, pleased with the view Mrs. Carter commended to him and by his encounter with her despite her response to his offer. He had established a rapport that would have been difficult with an older, sterner, worn-down woman. *Who was it I reminded her of?* he wondered. Yet, when he had broached the purchase of her uncle's property she immediately hardened. He swished the remains of his whiskey, took another swallow, savored the burn of the liquid down his throat, leaned back and closed his eyes.

He sensed the warmth and light of the sun, not yet at the horizon, through his lids. He would go to church tomorrow morning, hike up Mount Baker in the afternoon, and think through his strategy. On Monday, he would have to visit the Smead headquarters in Saranac Lake and arrange a visit to Axton Landing. Should he tell Charles Smead that Mary Carter was unlikely to sell her uncle's property in return for dropping the suit? He decided not to. He hoped he could charm Mary into changing her mind. Still with his eyes closed, he imagined riding out to the site of Corey's Inn with her. Some way of finding out whether she knew that Cyrus Carter had asked for Jean to be in the boat might occur to him, but so far he couldn't think of any.

———•———

*Looks like you've had company*, Tommy noted as Alice wheeled him into the kitchen.

Quickly Mary cleared the cups, pitcher, and sugar bowl from the table. "Yes. An unexpected one: Mr. Edward Green, from the company that insures Smead and the Adirondack Railroad." Alice went to her room, leaving Mary alone with Tommy. "He passed on an offer from Smead and the Adirondack Railroad to buy Uncle William's property." Mary saw Tommy looking at Mr. Green's copy of *The Nation*, on the kitchen table. "Oh, Mr. Green must have left that. He said Smead and Adirondack Railroad were worried about the bad publicity. Partly thanks to you, Tommy; you're widely read."

Tommy ignored his mother's flattery. *So you'll drop your lawsuit?* he wrote.

"Yes, that's what he suggested. He was making the offer for Smead," Mary said seeming to defend Edward.

*Maybe. If you win, the insurance company has to pay. They protect Smead against liability.*

Tommy was silent while Mary washed the teacups. Then he tore off the sheet he had been writing on and wrote in bold block letters on a fresh one: *D O N'T   S E L L!*

Lisa came in. She had been out with Peter O'Rourke, Jr. She looked at Tommy's latest note. "What's going on? Mary brought her up-to-date. Lisa's perspective was different from Tommy's. "Did he say how much?" Tommy shot his sister an angry glance.

"He said ten thousand was not an impossible price. He wants to survey uncle's property, for the companies I suppose."

"What did you tell him, Mama?" Lisa asked.

"I certainly didn't say yes—" Tommy clapped his hands and smiled at Lisa. "But I didn't come out and say no either." The smile left Tommy's face. *Why not?*

"I need more time to think, Tommy. A trial is no picnic. Mr. Venable's old. He told me last week that he's too weak to prepare the case and represent me. Your father, the only other lawyer I'd trust, is very busy. He has mixed feelings about the lawsuit."

*He doesn't like confrontation.*

"That's not fair, Tommy. You know that he's introduced bold legislation—the labor laws you wanted—and supported the 'forever wild' bill. He doesn't mind speaking up, he just doesn't like face-to-face confrontation." She glanced at Lisa. "Besides, there are other issues."

"Like your being a woman," Lisa said.

Mary smiled. Her daughter was learning. "Yes. A woman seeking redress for the destruction of a man's property will not have an easy time in court. Even Mr. Green mentioned that. And until uncle's will is probated, I don't have legal standing to bring the suit forward; his property is not yet mine. My opponents are likely to contest the will."

Mary took a towel off a hook near the stove and dried the teacups. "Ten thousand dollars without a battle over probate and a trial—that would be nice," she said dreamily.

Tommy wheeled himself into his room and slammed the door.

Mary had thought a lot about what she would do with the proceeds if they won their case. Now she could have it without a fight. She wanted to give Tommy more space and a real desk, maybe build another floor on to their house with additional bedrooms for visitors. If Alice continued to live with them she could have a room of her own, not Cyrus's study, which he would be glad to have back. Then there were less material things; expanding the activity of the suffragists was at the top of the list.

"How did you leave it with Mr. Green, Mama?" Lisa asked.

"I said, I'd get in touch with him if I had more to say. He's staying at Martin's Hotel." She looked at her daughter. "Do you think there's any harm in showing him uncle's property?"

"That's too big a question for me, Mama." Lisa stood. "We know how Tommy feels. What would Papa think?"

Mary smiled. "He'd say, 'Explore all the options.'"

The next day, Sunday, Mary sat at the kitchen table and composed a note.

Mr. Edward Green
Martin's Hotel
May 2, 1886

Dear Mr. Green,

I enjoyed our brief meeting yesterday. I think you would benefit from seeing the destruction caused by the Railroad's carelessness. Unfortunately, I am teaching this week. You and I could visit Uncle William's property together Saturday next.

I look forward to a favorable reply.
Mary Carter

She asked Alice, who by now knew the village quite well, to drop the note at the Hotel on Monday morning.

———•———

Edward had left to visit the Smead Company's headquarters in the village by the time Alice delivered the note. He arranged to go to Axton Landing with Charles on Tuesday to survey the damage to Smead's property in the forest fire. On returning to the Hotel, Edward read Mary's note carefully. It contained no hint that Mary had agreed to sell. Was the invitation simply to play on his conscience by showing him the desolation? If so, it meant that Mary thought he had a conscience. Maybe she truly was undecided and wanted to discuss it with him. On Saturday, he had been at pains to separate himself from the policies of Smead and the Railroad. If she trusted him, he might be able to get the information that Smead and the Lumber Association chairman wanted.

On the way out to Axton Landing on Tuesday, Edward told Charles of his contacts with Mary. "Of course you'll agree to see her next Saturday, won't you?" Edward nodded. "I'm sure you'll do your best to find out whether Mary knew that Cyrus plotted her lover's death."

"I wouldn't put it quite that way, Charles, but I'll try to find out whether Mary knew that Cyrus was responsible for Jean's being in the boat."

"Why don't you arrange a lunch with her at the foot of the Indian Carry, the south end of Upper Saranac Lake. It's a beautiful spot."

Edward sent a note to Mary that he would be delighted to visit Corey's property Saturday next and proposed to call for her at ten o'clock in a trap he would rent. Thinking that the trip and survey of Corey's property would take several hours, Lisa offered to prepare a picnic lunch for her mother and Mr. Green.

Although Mary tried not to show her nervousness as Saturday approached, Lisa noticed she was distracted. Lisa attributed it to the financial stakes of her impending meeting. Mary reassured herself that her seeing Edward Green again was only to show him Corey's property and to hear more about the companies' offer to buy it. That was not enough to make her nervous, she knew. Finally, she had to admit that Edward Green's resemblance to her first love made her jittery. Mary had come to love Cyrus dearly but the pleasant memories of her days and night with Jean, aroused by Edward Green's arrival, disturbed her conscience. She was determined to act with propriety on her visit with Edward to Corey's, where she and Jean had courted, but she trembled that she would not succeed. She told herself that beauty was not skin deep, that Edward Green was a potential enemy, and that she was being foolish, but still…

When Edward arrived, promptly at ten on Saturday, Lisa was stunned at how handsome he was. Her mother had not mentioned this to her, although she often commented to her daughter on people's physical attributes.

They sat side-by-side on the trap that Edward had hired at the livery, Mary holding the picnic basket on her lap. With the clatter of the wheels on the dirt road neither of them spoke very much. Mary pointed to the left when they were parallel to the eastern boundary of Corey's property. A few moments later she shouted above the din, "Pull in here," as they reached the remains of the inn. Holding the handles of the picnic basket in one hand she jumped from the trap before Edward could come around to help her.

"You're quite agile, I see."

"Remember, Mr. Green, I'm not as old as you expected. Besides, living up here one learns not to rely on others." She led Edward to the ruins of the inn. All that was left was the stone fireplace and fragments of the chimney. The stove had been hauled away. Already weeds and wild flowers were sprouting. The ashes had scattered or settled into the ground. Edward produced a small pad and pencil from his pocket and jotted some notes as he asked Mary questions about the inn: how many guest rooms; how many people could be served; the source of water; how many outhouses and so on.

Green asked, "Would you mind showing me where the four corners of the inn were situated so I can estimate its size?"

She looked at the fireplace and hesitantly walked to where she thought each of the corners had been. "It's difficult when there are no walls to give guidance." She led him around slowly, describing what had lain inside the walls that once stood. "This was the dining room." Her mind wandered back to the New Year's Eve fight there, started by Sean O'Rourke and Jean's retaliation in her defense. When they came to the far western side, Mary stopped. "It's complicated here. My uncle built a school room for me and a cabin, both attached to the inn." Mary silently recalled the time that Cyrus and Jean entered the schoolroom through the door from the inn, coming to the front of her desk, then turning to respond to the children's questions.

"There were also four cabins," Mary told him as they walked past the school, "each about the size of the school room."

"Look, Mrs. Carter, if your uncle had insured his property, we would have paid his estate the value of all those buildings. But I daresay that whoever comes into possession of this property is not going to be interested in replacing them."

"Why not? This is a perfect site for an inn: midway between Saranac and Tupper Lakes, close to the Raquette River. For the next one hundred years this land won't be worth much to Smead for lumbering, but it is worth a pretty penny for an inn or for a town to house lumberjacks working south of the river. I've read that company towns for workers and their families are springing up around the country."

Edward smiled. "You make a good point." Mary's astute observation made sense. More importantly, he might be able to advance his cause by agreeing with her.

"What about the value of Uncle's land surrounding the buildings?" Mary asked.

"I've checked the Harrietstown records. There is a proper deed in the name of Corey, but I'll have to arrange a survey. I'd guess he owned about one thousand acres. An offer of ten thousand dollars comes to ten dollars an acre, higher than you could get on the market, especially considering it's all burned over, except for the one forest tract in the northwest corner. Do I have your permission to arrange the survey?"

"Certainly, and I'd like a formal offer from Smead and the Railroad," Mary replied. Even if she decided not to accept the offer, an estimate of the property's worth would be useful if she decided to put the property on the market after Uncle William's will was probated.

Mary became pensive as they walked some more. The memories evoked by Edward Green's resemblance to Jean and by the tour around her uncle's inn, cabins, and the school made her feel guilty for even considering their sale. She looked at Edward. *Could she tell him this?* His hand-some face and serious demeanor almost persuaded her that he would be sympathetic, that he could cast aside his duty to his company and its clients. Still, what kind of a man would allow himself to be dragged into that kind of deceitful work?

The sun had passed its zenith when they returned to the trap, where Mary had left the picnic basket. "I've heard that the view up Upper Saranac Lake from the foot of Indian Carry is gorgeous," Mr. Green announced. "Is it far from here?"

"It's one of my favorite spots," Mary replied. "We can take the trap partway and walk the rest. The beach would be a lovely spot for our lunch. That reminds me, Mr. Green, did you enjoy the sunset from Martin's?"

"Spectacular," he answered as he helped Mary up to her seat. She did not resist. They parked the trap when the path became too narrow. Edward removed the traces and tethered the horse with a long rope so it could chew the stubble. Mary had taken the picnic basket and was walking toward the lake.

Walking briskly, Edward caught up to her and took the basket, admiring the fine wickerwork. He was surprised at its weight.

They emerged on Upper Saranac Lake, shimmering in the early afternoon sunlight. "Upper Saranac Lake is the source of the Saranac River and to my mind the most beautiful lake in the world," Mary told him.

After the business of the morning and the gloom of the forest through which they had walked, the shimmering waters stretching to the horizon were a welcome sight. Edward stood at Mary's side. "I can see why you feel that way." Mary stood for a few minutes, admiring the view. Shaking her reverie, she took the basket from Edward, set it on the ground, withdrew a large red and white-checkered tablecloth, and spread it before them. Mary continued to unload the basket. She withdrew a carving knife and cut slices of home-baked ham and bread on a small cutting board. She opened a jar of pickles preserved over the winter. The aroma of dill and vinegar filled the air. Finally, she removed two battered tin cups and chipped porcelain plates. While she arranged the food, Edward wandered around the sandy beach. Looking across the lake, he noticed two birds about one hundred yards out. Suddenly one disappeared, followed by the other. They reemerged nearer to the shore. He could make out the duck-shape of their black heads. They dived again. While they were submerged, Edward picked up some flat stones, no bigger than pebbles, and skimmed one across the water. It bounced several times before sinking. The birds surfaced again while Edward continued to skim rocks. Suddenly a quivering wail pierced the air.

Mary raised her head. "Loons! The first I've seen this spring. I'm afraid our presence is bothering them. Your rock-throwing probably doesn't help," she reprimanded. "If you look carefully you'll see the white dapples of their plumage."

Edward dropped the few remaining pebbles he held and sat next to Mary. "You've prepared quite a picnic. I'm famished."

They ate facing the lake. From under his jacket Edward produced a leather flask.

"You needn't have brought water, Mr. Green."

"It's wine, Mary, not water."

"Wine in the middle of the day? I'm afraid it will dull my wits."

"It will have to be very powerful to do that." He offered her the flask.

"Until I have some food in my stomach, I prefer water." She took off her shoes and stockings and raising her skirt to her knees with one hand, she waded a few feet out where she scooped water into the two tin cups in her other hand and returned. She set the cups in front of them.

"Is the water safe?"

Mary laughed. "I've been drinking it for years." Suddenly, she looked up, peering into the forest beyond the beach. "What was that?" She and Edward listened but neither heard anything. "I thought I heard a branch snap."

Sitting on the shore, alongside each other, they started to eat. "Is the lake inhabited—I mean with people, not animals?" Edward asked.

"There are a few cabins on both shores and at the top of the lake. A friend of ours, Jared Mason, built a cabin about ten years ago," she pointed up the eastern shore, "while he was recuperating from tuberculosis. He came up from New York City where he was a public health officer. The air here revived him."

"A doctor?" Mary nodded. "Does he still live here?"

"He married a young woman from Tupper Lake, Eleanor Weinberg, the daughter of a doctor, who also wanted to become a doctor. They left here for New York City where she went to medical school. They returned a couple of years ago when his tuberculosis flared up. They live in Tupper Lake but the cabin on the lake is their summer hide-a-way; two doctors can't be this isolated from their patients most of the time."

"'Weinberg'? Is she Jewish? I can't imagine going to a Jewish doctor, certainly not a woman." His mouth puckered as he bit into one of Mary's pickles.

Mary winced. She hadn't expected Edward Green to express such prejudices. "What difference should religion make when it comes to practicing medicine? Eleanor's father probably saved Cyrus's broken leg and he gave me very good advice when I was pregnant for the first time." She took a bite of bread and ham. "And why should it be any worse for a man to be seen by a woman doctor than for a woman to be seen by a man doctor? Maybe someday women will have a choice, but now we hardly ever do."

Ignoring Mary's remark, Edward finished his water and poured some wine into his cup. "When did Cyrus break his leg?"

"A long time ago, when he was a lumberjack."

"What happened?"

"He was trying to rescue, uhh, someone." The food stuck in her throat. She drained her cup of water. Without Mary's asking, Edward poured wine into her cup. He realized he had stumbled into what he was hoping to find, but that it was painful for Mary to remember. Having finished eating, Edward lay on his back, gazing at the azure sky.

Mary looked over the lake. *Should she continue? What was the point?* Searching for an answer, she undid her neatly tied bun, her auburn hair spilling to her waist. Her companion looked at her admiringly. Quickly, she gathered her hair and retied the bun. She turned to Edward uncertainly as he looked at her intently. Taking a sip of wine, she continued. "The other day, when you came to my home, I said you reminded me of someone." She searched his dark eyes. "It was Jean who Cyrus tried to rescue. I was supposed to marry him."

Edward sat up, resisting the impulse to take her hands. Yet he wanted to appear consoling, not probing. "Do you want to tell me what happened?"

"I don't mind. I've told the story before. "There was a massive logjam near Axton Landing, upstream on the Raquette from my uncle's property. The jobber, Ben Anderson, ordered Cyrus to take three men in his boat to the front of the jam, open up the boom, so the logs could flow out. They opened up the boom but the logs didn't move until a terrible storm came up that broke the jam. As Jean tried to row the boat away from the logs Cyrus fell overboard. Jean jumped in to try and rescue him. He never would have done that if he had more experience; he had never been in a jam before. A log hit him in the head, knocking him unconscious." She had repeated the story in a monotone, as if she had memorized it. "Some loggers found his body a few days later.

"Cyrus was able to avoid the logs. He kept his face upstream and was able to swim out of their way. But when he reached the boat and turned his head to grab on to the side a log rammed his leg into the boat, breaking the bone beneath his knee."

"How terrible," Edward sympathized. "Have some more wine." Mary held out her cup. "How come Jean was in the boat?"

"What do you mean?"

"It seems like an awfully dangerous job for someone with no experience."

Mary had wondered about this before. "You're right. I blame it on the incompetence of Ben Anderson, maybe even maliciousness; he was not fond of the French Canadians. It was on his order that Jean was in the boat."

Mary lay back and closed her eyes. Edward Green was on his feet, putting the cups and plates back in the basket, folding up the checkered table cloth. Opening her eyes, Mary sensed a change in Mr. Green. Although she didn't understand what accounted for it, she vaguely felt she had been violated.

They said little until they reached the Carter home. As she alighted Mary asked, "Will you let me know the results of the survey?"

"Of course."

"And if you care to submit a formal offer for the purchase of uncle's property, I'll consider it."

Edward handed her the picnic basket, considerably lighter now. "Thank you for a very lovely day, Mrs. Carter." Mary walked quickly up the path to the door.

———•———

Hearing the front door close, Tommy wheeled himself out of his room. Mary set the wicker basket on the kitchen table. Alice was helping Lisa prepare supper. They all looked at Mary expectantly. "Your face is flushed," Alice noted.

"It must have been the sun."

Tommy jotted a note and put it on the table: *He didn't try to seduce you, did he?*

They all laughed. Mary raised her right hand to the nape of her neck. "Not that I noticed," she demurred.

"What did you do, mama?"

"We walked around Uncle William's property. Mr. Green paced off the inn and said he'd arrange a survey of the entire property." Mary stopped for a moment. "Oh yes, he had checked the deed in the Harrietstown records. He said it was proper and in the Corey name, but he needed the survey to calculate the number of acres. He estimated one thousand. He told me last Saturday that Smead might offer ten dollars an acre, although that was above the market price."

Lisa announced, "Supper will be ready in five minutes. Everyone wash up and we can continue this at the table."

They ate silently for a few minutes. Then Lisa asked, "Where did you picnic?"

"He wanted to go down the Carry to Upper Saranac Lake." That's where we ate lunch.

"Did he like the ham I baked?" Lisa continued.

"It was delicious. We finished it! He must have liked it. The pickles, too."

"What did you talk about?" Lisa asked.

I told him that Jared had built a cabin up the lake and that got us talking about Eleanor and the Weinbergs. He said he couldn't see going to a Jewish, woman doctor."

*I'm sure you told him what you thought.*

"I certainly did." They all laughed but the rest of the meal was eaten in silence.

Before she went to bed that night, Mary wrote Cyrus of the day's events. She did not mention that Edward Green reminded her of Jean, but she told him they had picnicked on the shore of Upper Saranac Lake and that he was interested in how Cyrus broke his leg. The main reason she wrote was to tell her husband of the offer from Smead and the Adirondack Railroad in return for dropping the lawsuit. "Oh, Cyrus, I can't wait for your return so we can discuss this. I don't know what to do."

———•———

On the following Monday, Green arranged for a survey of the Corey property and then went to Smead headquarters where he asked to see Charles Smead. Charles greeted him warmly. "Ah, Edward, Saturday was lovely weather for a tryst, wasn't it?"

"Tryst? It was purely a business meeting."

"A picnic on the shore of Upper Saranac seems very romantic."

"You suggested it, as I recall."

Charles returned to his desk, took a seat in his high-backed swivel chair and beckoned to Edward to take a seat in front of the desk. He pulled out his key chain, found the right key, and opened the central desk drawer. He slid a five-by-seven inch daguerreotype across to Edward.

"My god! You had us followed." Edward flushed. He looked carefully at the fuzzy picture. In black and white, the glory of the lake and sky were muted. In the foreground, Edward lay on his back. Mary, her hair loosened, was looking at him over her left shoulder. He was lying very close to her.

Charles pulled out another print. This one showed Mary holding her skirts above her knees and smiling at Edward, as she emerged barefoot from the lake. Suddenly Edward recalled that was the moment when Mary thought she heard a branch snap. Angrily, he asked Smead, "What do you intend to do with these? Do you have the original plates?"

Charles retrieved the prints, put them back in the drawer, and locked it. "Have no fear, Edward. They are not to be used to blackmail you if, by chance, you have a relationship with another woman. I doubt such a person will ever see them. However, they may come in handy to defeat Cyrus Carter's bid for reelection. That depends on what you learned from Mary. My agent dared not come close enough to hear what the two of you discussed. If they turn out to be of no use, I will destroy them and the plates."

Edward had underestimated how sordid his mission would become. He had a pang of regret for Mary, and for Cyrus too, but proceeded to tell Charles of his conversation with Mary.

"So, Mary was not aware that Cyrus ordered Jean into his boat?"

"No, she wasn't," Edward replied. "What will you do now?"

"Well, I think we'll see if Cyrus wants his wife to know what he did. Maybe he'll decide not to file for re-election."

"Will you tell him how you found out?"

"I don't think that will be necessary."

"What if he doesn't pull out?"

"Well, then." He patted his desk above the central drawer. "We'll try to make him look like he's been cuckolded. That will lose him a few votes around here. A real man doesn't tolerate his wife's fooling around. It will also show men what this suffragist activity leads to. They won't stand for it."

"You mean you'll use the pictures."

"Only if it becomes necessary. His Republican opponent will make the accusation that Cyrus's wife was seen dallying on the shores of Upper Saranac; that will be easy enough for us to arrange. If Mary denies it, he can wave the photographs around, but still not show them." Charles stood, signaling their meeting was over.

Edward realized at once what Smead wanted from his visit to Saranac Lake. "I don't suppose you're much interested," he said sarcastically, "but Mrs. Carter has not turned down the companies' offer. She agreed to the survey of the Corey property and asked that I submit a formal offer from you and the railroad. I wanted to discuss that with you this morning."

"There's nothing to discuss. Let me know when you've got the results of the survey. The formal offer should come from Mr. Durant and me." He stopped to shake Edward's hand. "You've performed invaluable service, Mr. Green. You will be amply rewarded."

"Thank you, Sir," Edward Green said meekly and then left.

# 5

# The 1886 Election

TOBIAS Brown, whom Cyrus had humiliated in his bid to become a Harrietstown Councilman in 1874, was chosen by the Republican Party of Franklin County to oppose Cyrus Carter in the 1886 elections for State Assemblyman. Brown owned a profitable hardware store in Saranac Lake Village but he did not have to dip into his personal savings for the campaign. Smead and other lumber companies in the county saw to that. They were particularly happy that a popular citizen from the Village would neutralize Carter's hometown advantage, but from the start of the campaign, Cyrus drew bigger crowds than Brown.

In September, Charles Smead arranged for a sequence of anonymous letters to be mailed to Cyrus. The first simply read, "Do you want this election to destroy your family? Withdraw!" Cyrus had received crank notes before and did not pay much attention. When he received the second a few days later, written in the same hand, he began to worry. Cryptically, it said, "Your secret will be disclosed if you don't withdraw." *What secret do I have?* The next day he left for a swing through the County all the way up to Malone. When he returned a third letter was waiting. He tore open the familiar envelope and removed the same type of paper, neatly folded, as had been the others. In the same hand it said, "Does Mary know?" This time he blanched. His hands turned cold. He recalled the letter Mary sent him as the legislative session was winding down. She had written that the man from the insurance company—Cyrus couldn't recall his name—had asked how Cyrus had broken his leg. *Should I ask Mary what she told him?* All these years, Cyrus's conscience had been nagged by his never having told Mary that he, Cyrus, was responsible for Jean being in the boat, not Anderson. *If I tell her now, what will Mary think? That I was jealous of Jean?* Cyrus thought their marriage was solid, that Mary loved him almost as much as he loved her, but he hesitated to act.

When he was not campaigning elsewhere, Cyrus sorted the mail before Mary returned from the schoolhouse. On the first Tuesday in October, the mail contained a letter addressed to Mary in the same hand as the previous letters addressed to him. The envelope was also the same as the previous ones. He carried the envelope to his desk in the parlor, placed it face up, sat down, and stared at it without touching for a minute. Finally, he turned the envelope over. With his penknife he slit it open and unfolded the single sheet of paper. "Your husband has not played fair with you." Cyrus went to the fireplace, lit a match and burned the envelope and the paper.

He knew that he could not be present to intercept the mail every day. He also wondered if the message, although addressed to Mary, was really meant for him.

At dinner that night, Lisa commented, "You seem very quiet tonight, Papa."

"The campaign is wearing him down," Mary replied. "You're already sixty, Cyrus. Not exactly a spring chicken." Lisa laughed and Tommy smiled. Alice kept discreetly quiet.

"I guess I'm not," Cyrus said, suddenly feeling his age.

On Friday, another letter addressed to Cyrus arrived. "If you don't announce your withdrawal by Monday, Mary will be told."

As soon as Alice left for work that Saturday, Cyrus gathered his family around the kitchen table. Tommy wrote out a note: *You're not going to ask Alice to leave, are you?*

"No, that never occurred to me." Tommy grinned with relief.

Cyrus ran his hand through his still-thick white hair, reluctant to begin. Finally, "Do you remember that insurance man who said that Smead wanted to buy your uncle's property?"

"Edward Green, yes, of course, I remember him, "Mary said. "He was going to have it surveyed and then Smead and the Railroad would make me an offer."

"I don't recall your having received an offer."

"No, I haven't," Mary replied.

Cyrus was pensive. "I think your Mr. Green—"

"He's not my Mr. Green." Mary was offended.

"No. Of course not. I think Mr. Green was after something else. You told me he was very interested in—" he hesitated, "in how I broke my leg."

"Yes. I told him the whole story, of how Ben Anderson ordered Jean into your boat and—"

"That's enough," Cyrus said irritably. There was silence around the table.

Finally, Cyrus said, "I think Mr. Green was collecting evidence to blackmail me."

None of them expected that. "Cyrus, what are you talking about?" Mary asked incredulously. Cyrus went to his desk in the parlor and returned with the anonymous letters, which he had not destroyed, arranged in chronological order. He passed them one at a time to Mary who read them and passed them to Tommy and he to Lisa.

When they finished reading, more puzzled than ever, Cyrus turned fully to Mary. His face was ashen above his beard. He took Mary's hands. "Ben Anderson did not order Jean into my boat. Jean was in the boat because I trusted him more than Sean O'Rourke, the man Anderson chose. Anderson agreed with my request that Jean take Sean's place."

Mary gasped, released Cyrus's hands, and raised one hand to her mouth. "Oh my god! If you hadn't—"

"Yes, I know. Jean might be alive today and would probably be your husband." No one spoke.

Tommy reached for his pad and pencil and wrote hurriedly: *And neither Lisa nor I would be here. That would be terrible.* He shoved the pad around so all the others could see. That broke the tension.

Crying, Mary got up, hugged Tommy and then Lisa. "You're right. I can't bear the thought of not having you and Lisa." Cyrus also arose. Mary let go of Lisa, grabbed him by the arm and turned him toward her. Hugging him tightly, she kissed him on the lips. "Cyrus, I wouldn't trade this family for anything—or anyone." She hesitated, "But why didn't you tell me before now?"

Cyrus nodded. "Guilt, I suppose." He paused. "I have no other excuse. I am sorry."

———•———

The Town Council held a picnic that Sunday afternoon and had invited both candidates for the Assembly to speak. As had happened twelve years earlier when they first faced each other, Tobias Brown spoke first. This time he made no personal accusations. He launched into an attack on the "forever wild" law, saying it would impoverish the county. "Lumber is our most important industry. Wealthy downstaters are buying up choice forest that the state has not yet sunk its claws into. They want this land for their own preserves. There won't be many jobs in that." He turned to Cyrus. "My worthy opponent here," he said sneeringly, "supported 'forever wild.'" He turned back to face the audience. "Surely you can do better this time." Surprisingly, he didn't get much applause. There weren't many laborers present; they could not afford houses in the village. Although some of the residents—shopkeepers—profited from the lumber companies, more of them were concerned about the woods. They were beginning to make as much money from tourists and patients coming to the Trudeau Sanitarium as from the lumber companies. If the woods were destroyed, both would falter.

Cyrus stood and faced the crowd. Patiently he explained why he supported the "forever wild" bill. He paused before changing the subject. "The lumber companies want to see me defeated." He reached into his pocket and pulled out the anonymous letters he had received. He waved them. "I don't know who sent these letters." He turned to Tobias Brown. "I'm quite certain Mr. Brown didn't. He is too honorable for that," he added with a sardonic flair. "These letters, ladies and gentlemen—and I will be pleased to pass them around—contain a threat to blackmail me if I don't withdraw." He opened the last one and read it aloud. "'If you don't announce your withdrawal by Monday, Mary will be told.'" The crowd murmured. "The letter was referring to an incident that happened almost thirty years ago in which a good friend of Mary's and mine was killed breaking a log-jam." He paused and looked at the crowd. They realized the gravity of the threat. "Ladies and gentlemen, Mary has been told." He paused. "By me!" The crowd seemed to sigh with relief. He was not quite finished. "I am not going to with-draw." He sat down. The applause started slowly and then became thunderous.

---

Smead's agents were present at the picnic. Charles knew before the day was out. He got word to Tobias Brown that he wanted to see him. Tobias was shown into Charles's office promptly at nine on Monday morning, October 1lth. "You want to win this race, don't you Tobias?"

"I wouldn't be running if I didn't. I'd like to settle an old score with Carter. He beat me for town councilman in 1874."

"Are you prepared to go to any length?"

Tobias had suspected that Smead was behind the blackmail attempt that Cyrus alleged. Charles's question confirmed that it was not beneath him. He must have some-thing else in mind, Tobias thought. Vaguely, he nodded.

Charles pulled out his keychain and opened his desk drawer. He took out two photographs, turned them to face Tobias and slid them across the desk. Tobias peered at them.

"I can't quite make out the woman. She looks familiar."

"It's Mary Carter."

"Are you sure?" Charles nodded. Tobias looked some more. "Who's the man? It's not Cyrus Carter, is it?"

"No. This man is clean-shaven and much younger."

Tobias sat back. "You're not suggesting…"

"The pictures speak for themselves, don't you think?"

"Surely there must be another explanation. That's not like Mary Carter."

"It's not? The whole town knows she had a bastard son before Cyrus married her. The whole town knows she's a suffragist. One of those uppity women. What more proof do you need?"

Tobias knew all this. He also knew that he and the other parents trusted their children to Mary's tutelage. He looked from the pictures to Charles. He was smirking. "I don't see what I can do," Tobias said.

Charles opened a side drawer and took out a large envelope. He inserted the pictures in it, licked the envelope shut and handed it to Tobias Brown. "Don't let these photographs out of your hands, but if they happen to uh, get lost, I have the plates." He stood, ushering Tobias out.

Tobias remembered 1874 very well. He had not carefully researched the exact location of the Carter residence and Carter had ridiculed and humiliated him as a result. He was glad that Smead had not told him of the attempt to blackmail Cyrus. If he had, Tobias might again have used the information and again been humiliated. He rode back into town and went straight to the Carter house.

Cyrus answered the door. "Tobias Brown. What a surprise!"

Tobias did not smile. "I have something important to discuss with you. Is Mary home?"

"No. She's teaching." He showed Tobias into the parlor. They sat facing each other. Cyrus noticed the envelope.

"You know, Cyrus, I want to win this election."

"So do I."

"You also know that I had nothing to do with the attempt to blackmail you." Cyrus nodded. Tobias raised the envelope. "Do you have a letter opener?" Cyrus handed Tobias his penknife. Carefully he slit the envelope open. He rose, "Perhaps we should go to where the light is better." Cyrus led Tobias to the kitchen. Carefully Tobias laid the photos on the table. Cyrus looked down at them. He put his bifocals on and looked again. He knew instantly when they must have been taken.

Facing Tobias, he asked, "You got these from Smead, didn't you?"

"How did you know?"

Cyrus was angry. "The company will stop at nothing to see me defeated. They used this man"—he pointed to the man in one of the photos—"to trick my wife. Smead must have had a photographer follow them."

Tobias resumed his seat. Cyrus paced around the room. After a few moments he calmed down and slumped into a kitchen chair. "What are you going to do with these photos, Tobias?"

"Before I do anything, Cyrus, I came here to see if you— or your wife—could explain the pictures."

"Indeed I can. This man—" he pointed again to the picture with Edward lying on his back—"is an insurance agent representing the Smead Lumber Company. He was here ostensibly to reach a settlement with Mary so she would drop her lawsuit against Smead and the Adirondack Railroad for the fire that killed her uncle, William Corey, and destroyed most of his property. "He was also here to see if he could compromise Mary one way or the other and force me out of my campaign for reelection. " He looked at the pictures again. Now he was angry with Mary. How could she have been so foolish? "If the two of them had gone any further, I'm sure there'd be a picture." He sat silently for a moment. "What are you going to do, Tobias?"

Tobias held out his hand for the pictures. Cyrus passed them over. Tobias put one on top of the other and tore them up first one way and then the other. He handed the pieces back to Cyrus. "You can dispose of them." He got up to leave. "Cyrus, if I had done what Smead wanted of me, you would have got the better of me again. I thought there must be an explanation. If this comes out—Smead says he has the plates—you'll be sure I had nothing to do with it. You'd get the better of me again. Good day."

———•———

After supper that evening, Mary and Cyrus were alone at the kitchen table, Mary preparing her lessons for the next day and Cyrus making notes for a speech. The kerosene lamp at the center of the table cast their shadows on the wall. Cyrus had fought off saying anything until Lisa and Tommy had gone to bed. "Tobias Brown dropped by this morning," he said as evenly as possible.

Mary put her pencil down. "Really. What a surprise."

"That's what I said." He looked at Mary. "He had two photographs of you with that insurance man."

"Edward Green."

"Yes. Why can't I remember his name?" Cyrus chided himself.

"Photographs? That can't be."

Cyrus got up, unable to contain himself any longer.

"Charles Smead arranged the whole thing. He had some-one follow you down the Indian Carry who then hid in the forest. He took a photograph of you wading, holding your skirt above your knees, and another of you looking down at a supine Mr., uhh, Green."

Mary was speechless. Her heart was pounding. She could feel the blood rushing in her ears. Above it all she heard Cyrus.

"Why couldn't you be more discreet? Why did you have to go down to the lake for your picnic? Do you have an attraction to the man?"

"Discreet? It was his idea to go down to the lake. I can't believe he knew Smead had hidden a photographer there. It's all, it's all too, too demeaning. I did nothing wrong, Cyrus," she argued. Cyrus turned his back and walked into the parlor. Mary tried to resume preparing her lessons, but she quickly threw her pencil down and gave up. *I did do something wrong,* Mary admitted to herself. *Just because he reminded me of Jean was no reason to tell him what I did. Cyrus would never understand—and I'm not sure I know why I did it either. Looks are deceiving.*

She and Cyrus said little to each other over the next few days. Lisa, Tommy and Alice attributed their rift to the strain of the campaign. Cyrus had not told Mary that Tobias had torn up the photos, and she wondered whether rumors were abroad about them; she would be the last to know. If they got out, Cyrus would lose the election, branded as a cuckold, and she an adulteress.

———•———

October ended. Charles Smead waited for Tobias Brown to make known the character of Cyrus's wife, but he did not mention the 'evidence' in his speeches. The implications of the photographs needed time to spread through the county, Smead knew. Smead considered having his own men release the photographs, but he needed another set of prints and he did not have time to get them from the photographer who took the pictures who he brought in from Elizabethtown; no photographer closer was trustworthy. Nor did Smead want to arouse suspicion by going to see Brown or having Brown come to his office again. Election day came and Tobias remained silent. Smead was infuriated, but it was too late for him to do anything.

———•———

Mary accompanied Cyrus to the Town Hall to witness the vote counting. When it became evident that Cyrus had won overwhelmingly in Harrietstown and Santa Clara and the nearby townships, she smiled broadly and took his hand as people gathered round to congratulate him. When he had some breathing space he turned to her. "We have to talk, don't we?"

She gripped his hand even more tightly as her eyes teared. "Yes," she whispered. His victory was clinched when a telegram arrived from the Democratic Party in Malone; he had won there, too.

In the darkness they walked home arm-in-arm. Almost simultaneously, each apologized. "I was foolish to show Mr. Green uncle's property. Remember, I wrote you after my first meeting with him that I didn't know what to do. My first reaction, and Tommy reinforced it, was to refuse the offer, but it did have its bright side."

"The settlement would have made our lives easier, but you're right, Mary dear: we'd always regret that the lumber and railroad companies had got the better of us." Unseemly for an aging couple, they stopped on the street to hug and kiss. "I want as little to do with Smead as possible," Cyrus said as they resumed their walk.

"As soon as Uncle's will is probated, I will put the property on the market, but I won't accept an offer from Smead."

"If we withdraw the suit, they're not likely to want the property."

Mary repeated what she had told Cyrus the previous spring, but with a flourish. "Now that you're so well-known, we'll be having more visitors. I'll use the money from the sale to add on to our house."

Cyrus agreed, but added, "Maybe you'll have some left over for the suffrage movement."

They reached home and found Peter O'Rourke, Jr. there with Lisa, as well as Tommy and Alice. They looked at Cyrus and Mary anxiously. Mary exclaimed, "Cyrus won!" When the excitement simmered down, Lisa banged her hand on the kitchen table a few times. "I have another announcement." They turned to her expectantly. "Peter and I are going to get married. We've waited long enough what with Uncle William's death and then the death of Peter's grandfather."

The excitement returned. Although she wasn't surprised, Mary beamed and hugged Lisa and then Peter. Lisa bent over Tommy's wheelchair so he could hug her. "It's too bad John's not here." Then Tommy shook Peter's hand. He wrote, *If it weren't for you I wouldn't be here to celebrate.* Peter bent over and hugged him.

Cyrus never expected that his youngest child, albeit his only daughter, would be the first to marry. Now he just hoped that Tommy would remain healthy despite his paraplegia and that John would not fall victim to violence and would eventually return to Saranac Lake.

"We'd like to have a Christmas wedding," Lisa continued.

"Where will you live?" Cyrus asked.

"We'll move in with Peter's mother until we can build our own house. There's a lot on Helen Street near Pine that's for sale. Between Peter's salary and mine we probably can get a mortgage on the property."

"When I sell Uncle William's property, I'll be able to help you," Mary said.

Mary and Cyrus slept with their arms around each other that night for the first time since Tobias Brown's visit.

<hr />

William Corey's will cleared probate shortly after the election. Mary arranged for "For Sale" signs to go up on the property and advertised in the local newspapers. Smead offered her five dollars an acre for the northwest corner of the property that had escaped the fire and had first growth conifers and mixed hardwoods. She and Cyrus took their sleigh out there one bright early winter day to have a look at it. According to the plat, it ran from the bank of the Raquette north to the road between Saranac and Tupper Lakes. The temperature had risen above freezing and the heavy wet snow caused the pine boughs to droop downward, dripping water off their branches. The couple left their trap on the road and sloshed southward through the snow on the western edge of the forest.

"No wonder Smead wants to get its hands on this," Cyrus said. "Virgin white pines and spruce. Plenty of birch, maple, and beech too. They'd make a fortune on lumber and pulp wood for paper here. That explains their generous offer."

Cyrus was stomping ahead of Mary. She bent to pick up some snow, compacted it into a ball and threw it at Cyrus. "If you think I'm going to sell to Smead, you've got another guess coming, Mr. Carter." She lobbed another snowball at him. This one he caught, tossing it back to her. She easily deflected it. For a few minutes the aging couple cavorted in the snow like children, throwing snowballs playfully at each other. "Seriously, Cyrus," Mary said when they started to walk back to the sleigh, "it would be a crime for any company to raze this forest. I'd sell it to the state to add it to the Forest Preserve."

"You'll only get a dollar an acre," Cyrus replied. They walked on silently for a few moments. Then Cyrus added, "But its unspoiled beauty is worth a lot more to us, isn't it?" Mary did not answer but caught up to Cyrus, who had stopped walking, and kissed him on the lips.

Soon after, Mary contacted an agent of the Forest Commission to have the forest surveyed. It came to three hundred and twenty acres for which she received three hundred and twenty dollars. The State of New York obtained the funds by the sale of land outside the preserve in order to purchase land in it. Thus, Mary and Cyrus believed that this parcel of land once the property of William Corey was to remain forever wild, as he would have wanted.

Mary had several private offers for the remainder of the land, including the site of Corey's inn. She sold it for two thousand dollars to a young couple from Syracuse who wanted to rebuild the inn. She was thrilled when they asked if they could name the inn for her uncle. The couple sold surrounding two-acre parcels on which homesteads could be built. They used the proceeds to rebuild Corey's Inn. In a few years, a small village, with its own post office, also called Corey's, was established just south of the inn.

Mary gave part of the proceeds to Lisa and Peter. She planned to use most of the rest to add on to the Carter house on Helen Street, enlarging the parlor, adding a dining room, a second floor with a bedroom for Alice, and another for John when he returned. She wanted to add another bedroom and an attic to insulate from the winter cold and summer heat as well as for storage. But instead she gave the remainder to the National American Woman Suffrage Association.

# PART II

# 6

# Life Death Life Death

J ARED and Eleanor Mason returned to the Adirondacks in 1884, Jared once again weakened by tuberculosis. This time Jared would stay. They moved into Eleanor's old room in the Weinberg house. Pregnant for the first time, Eleanor expected to take over her father's medical practice when her baby was old enough. Freda was looking forward to helping raise her grandchild, Ruben, who was born in August. Henry was in attendance and cut and tied the umbilical cord, bathed and swaddled the baby. As he laid Ruben across Eleanor's chest both he and Eleanor noticed that his lips were faintly blue, although he was breathing normally for a newborn, but over the next few weeks, Ruben had spells in which he became intensely blue. He would cry, stop breathing, and begin again with a gasp, his color soon returning to normal. Taking turns listening to the baby's heart with Henry's stethoscope, the doctors agreed he had a heart murmur and concluded inescapably that he had been born with a heart defect and they could do nothing about it. He nursed well until one of his spells started, but gained weight poorly. Ruben died when he was not quite three months old.

Ruben's grave was one of the first in the Jewish cemetery in Tupper Lake. As the village had grown, a small number of Jews had joined the Weinbergs there, most of them setting up small businesses in dry goods, hardware, furniture. Some of them brought their aging parents who did not accommodate well to the harsh winters. Freda had been after Henry to meet with members of the Beth Joseph congregation to establish a cemetery. About the time when Eleanor and Jared returned to Tupper Lake, the congregation purchased, with Henry's help, a one-acre plot located between the Catholic and Protestant cemeteries close to the Raquette River shortly before it flowed into Tupper Lake.

Cyrus and Mary attended the funeral, giving comfort to the bereaved parents and Freda and Henry Weinberg, the grandparents. In the hope of giving Jared some good news, Cyrus pulled him aside and told him that he had heard that at Dickinson Center, north of Tupper Lake on the Raquette, people were concerned about the chemicals that were pouring into the river from the pulp mills. He thought the county might be interested in having a man with Jared's experience investigate, although the mills were an important source of revenue for the county. Jared, whose health had not showed much sign of returning, probably because of the strain of Ruben's sickness, demurred. "Cyrus, I'm too weak to think of it now. I can't walk a few steps without getting short of breath and I still have bouts of coughing."

"Have you been out to your cabin on Upper Saranac?" Cyrus's boys had helped Jared build it in 1875. "The fresh air out there should help."

"I haven't had the strength, but maybe now that Ruben—" he paused, his face crinkled. "Maybe now that Eleanor has more time, she can help get me out there before the lake freezes." He paused for a moment, then took hold of Cyrus's sleeve and pulled him closer so Freda and Henry Weinberg could not hear. "But you know, Cyrus, Freda is not doing well. She loved little Ruben but his illness and death took a toll on her. Eleanor feels we can't live with the Weinbergs without her doing more of the household chores and taking over most of the cooking. She's also started to see some of Henry's patients. He's getting old, too. I need more time to regain my strength, Cyrus, but I hope by the spring I'll be ready to pursue a job." The two men hugged.

While Cyrus and Jared talked, Eleanor expressed her worry to Mary over her husband's slow recovery. "Ruben's death was almost as hard on Jared as on me. I hope now he'll be able to rest more and get his strength back." She glanced at the two men and saw more interest in her husband's eyes than she had seen for a while. "Maybe Cyrus has some good news for Jared, something to make him look forward to." She paused for a moment and then glanced at Mary, who looked almost as young as Eleanor despite being thirteen years older. "Are you still a suffragist, Mary?"

"More than ever! The Wyoming Territory has given women the right to vote and campaigns are close to succeeding in a number of states, mostly out west. The movement really started in New York at Seneca Falls, but we haven't gotten very far in this state. Cyrus is one of the few pro-suffrage voices in the Assembly. Men will not grant us the right to vote unless we unite and demand it."

"I'll be pleased to help any way I can," Eleanor replied. "Now, without the baby, I'll have more time, and I don't mind speaking out about what women have suffered." She paused, thinking about the similarity of *suffer* and *suffrage*. "Getting women the vote is one answer."

Shortly before Cyrus's re-election in 1886, Lisa Carter confided to her mother that she had missed two periods. At first, Mary was annoyed and upset; there was enough going on in her life without this complication, but when she realized that Lisa had known Peter longer and better than she had known Jean when they made love the only time, she softened. She was also grateful that her daughter would not have to wait until after her child was born to find a husband and that the man Lisa loved and married was truly the father. Torn between her daughter's behavior (not too different from her own twenty-eight years earlier) and the prospect of becoming a grandmother, Mary asked, "What do you propose to do about it?"

"Peter and I have talked about it. We'd like to get married before I begin to show, around Christmas or New Years, maybe."

Mary thought about it and concluded that would be reasonable.

Cyrus had found it prudent to join St. Luke's Church in the village when he had first run for office; it had the largest congregation. He and Mary put in a Sunday morning appearance from time to time, and when Reverend Lindy took over from Reverend Jones they made sure to congratulate him. Lisa's wedding took place at the church on the Sunday after Christmas.

As he made clear through numerous notes, Tommy disapproved of his sister's getting married at St. Luke's. He admitted that an outdoor wedding—he had heard the story of his parents' wedding on the knoll at Bartlett's Sportsmen's Club many times—was impractical in winter. After his third note to his sister suggesting she and Peter wait for warmer weather when they could have an outdoor wedding, Lisa got angry, tore up the note, and told him to mind his own business. He began to wonder whether there was some reason she was in a hurry.

As the day approached, Mary asked Alice if she would help Tommy get ready for the wedding, as Mary would be busy helping Lisa. As Alice did not work Sundays, she could not refuse. On the morning of the wedding, she lifted Tommy from his bed without mishap, helped him put on his Sunday best, and then his overcoat. Tommy wheeled himself down the ramp, and then Alice pushed him through the snow-covered paths to the Church. Cyrus, Mary, and Lisa had already left. She wheeled him down the side aisle, placing the wheelchair just outside the first row, and took the aisle seat next to Tommy. When Peter raised Lisa's veil Tommy could not believe how beautiful his sister looked.

———•———

The reception in the ballroom at The Riverside Inn started quietly. Cyrus and Mary, and Peter's mother, Susie, greeted the invited guests, soon joined by Lisa and Peter. Jared and Eleanor were near the front of the line. One look told Cyrus that Jared had not recovered as completely as in 1871. Stooped, face deeply lined and gaunt, hair thin and a dirty gray, skin sallow, jacket fitting loosely, he was hardly recognizable. "I heard that you did such a good job investigating contamination of the pulp mill at Dickinson Center that the county made you Deputy Health Commissioner."

"That's because I didn't find evidence for the claims that the switchover to the sulfite process was killing off fishes or people downstream. The mill and the county were very relieved. Now, I've got more of an office job that's worse than working in the field."

Eleanor came alongside Jared and took his arm. "But it's not as demanding on him physically." She turned to Jared, "Come on, darling, you're holding up the line. You can talk to Cyrus later." They moved on.

The room was still quiet as the waiters circulated with trays of cider, spiked punch, and hors d'oeuvres. Soon the room warmed and the noise level picked up. Alan Phillips, who had been one of Mary's first students at Axton Landing in 1859, and ten years later ran afoul of Reverend Jones in her school in the village, asked Tommy if he ever heard from his brother John. Tommy nodded. Alan tried to keep his questions simple so Tommy would not have to write too much. "Where is he?"

*Chicago.*

"Is he working?"

*McCormick Harvesting Machine.*

"That's where there was a big strike, wasn't it? And then the bombing that killed several people last May."

*Haymarket,* Tommy wrote.

"Is John coming home soon?" Tommy shrugged in response. "Write him that there are going to be plenty of jobs around here." Tommy looked at Alan expectantly. "Paul Smith's bought thousands of acres in Franklin County and is selling off large parcels to millionaires who want to build Great Camps."

*Who is Paul Smith?*

"He has a hotel on Lower St. Regis Lake, north of here."

"What do you mean by 'great camps'?" another man asked.

Tommy started to write his answer. *Durant's plush Camp Pine Knot on Raquette Lake is one.*

"That's what they are," Alan said. "I've heard that J.J. Schuyler, a wealthy banker in New York City, is negotiating with Smith to buy a large plot on the west side of Upper Saranac; it's very close to our family's farm. He intends to build a great lodge to house his family and friends, take them hunting and fishing in his own private woods and lakes. He wants all the comforts he's got in New York City. Schuyler will need men to clear and level the place. He'll need carpenters and stonemasons and ordinary workers to build his mansion and fit it with the most modern conveniences." Alan was an expert furniture maker and hoped that Schuyler would be an avid customer. "I've heard he wants to build a bowling alley; he's got money to burn."

*Not like the rest of us,* Tommy wrote.

The noise built up gradually so that people didn't realize they were shouting, but it quickly subsided when Cyrus led Lisa to the dance floor, soon joined by Peter and Mary and then others. Tommy kept scribbling and showed his new note to Alan. *Where d'ya think that money came from?*

Alan glanced at Tommy's immobile legs. "Off the backs of fellas like you and me." Alan beckoned for a waitress with a tray of cider. He took a swig and wiped his lips on the little napkin she offered. "But look, Tommy, if they want to part with some of their wealth to improve their comfort and contribute to mine at the same time, I'll forgive them their trespasses."

"Forgive them?" asked Jared Mason, who had stepped into the circle of younger men. "You don't see the point, Alan. If we go hat in hand begging for jobs, your Mr. Schuyler will pay just enough to keep us coming to work. You won't get much comfort out of that."

"It's better than starving, don't you think?" Alan looked for his wife across the floor. "I promised my gal I'd give her a dance."

Tommy wrote another note. *If you organized, you'd neither starve nor work like a dog.*

Alan stood up. "Don't talk organizing around here. After what happened to you, Tommy, the men are too scared to say 'boo' to the bosses."

Peter O'Rourke had finished his dance with Mary and was circulating around the floor. He approached as Jared, Tommy, and Alan were having their exchange. Peter had been promoted to Stationmaster at the Axton Landing station, a lonely job since it was merely a stop for the trains that serviced the Smead lumber camp to take on water and wood to generate steam and to load its flat cars with logs. A small lad—Lisa was almost as tall—he was fiercely loyal to Tommy; Tommy had helped get him a job on the railroad and it was Peter who had organized Tommy's rescue after he was forced to jump from the trestle near Axton Landing.

"It only takes one wrong move to get the company's ire," Peter heard Alan say as he started across the floor. "What makes you think times have changed?"

Tommy, who had already had a couple of ciders, startled Peter with his note. *I don't see how you can keep working for the Railroad, Peter.* Peter felt queasy as he tried to formulate a response. "Jobs aren't easy to find around these parts, Tommy. Now I've got two mouths to feed." Another note: *And maybe three soon?* Peter turned red momentarily, then continued. "Besides, I try to make sure there's no repeat of what killed Corey and destroyed his property. I won't let a train through to Tupper Lake unless it's equipped with a spark catcher. The engineers grumble but they know I'm right. They don't want to be responsible for more fires. And the lumber companies, of course, don't want their property to go up in flames." Peter had no illusion that he'd keep his job if he stepped out of line with the company's interests. He excused himself from the conversation, saying, "I've got to make sure everyone here's happy."

By the time Alan brought his wife on to the floor, it was crowded with merrily twirling partners.

———•———

In June, Eleanor and Jared helped celebrate the Carters' wedding anniversary at Bartlett's, the site of their wedding twenty-eight years earlier. Virgil Bartlett had died three years earlier, but Caroline continued to run the hotel. Eleanor was surprised to see that Lisa O'Rourke was pregnant and, to Eleanor's expert eye, close to delivering. Lisa took her aside and told her that the midwife who had seen her a few days earlier said that the baby had not yet turned head down and was worried it might not before Lisa went into labor. At Eleanor's request, Mrs. Bartlett allowed them to use an unoccupied guest room. There, Eleanor examined Lisa, confirming that the head was not down, a breech. She helped Lisa dress and hugged her after she got up. "Of course, I'll help," she said reassuringly.

Eleanor consulted with Henry and Jared about breech presentations, but neither of them had as much experience in managing confinements as Eleanor. She had established a small reputation among expecting mothers in the City as a sympathetic and expert obstetrician, although she did not limit her practice to that specialty. Ever since graduating from medical school Eleanor had anticipated that she would end up practicing in the Adirondacks; she knew she had to master a wide range of skills, including orthopedics and obstetrics, if she was to serve the needs of the local population.

When Lisa went into labor on a warm afternoon in June, Peter ran over to the Carters' house, borrowed their small trap, and took off for Tupper Lake to bring Eleanor back. As soon as he left, Mary gathered a basin and some clean sheets and walked briskly to the small house the young couple had purchased on Helen Street. Peter's mother Susie was holding Lisa's hand as she writhed with contractions, sweat sprinkling her brow. From the pump outside, Mary filled the basin with water, set it on the stove, which she stoked with wood Peter had chopped, and attended her daughter, arranging the clean sheets under her.

It was almost dark by the time Peter arrived at the Weinbergs' house in Tupper Lake. Eleanor answered the door and knew immediately why he was there. She shouted to Henry, Freda, and Jared where she was headed, grabbed her medical bag, and climbed into the trap beside Peter. Twilight lasted long enough to guide them out of the village and on to the road between Tupper and Saranac Lakes. Peter stopped to light kerosene lanterns on either side of the trap but they did little to illuminate the road. It had taken Peter almost two hours to cover the twenty miles between the two villages. Now that it was dark and the horse lathered, he could not expect to be as fast returning. Sporadically, their way was lit by streaks of lightning, which, they hoped was merely heat lightning. As they passed the place where the new Corey's

Inn was being constructed, large drops pelted them. Soon the rain poured steadily and the road quickly turned to mud.

They arrived at the O'Rourkes' house after midnight. Eleanor jumped down and ran toward the house while Peter tied the horses. Brushing as much water from her clothes as possible and removing her shoes, she entered to see Mary holding a small, tightly swathed bundle in her lap rocking gently in front of the fire, which she had built to fend off the night chill. Eleanor stopped and a smile crept across her face. Peter ran in and without stopping ran to the back of the house to see his wife.

"What happened?" Eleanor asked Mary.

"I don't remember my labors being so difficult. For the first few hours nothing seemed to change. Then Lisa told us she felt it was time. She gave a few more good pushes and out came this beautiful baby girl."

"Feet first?" asked Eleanor incredulously.

"No, head first and face down. I guess the young lady had turned herself around."

Peter ran out and peeked at his daughter dozing contentedly in Mary's lap. "She's so small," he exclaimed wondrously.

"What did you expect?" Mary and Eleanor said in unison. They all returned to Lisa's bed where Susie had bathed Lisa and changed the sheets. Mary started to give her granddaughter, who they named Rebecca, back to her daughter.

Lisa interrupted. "If you don't mind, I'd like Eleanor to examine her, that is, if it's all right with her."

Eleanor opened her bag and pulled out her stethoscope. Gently she unwrapped the baby, rubbed her hand over the bell of the instrument to warm it and placed it gingerly on the infant's chest. She listened intently and then looked up with a broad grin. "Sounds perfectly normal and she's a lovely pink." Never remorseful or resentful, Eleanor was genuinely happy at other women's good fortune. She wrapped Rebecca and handed her back to Lisa.

———•———

Freda Weinberg had grown progressively frail since her daughter and Jared had moved in. When Ruben was born, Freda and Henry gave their bigger bedroom to the growing family and moved into Eleanor's old room. Freda became too weak to get out of bed and succumbed to pneumonia on New Year's Day, 1888. She had lit Sabbath candles every Friday night, swept their house clean of bread before each Passover, and often attended services at the Beth Joseph synagogue, sitting upstairs in the women's section. Although Henry was not active in the congregation, he was glad he had helped establish the Jewish cemetery. Freda had wanted a Jewish burial and to have the *Kaddish* read. Even less observant than her father, Eleanor acceded to her mother's wish, but she told her father she would not sit Shiva nor promise to light a yahrzeit candle on the anniversary of her death. "Why is it, Papa, that the Jewish religion shows so little respect for women when they're alive, but treats them equally when they're dead?" Her father had no reply.

The Carters attended the funeral. So did George and Ann Phillips with their sons Tom and Alan and their families. Henry had saved Alan Phillips from croup over thirty years earlier and continued to care for the entire family. Most of the congregation was there, although the Weinbergs seldom socialized with them. One member led the mourners in prayers, concluding with the *Kaddish*. Henry wept as he tossed the first handful of dirt over the coffin. He had aged in the days since Cyrus had last seen him. Eleanor held his arm firmly to prevent her father from falling.

Jared Mason walked back toward the Raquette as the service continued. Looking at the river, its banks lined with snow, snow capping the rocks protruding from its surface, snow weighing down the limbs of overarching pine and hemlock, he heard only the gentle murmur of the flowing water. *How deceptively peaceful it seems. Where in the world can one find true peace?* he wondered.

When the grave had been covered, each mourner placed a rock at its head, making a small pile, as was the Jewish custom.

———•———

Pleased to have Eleanor and Jared to keep him company, Henry wanted to continue to see patients. Staying home only made him lonely for Freda. Eleanor often was with Henry in his clinic, meeting his patients and consulting with her father on their treatment. The old man recognized that his daughter was up to date on medical advances and was glad to learn from her. Eleanor had handled obstetrics from the start and her father gradually turned the rest of his practice over to her.

Despite his weakened condition, Jared harbored the hope that he and Eleanor would return to the city where he would resume his job as Inspector for the Health Department, grueling though it was. Jared's job with Franklin County was much less demanding except when an epidemic developed and he was called on to supervise quarantine or other measures. Patiently and subtly, Eleanor persuaded him that he

was much better off in the Adirondacks. Finally, he acqui-
esced on one condition: That they would spend the summer
in the cabin on Upper Saranac Lake that John and Tommy
Carter had helped him build. Eleanor countered, saying she
would agree only if the cabin was enlarged to accommodate her father and make cooking easy. Jared agreed to these
terms, although he knew he could not make the additions
himself.

# 7

# Homecoming, December 1887

THE Carters were eating dinner when Cyrus heard the outside door open. It was already dark out. He went to the vestibule, followed immediately by Mary who held the candelabrum she used to illuminate the kitchen table. A tall figure loomed over them.

"Hello, Cyrus," the voice said softly. "Hello Mama."

"John!" Mary burst out. Standing on tiptoe she hugged him. "We didn't expect you until tomorrow."

John embraced her. "I am glad to be home." Mary was still holding the candelabrum. John took it from her and placed it on a small table in the hall. "Be careful, Mama, or you'll set us all on fire." John walked into the kitchen, bent down, and gave Tommy a long tight hug, which Tommy vigorously reciprocated. "Ow," John said. "You've made up for your legs by the strength of your arms. I think you've broken my ribs," he said playfully.

Mary picked up the candelabrum, followed John into the kitchen, and inspected him closely. "You're too thin, John. Have you not been eating?"

"If I ate the way you fed me, Mama, it would use up my entire salary. I manage, but I had too little money left to eat much on the train; I'm starved."

"There's plenty to eat here. We'll begin to fatten you up

right now." Mary pulled out the chair in front of the setting saved for Alice next to Mary's at one end of the table.

"You've set a place for me, Mama. I thought you wouldn't expect me until tomorrow."

"That place is Alice Massing's. She's working at Trudeau's. She'll be here any minute."

"Oh, I forgot. Tommy wrote me about her." Hurriedly, Mary set another place for Alice on John's other side.

John was eating hungrily, talking little, when Alice entered. Swallowing his last mouthful, he stood politely as Mary introduced her and John shook Alice's hand. "Alice is from Glens Falls. I've known her since she visited the Adirondacks the summer Uncle William's place burned. She's a fellow suffragist." For fear of upsetting Alice, Mary decided not to explain her presence further. From Tommy's letters, John knew more. He cast a glance at Tommy as Mary introduced Alice and noticed a slight change in his complexion.

Alice released John's hand, and he helped her into her chair. "Your mother and Cyrus have been extremely kind to me." Tommy had already explained to Alice that Cyrus was not John's father. Tommy looked at Alice and she quickly added, "And Tommy and Lisa, too." Swallowing a mouthful, John offered the platters with roasted venison and potatoes to Alice.

Mary gave John a second careful look. She brushed his long black hair away from his temple. "My god, John! How did you get that scar?" She ran her finger over a thin white line that stood out from his darker skin, running from under his hairline down to his eyebrow. John's deep dark eyes, his straight nose, firm mouth and chin—in short his handsome face—were sure to draw attention away from the faint scar.

He finished chewing. "The McCormick strike, a police-man's nightstick. I wrote Tommy that McCormick wouldn't budge on the Union's demand for an eight-hour work day." Tommy nodded. John was ready to go into details but he glanced at his mother; she had put her hand over her mouth, staring at him, her eyes open wide with fear, her face, he thought, pale. He realized she would be even more distraught if he told her that one of the two workers who was shot dead by the police had stood next to him. He tried to extricate himself as gently as possible. "It was just a fight between us and the cops," he said, "but it led to the dem-onstration the next evening in Haymarket Square." John noticed that Tommy was taking notes.

Cyrus interrupted. "We've heard about the Haymarket. I suppose you were there?" he asked with some annoyance. "There's not much sympathy for that kind of action in these parts. People here seem willing to let nature take its course." The conversation stopped as the diners saw that Tommy had something to say. He showed his pad to Cyrus who passed it around. *It's not nature that sets the course, Dad. It's the bankers and manufacturers.*

"That's not my position, mind you," Cyrus continued, disregarding Tommy's note. "In Albany, I try to get the leg-islature to give nature a push." (Tommy wrote again, his pad on his lap so no one could see. He slipped it to John. *Not with much success.*

John answered Cyrus's question that preceded his little speech. "Yes, I was there. The gathering in Haymarket was supposed to be a peaceful demonstration in support of the workers striking for an eight-hour day and to mourn for the two workers who had been killed the previous day outside the McCormick factory. Only after the speeches were finished did the police try to disperse us. Then someone threw a bomb—I have no idea who threw it, maybe a police spy—and the police opened fire. Seven people were killed, including policemen, and scores were injured." He put his fork down. His face was gray and solemn. After a few moments he resumed. "Seven men were convicted of a conspiracy. At their trial no evidence linked them directly to the bombing. I helped raise money for the defendants' appeal. The Illinois Supreme Court turned them down in October. Four of them were hanged last month."

No one spoke for a moment. Tommy scribbled a fast note and circulated it. *How can we eat when these men were unjustly punished?*

"If we fasted in public, Tommy," John replied, "to show our support, that would be one thing. But fasting in private accomplishes nothing and only weakens us." He picked up his fork.

Tommy was not finished. *You're right, John. We must have the strength to fight back even if it means violence.*

This was too much for Cyrus. "I never thought a son of mine would say that. I only hope no son of mine would instigate violence."

Looking at his useless legs, Tommy wrote, *Don't worry, Dad, it's unlikely.* John said nothing.

The remainder of the meal was eaten in silence. Immediately afterward, Cyrus went to the parlor where he added a few logs to the smoldering fire. John's early arrival had left him uneasy. As he tended the fire he debated telling John about his role in Jean's fatal accident. Withholding the information from Mary had almost had dire consequences, with

Smead's attempt at blackmail. He thought, too, that Tommy or one of the others might tell John. His mind made up, he stood and turned to face John who had followed Cyrus into the parlor. "It's good to have you back, John. Your mother and I will be pleased if you stay for a while. Lisa and Peter will be building a house soon and your mother is going to add on to this one in the spring. You wouldn't have to go far to get work."

"I've thought of going to work in one of the sawmills near here, try my hand at organizing my fellow workers, and maybe making a little money."

Cyrus winced inwardly when John mentioned organizing. "I was thinking about your mother's project to enlarge this house. You'll have to discuss wages with her, but she's quite generous you know, especially where her children are involved." Cyrus got up and drew the curtains over the front window. "There is something I need to tell you, John. Your mother, brother, and sister already know." Cyrus first apologized for not having told John, or his mother, the complete story about the logjam long before. He then explained, as he had told them before the 1886 election, exactly what happened.

John sat quietly for a few minutes, looking into the fire. Finally, he said, "Cyrus, I can understand how badly you felt and that your not telling Mama wasn't because you wanted to marry her."

"The thought of marriage never entered my mind until after you were born."

John smiled. "I don't know if telling Mama before you were married would have kept her from marrying you, but I'm glad she married you. I don't know where I'd be today if it wasn't for you, Cyrus. The injustice in the world upsets me, but I can't claim that I've suffered any as a result of my upbringing." He rubbed his eyes. "Thanks for telling me."

Mary poked her head in the doorway. "Cyrus, dear, we best be going to bed." She turned to John. "I know it's a bit cramped, dear, what with the wheelchair and all, but it will be like old times sharing your room with Tommy. At this time next year, you can have a room of your own if the renovation is finished."

"What renovation?" John asked innocently.

"From what your mother got for the sale of Uncle William's property. I guess I didn't write you that we'd found a buyer."

Tommy had wheeled himself into the parlor. Mary addressed him. "If you are ready to turn in, Tommy, I can give you a hand. If you're not ready, Alice can help before she goes to bed."

"Why can't I help?" John asked.

"Of course you can, John, but someone has to show you what to do."

Tommy jotted a note. *Let's go, Mama. You can show John what to do.*

Everyone was leaving the parlor as Alice entered. "I was just going to read for awhile," she announced. John gave her a warm smile as he passed her and seemed to be on the verge of saying something, but he remained silent.

Cyrus headed straight for his and Mary's bedroom. Mary came in a few minutes later. "The boys seem happy to see each other. Tommy's been peppering John with questions. John will surely tell him more about the labor struggles in Chicago. I thought he held back on account of me." She noticed Cyrus scowling as they prepared for bed. "Aren't you glad to have John home?"

He did not respond immediately, nor answer her question when he did. "I told him that I ordered Jean into the boat."

"How did he take it?"

"Very well. He doesn't hold it against me."

"Then you should be pleased. What is the trouble?"

While Mary got into bed, Cyrus paced the floor of their bedroom. "Of course, I'm glad John's back and in one piece, too, except for that scar. I don't want another son maimed by those robber barons." (He realized he had called John a son.) "John came close to getting himself killed by McCormick's goons. I'm sure that bothers you, too, but what are we to do? Maybe strikes are more effective than legislating when it comes to protecting laborers," Cyrus speculated. "I'm no longer sure I know what works. Passing laws to save trees—we can muster the votes for that—but not for saving workers."

Mary knew she could not soothe Cyrus. With both of her sons marred by industrial strife, she, too, had come to recognize that saving trees was not the whole story. Cyrus soon stopped pacing and prepared for bed. Mary blew the candle out when he climbed in beside her.

———•———

After he helped Mary with Tommy, John went back to the parlor. Alice looked up from her reading. John was as tall as Lloyd. She saw traces of Mary in his face. He took the cushioned chair opposite her. The fire illuminated their faces. "Tommy wrote me that you and he were real friends."

As he looked at her face, ringed by dark hair, John saw Alice color momentarily. (Tommy had not written John that he had declared his love for Alice.) "He said that a tragic turn of events brought you to the village here, but he didn't write what happened." John worried that his curiosity had gotten the better of him. "If it's too painful, you don't have to tell me."

"It's a long story."

"That's all right. I've nowhere to go and I'm not tired."

"Cyrus invited my husband and me and our two children up here three years ago. My husband was a lobbyist for the Lumberman's Association."

John's face showed surprise. "Really? That doesn't sound like Cyrus."

"He was hoping to show Lloyd—my husband—how the lumber companies were doing harm."

"Did he succeed?"

"Yes. But not the way Cyrus had hoped. Lloyd became terribly conflicted. He started to drink. He took it out on me."

John had a fleeting image of a big brutish man striking this petite woman.

"He couldn't control himself. The Lumberman's Association fired him at the end of the legislative session in 1885. Either he jumped or fell off the bridge in Glens Falls. He was probably drunk at the time." Here she paused. She could feel a lump rising in her throat and swallowed hard.

"Lloyd came from a wealthy family. His parents blamed me for his death and took my children away." She paused once more to regain her composure. "Cyrus says the law will not be on my side to get them back. He went to Glens Falls last spring and located the school that Donald and Elizabeth were attending. The headmaster told Cyrus that he had orders from Lloyd's father not to allow anyone to visit them nor to receive letters except from their grandparents. Cyrus carried a letter I had written to them; he was unable to deliver it." She stood up.

John rose and stepped towards her and took her hands. Almost imperceptibly, she leaned toward him. "I'm so sorry," he said, shaking his head angrily. "These magnates—they can commit violence, rend families apart one way or the other, and get away with it. Will we always be impotent?" As John let go of her hands they both turned to look into the dwindling fire. "You know, Tommy may be the most powerful of us all. With his writing, he can reach more people than we ever can."

Alice turned to the doorway. "Yes, I greatly admire Tommy. He's been very kind to me." She paused as if to say something more. Finally, she simply said, "I have to work tomorrow; I best be going to bed. Good night." They shook hands. John returned to his seat, remaining until the glowing embers disappeared and a chill entered the room.

———— • ————

Tommy was glad John had come home. To have participated in the McCormick strike and Haymarket and come out unshaken in his determination to see labor triumph made John a hero in Tommy's eyes. He was pleased to have an ally in his arguments with Cyrus, who refused to see the need for direct action and insisted laws could eventually improve working conditions without resort to violence. He brushed aside his mother's horror of what had happened to her sons at the hands of labor's enemies. If sacrificing lives was necessary, so be it.

*It must be tough when you've got so many men who'll scab,* Tommy wrote when John talked to him about the McCormick strike.

John thought back to Tommy's description of his triumph over Durant and the Adirondack Railroad. "You know it's possible, Tommy. You got your ten-hour day and hourly wage despite the scabs."

*Only because the railroad engineers helped us. The scabs never had a chance.*

"We call that 'solidarity,'" John told Tommy, who wrote the term in his notebook.

John could stand to fight another day but Tommy's organizing career, illustrious as it may have been, was finished. Tommy despaired that he could not accomplish as much by writing as he could by direct action, hoping by some miracle that the nerves and muscles that controlled his lower limbs would function again. In the meantime, he had done what he could to strengthen his upper body, first with rowing and then with sawing—both with his father's help. Cyrus helped Tommy into and out of his old guideboat. The first time he did this, he told Mary he felt like a king being transported by his prince. The blisters on Tommy's hands turned to callus, and his shoulders, arms, and back bulged under his shirt. When the weather turned cold, Tommy feared all the strength he had gained during the summer would be lost as he spent most of the day writing or reading in front of the fire. Recognizing his son's disquiet, Cyrus solved the problem. He built a long sturdy table out of durable pine planks, cutting a large U-shaped notch out of the top surface, and assembled it in the shed. He piled logs that needed cutting to firewood alongside the table. In his wheelchair, Tommy could pick up a log from the pile, lay it across the table and saw it in two, making a pile of sawn logs on the other side. He taught himself to hold the saw in his left hand as well as his right so he could strengthen the muscles of both arms. He sawed so vigorously that he seldom got cold.

While Tommy sawed logs for firewood, John hunted, using Cyrus's old muzzle-loading rifle. The ducks and geese were gone, but partridge, rabbit, and deer still inhabited the woods. The family was pleased to have variety on the table.

Tommy wished he could hunt. He had not held a rifle since he had been in school. He asked his father if he could use his rifle to sharpen his aim so eventually he might hunt. He had John set up tin cans along the fence the Carters had put around their property. Though they were far away, he let the neighbors know that he was taking target practice so the shots would not alarm them, and he promised to shoot only when no one was out and about.

Some evenings Alice, John, and Tommy sat around the kitchen table, playing cards. Alice taught the brothers to play hearts (a game Lloyd had taught her) and other games three could play. John had learned to play poker in Chicago, but three was hardly enough to make a game, and to gamble with a young woman was unseemly. Tommy quickly noticed that Alice adopted the same friendliness to John as she did to him. John teased Alice about her being too serious, knowing full well she had worries that neither he nor his brother had; she was good natured about it, breaking into a smile and even poking John in the ribs. Tommy sometimes teased in private notes to Alice. Then she slapped his hands playfully.

Alice began to feel the two brothers were vying for her attention. More coquettish than she had been for many years, she did nothing to dissuade them. The memory of Tommy's kiss and declaration of love seemed less threatening. He seemed content to share her with his older brother.

By winter's end, Tommy hardly ever missed his targets, even from a distance of fifty yards. One Saturday he invited Alice and John to admire his marksmanship. He did not miss one can; they were duly impressed. Tommy wrote, *Why don't you try, John?* With Alice standing by, John took up the challenge. The brothers arranged a contest. Starting twenty-five yards from the fence, they took turns shooting. Neither missed and they had Alice set up the cans as John wheeled Tommy back another twenty-five yards. Neither had yet missed when John wheeled Tommy back to one hundred yards from the fence, almost the other end of the Carter's property. By this time dusk had settled. John shot first, his bullet knocking the can down. Tommy took careful aim but missed. Alice rewarded John with a kiss on the cheek. When she saw the anger in Tommy's eyes, she bent and kissed him too.

———•———

In the spring, when mud had replaced snow in the streets, John wheeled Tommy down to the Watering Hole where they met some of their old friends and talked over a couple of beers. Tommy had not had one since he had celebrated his eighteenth birthday with Peter O'Rourke junior, eight years earlier. The men quickly got used to Tommy's written repartee and made sure he was included in the conversation. John had gotten some of them to help with the additions Mary was putting on to the Carter home on Helen Street. When the Masons asked him to expand their camp he hired some of them to help. Some days, instead of going directly to the worksite through Caroline Bartlett's, John would drive Tommy in Cyrus's wagon to the Indian Carry and have Tommy row him to the worksite from the termination of the Indian Carry. Tommy would row up the lake, returning later to pick up his brother.

# 8

# The Great Camp

THE three story brownstone on the east side of Fifth Avenue a block north of Madison Square Park looked no different from the adjacent houses except for the brass plaque above the steps to the right of the door, which read "Union Club." Such names in the eighteen eighties denoted wealth, not workingmen's associations. The main lounge on the second floor was the central room of the Club, replete with overstuffed leather chairs and sofas, richly carved mahogany coffee and end tables (some with heavily shaded gas lamps, others with humidors or scattered newspapers and magazines, all with heavy glass ash trays), book cases filled with leather bound first editions along the walls, luxurious oriental carpets over the dark Oakwood floors, hunting trophies adorning the walls, and high-ceilinged chandeliers. Heavily draped, the windows emitted little natural light even in the middle of the day. No wonder the room had a faint musty, smoky odor. Six feet out from the longer north and south sides of the lounge the lower ceilings were each supported by a row of smooth Romanesque columns, which formed the outside of two corridors that ran parallel to these walls. On the other sides, heavy oak doors, each one centered between two adjacent columns, interrupted the solid wood paneled wall. The doors opened into smaller rooms that the members used for private meetings, card games, or other forms of amusement. No women were permitted in the Club.

In one of these rooms in June 1887, J.J. Schuyler, a wealthy New York banker, and three of his colleagues met with Paul Smith, principal land owner, hotelier, and developer of land near the St. Regis and Saranac lakes. Using a private railroad car at his disposal, Schuyler had invited Smith to come down to the City to discuss a business opportunity with a few members who were his close friends. He had met Smith the previous summer when he and his daughter had camped on one of the islands on Lower St. Regis owned by Smith. Smith, a large man whose watch fob arched across his prominent abdomen, had just brought on gales of laughter with a story of one of his encounters on his recent trip to Europe. When the laughter subsided and the men had relit their cigars, Schuyler spoke. "Gentlemen, we have a rare opportunity to purchase unspoiled land in the Adirondacks from Mr. Smith. The opportunity will not be there forever. New York State is being pressured by the conservationists to buy more wild land to add it to the forest preserve, which the law now requires be left forever wild. Mr. Smith had the foresight over the years to buy up prime land near the St. Regis Lakes and more recently on the western shores of Upper Saranac Lake."

"What's this I hear of an Adirondack Park?" one of the other men interrupted. They all turned to Paul Smith.

"Yes, I've heard those rumors," Smith replied. There's much more talk of that in the City than upstate. Some of your brethren down here are worried that if the lumber companies strip the forests up there your water supply will be imperiled. If they get the State to create a park—or get the Federal Government to make it a National Park—then all the land will be public."

"We wouldn't want that, would we?" Schuyler interjected.

"No," responded a third man, who owned a large share of the railroads being constructed in the northeast. "We'd have little reason to have railroads up there if the lumber companies were shut down."

"On the contrary," replied Smith. "You'd do a brisk business carrying tourists to and from the Adirondacks."

"I hadn't thought of that," muttered the railroad magnate.

"But, gentlemen," Smith continued, "your own peace and quiet, your ability to hunt and fish without intrusion by the riff raff, would be lost."

Schuyler spoke again. "Mr. Smith wants to see the beauty and the tranquility of the northwoods preserved, gentlemen, but not by the State. He is putting large tracts of virgin land for sale to the likes of us. I've already put a deposit down on one thousand acres with almost a mile of shorefront on Upper Saranac." He turned to Smith, "Why don't you show them what's available, Paul?"

Smith reached down alongside his chair and from a leather portmanteau pulled out a sheath of maps and other papers. The men gathered round his side of the table to peruse them. While they were doing so there was a knock on the door and a uniformed attendant announced to Mr. Schuyler that his daughter had arrived and was waiting for him in front of the Club in their carriage.

"Gentlemen, excuse me. I'm glad I've had the opportunity to introduce you to Mr. Smith. I'm sure you can carry on amiably without me. I bid you good day."

When Schuyler emerged in the twilight a crescent moon

and Venus were rising. A finely polished Hansom was waiting at the curb. The liveried driver jumped down from his
seat above and to the rear of the compartment. "Evenin' Mr.
Schuyler," he called to his boss, opened the door, and helped
him up. "Home, Sir?" Schuyler grunted affirmatively.

His daughter stopped fanning herself as he entered. In the
dim light her features or her figure could not be discerned.

"Excellent timing, my dear. As he sat he bent and kissed
her lightly on her smooth cheek. "Paul was just showing the
others the lands he has for sale. No one had asked whether
I was getting a commission and your arrival eliminated the
possibility they would learn my self-interest."

"Unless Mr. Smith reveals it," she observed shrewdly.

"He's too good a businessman for that, Ophelia."

"Oh, I can hardly wait, Daddy, to get out of this oppres-
sive heat. Will we see what we've purchased this summer?"

"Of course, darling. I've arranged with Phidias Wright
to visit us to survey the property and prepare a plan for the
buildings. He tells me if all goes well he should have the
plans by the end of the year and construction can start as
soon as the weather allows it. The winter is a blessing up
there for the lumber can be transported on the snow."

"Will he accompany us on our railroad car? Or will he
arrive later?"

"He has a job to finish up so he'll join us in a few weeks.
Mr. Smith will build us a tent platform and provide the
necessities as soon as I pay the balance. We'll bring our own
supplies."

Accustomed to having her needs met, Ophelia Schuyler
did not worry about roughing it. "Is this Mr. Wright handsome, Daddy?"

Schuyler laughed uneasily. "He's more than twice your age dear, bald as a billiard. He has a son who's about your age."

"Will he bring his son?"

"Oh, I doubt that." Schuyler cursed himself for even mentioning it.

John Carter remained in Saranac Lake Village, serving as his mother's agent to purchase lumber and other supplies for the addition to the Carter house on Helen Street. Together the family laid out the plans for the enlargement of the parlor and an adjacent dining room below and two bedrooms above. On top of these structures they laid out three bedrooms and, above the expanded second floor, an attic. Hiring a few young men from the village, John led the construction starting in the spring. On the ground floor they did not break through the outside wall until the parlor and dining room were framed and the clapboards hammered in place. On a warm day in May, they broke through, bringing a storm of written complaint from Tommy who earlier had feigned anger about the noise and now complained of the drafts and cold. By July the second floor additions were complete and the new roof, whose beams and joists had been constructed on the adjacent ground, was ready to be raised. Home from Albany, Cyrus and his friends and John and his crew helped on the historic occasion. The Carter house was now one of the largest in the Village.

One immediate benefit of the construction was that Cyrus could now reclaim his study and Alice, who Mary had persuaded not to move out after she went to work for Dr. Trudeau, had her own bedroom on the second floor.

John had earned the friendship of the crew he had assembled. They were a tough bunch, used to long periods of unemployment during which they hunted and fished to keep themselves, and for those who had them, their families, fed and clothed. From the money Mary advanced to him, John paid them weekly at an hourly wage higher than the going rate in the Village. He worked alongside the men, often taking the most dangerous jobs. Work started at eight o'clock every morning except Sunday and stopped promptly at five, with an hour for lunch. He insisted the men appear promptly; he always had their work prepared by the time they arrived. When one of the workers appeared unsteady an hour late one Monday morning—his tardiness had held up the work the others were scheduled to do—John warned him if it happened again, he'd have to fire him. The others grunted in agreement with John and let the tardy man know they had no sympathy for him. Neither he nor anyone else was late again. If one of the men was sick, he sent word ahead and John would visit him after work to make sure he was being cared for adequately.

When Eleanor and Jared Mason heard of John's prowess as a carpenter and foreman they asked if he would repair and enlarge the little cabin that John and Tommy had helped Jared build twelve years earlier. Smiling, John reminded Jared that he and Tommy had formed the Brotherhood of Brothers to negotiate a living wage. Jared complained, "Now that you're so experienced, I suppose your price has gone up, along with the cost of wood."

"Mostly because subsistence costs for our labor power have risen," John rejoindered.

"Sounds like you've been reading Marx," Jared replied. "I can't argue with that. I'm afraid, John, I won't be around to make sure you do the job right, but I'll get there when my strength allows, and when it's done, Eleanor and I will spend our weekends there, and we'll try to bring Henry along too, as long as snow and ice don't stand in our way."

As the work on the Carter house neared completion, John brought some of his crew to Upper Saranac Lake (obtaining permission from Caroline Bartlett to go up the Carry trail between the Middle and Upper Lakes) to expand the Masons' modest camp. They extended the log structure in the back to make a separate bedroom and knocked through what had been the outside stone wall of the fireplace so that the same chimney served as a fireplace in the bedroom as well as the original entry room, which now served as a small parlor. On the north side of the parlor, they broke through the logs to build a small kitchen with a separate flue for the cast iron stove that was delivered by train to the station at Axton Landing; Peter O'Rourke, the stationmaster, arranged the special stop. Getting the stove from the station to the cabin was not easy. John and his men, with Jared Mason's approval, brought it down Indian Carry to the south shore of the Lake and built a sturdy raft to carry it to the Masons' cabin. When a sudden squall turned the raft around they feared the raft would capsize, sending the stove to the bottom of the lake. Fortunately, the wind abated and they landed successfully.

————•————

While John and his crew were working on the Mason camp, Phidias Wright was visiting J.J. Schuyler's rustic camp on the opposite shore of Upper Saranac. After Schuyler paid the balance of his bill, deducting the commission he earned by inducing others to buy land, Paul Smith had erected five tents on the property; one for Mr. Schuyler, a second for Phidias Wright, another for Ophelia and her girlfriends, a fourth for a mess hall with an open air kitchen covered only by a canvas tarpaulin, and finally one for the Schuylers' cook, maids, and servants, partitioned to allow separate quarters for men and women. Ophelia's mother had died when Ophelia, her only child, was eight years old. J.J., very fond of his daughter, kept her close to him. She had been taught by a series of governesses before she left for Smith College at the age of seventeen.

To the Schuylers, the Adirondack summer, though unusually warm, was a relief after the stifling heat of Manhattan. Schuyler was tall and husky, with a mane of white hair. Wright was short and stout, his baldpate gleaming in the sun when they were out. The two men spent most of a week tramping to select sites for Schuyler's Great Camp. Both of them had visited the Great Camps built by W.W. Durant on Raquette Lake to get ideas about their own camp. For the main lodge they selected the top of a knoll from which Upper Saranac Lake could be seen and easily reached, a quarter of a mile below. To the southeast the long shoulder of Ampersand Mountain was visible from the site while to the north, seemingly at the head of the lake, St. Regis Mountain stood out.

Ophelia, who spent most of her days with one of her classmates from Smith College—they had graduated the previous year—told her father she did not want to live in the main lodge and have to trudge up the hill after swimming or boating. She preferred to be near the water. Wright said he could design a boathouse with living quarters and all the modern conveniences that she could use when not occupying her quarters in the main lodge. The other buildings they planned were a kitchen and dining hall, guesthouse, a long low building housing a small theatre, a bowling alley, and a billiards room. The servants' quarters would stand a quarter-mile distant from this compound.

One afternoon as Phidias, J.J., and Ophelia stood on the shore of Upper Saranac near where they planned the boathouse, they heard the ring of axes and the beat of hammers across the lake. They could not see any activity and concluded that it was coming from up Bartlett's Bay. Paul Smith had provided a guide and a boat for the Schuylers, and Phidias proposed that the guide row them across the lake to investigate. Unusual for that time of year, the wind was coming from the east, which probably explained why they heard the work. Saying he'd had enough fresh air for one day, J.J. demurred. Ophelia and Phidias embarked with the guide. Rowing against the wind—there were white caps on the lake—it took them about twenty minutes to enter the bay and another ten minutes to locate the source of the sounds. It was about four-thirty when they reached the large rock near the Mason's cabin and asked if they could land. Jared was not present and John, who had walked down to the edge of the lake, saw no reason to refuse. He recognized the guide as one from Saranac Lake. When the boat beached, Phidias rose, stepped ashore, and then helped Ophelia. She was wearing a wide-brimmed straw hat fastened around her throat by a pale blue silk scarf. A wisp of blonde hair peeked out from under the brim. Ophelia lifted her white linen dress to her knees as she stepped over the gunwale and stood barefoot on the sand, her naked feet whiter than the lace dress she was wearing.

"Thanks for allowing us to visit," Phidias addressed John. "Is this your cabin, young man?"

John was stripped to the waist, his broad shoulders and muscular arms glistening with sweat. Quickly he put his shirt on. He was stunned to see a beautiful, stylish young woman in the primitive surroundings. Still looking at her after Phidias asked his question, John regained his composure and quickly recollected the words just spoken. "No, Sir. We're expanding it for the Masons, medical doctors whose principal residence is in Tupper Lake." He paused. "I'm sorry, I didn't catch your name."

"Phidias Wright, Architect, young man. And your name?"

"John Carter." He glanced again at the young woman who had started to walk up the beach toward the cabin, seemingly ignoring John. Her dress fit tightly over her narrow hips and he could make out the rounded contours of her buttocks as she glided to the cabin. The workers there put down their hammers and saws and watched her approach.

"Are you in charge of the construction here?" Wright continued, oblivious to the effect Ophelia had on the men.

"I suppose you could say that. I work along with them."

Without invitation, Wright started up the gentle slope, trailing Ophelia, with John trailing him. When Ophelia reached the door she had no hesitation of stepping inside, as if the place was hers. "How charming," she said to Wright, who had caught up with her. "Will our place be like this?"

Wright laughed. "One hundred times bigger and much

more comfortable, with rugs on the floor, moose heads and other trophies on the walls, and solid chairs and tables."

"But this is so quaint and charming."

Wright was examining the new construction, the bedroom and kitchen, peering closely at the seams and joints. "Is this your work?" he turned to John.

"Yes, Sir. The men and I, we're building it."

"I wouldn't have expected such high quality from—" he caught himself before he insulted John, "from someone so young."

"Thank you. We have to build solidly up here to withstand the snow and cold."

"Do you do this work all year round?"

John laughed. "We don't get much call for construction hereabouts. There's not that many folks with money. The boys and I spend a lot of time hunting and fishing—that's how we feed our families," he said, glancing out the window at the guide who had stayed with the boat, "and guiding when we get the opportunity."

"Do you have a family?" Ophelia stood alongside Wright.

"Of course, Miss."

"Do you have children, I meant?"

"No Miss, I'm not married."

"Don't call me 'Miss,'" she commanded. "My name is Ophelia. Ophelia Schuyler."

"Ophelia's father has just purchased one thousand acres on the western shore," Wright said, interrupting their dialog. "Opposite Bartlett Bay, extending west towards Tupper Lake. He's planning to build a Great Camp there. I'm surveying and drawing up plans for the buildings. We could use some good workers."

"Well, if I'm around when you're ready to begin, let me

know. I live with my parents on Helen Street in Saranac Lake Village. You won't have trouble finding me, unless I decide to go west again."

Ophelia, who had walked out of the cabin heading towards the boat, turned her head to address John, "How far west have you been?"

"Chicago," John stopped. He didn't want to offend her by using 'Miss,' but he didn't think it proper to call her 'Ophelia.'

"I haven't been that far," she replied, not bothered by the lack of appellation. "Only to Europe. Is it like New York City?"

John reflected a moment. He did not know the elegant side of Chicago and had never heard people speak about it with the same awe as they spoke about Manhattan.

"I wouldn't say so. It's brutish and dirty." He was thinking of the slaughterhouses, the McCormick strike, the Haymarket bombing, and the trial.

They reached the boat. In the late afternoon the wind had abated and the water in the cove was mirror smooth. Wright offered his hand to Ophelia as she stepped into the boat. Only after the boat disappeared behind the point of the cove did the men resume their work.

———•———

When the weather turned cool in September, Schuyler, his daughter, and their retinue returned to the City, leaving Wright and his assistant to survey the property, laying out boundary markers and siting the buildings of the Great Camp. In surveying the boundaries, Wright and his assistant trudged on to a small farm near the southwest corner. The forest had thinned out and about ten acres of land was yielding potatoes, corn, and leafy vegetables. Their survey indicated that the farmhouse and part of the farm lay within the boundaries of Schuyler's property. Wright took it on himself to notify the farmer.

A few days later, on a cool sunny morning, he knocked on the door of the farmhouse. George Phillips, father of Alan and Tom, responded. Wright introduced himself and as politely as possible informed Phillips that part of his land now belonged to J.J. Schuyler. George offered Wright a seat. The architect was surprised that the furniture in the room was artistically designed out of local woods, retaining the natural curves of the branches for chair arms and table legs, while twigs, still with their bark, ornamented the table edges, bureaus, and chair backs. "Your furniture is stunning, Mr. Phillips. Who built it?"

"My younger son Alan. He's loved to carve since his mother and I gave him his first knife. He's carved an entire bed for himself and his wife. They live just west of here."

Tom, who had been digging potatoes, interrupted their conversation. He had come up to the house, pumped water from the well, wiped his hands on his overalls, clomped the mud off his boots, and entered. He offered his still damp hand to Mr. Wright who shook it gingerly and then dried his hand on his trousers. The elder Phillips related the situation to his son.

"What does Mr. Schuyler propose to do about it?" Tom asked.

"I don't know. I just discovered the situation yesterday. He's back in New York City. I will have to write him, or wait until I return and speak to him directly."

"I bought this land when I married forty-two years ago. Got the deed to prove it," George said.

"Surveying wasn't so accurate then, Mr. Phillips. I'm sure the County surveyors will confirm my results. To put it bluntly," he turned from father to son and back again, "you're trespassing!"

"We'll see about that," the elder Phillips muttered inaudibly into his long white beard. In a louder voice, he replied "Guess there's nothing else to be said for now, Mr. Wright." The men stood.

"There is one more thing I'd like to ask you, George." Wright was surprised he used Phillips' first name. "The furniture your son makes, does he do it commercially?"

"You mean does he sell it?" Tom interjected.

"Yes. That's what I mean."

"Not so far as I know," George replied. Tom nodded in agreement.

"He should think about it. It's really quite marvelous and unique. In fact, I've been thinking about the furnishings for Mr. Wright's camp. Alan's work would do very nicely."

"We'll have to settle the land matter first," Tom replied. There was no shaking of hands as Phidias Wright departed.

# 9

# Disputed Land

RETURNING to the City in late September, Wright spent most of the fall working on the blueprints for the various buildings. Only when he came to review the plat for the entire property did he remember George Phillip's farm and the dispute that might be brewing. He immediately notified J.J. Schuyler who consulted his lawyers. They advised that Schuyler register the deed with Franklin County.

Phillips had moved faster. Shortly after Wright's visit he had gone to see Cyrus Carter. Suspicious of Schuyler's claim, Cyrus went to the Courthouse and examined the deeds. The land was still registered under Paul Smith's name. Carefully examining the boundaries, Cyrus discovered an overlap between Smith's claim and the land registered by Phillips. He was in a quandary. Smith, the consummate diplomat, had contributed to both Cyrus's campaign and Tobias Brown's in 1886. In the current campaign, in which Cyrus was not contested for Assemblyman, Smith was a major contributor. Cyrus had also done legal work for Smith before being elected to the Assembly. Still, Phillips was a loyal friend and undoubtedly had the prior claim.

Cyrus expected that Smith's surveyor had made a mistake and rode up to Smith's resort on Lower St. Regis Lake with the hope that an amicable settlement could be reached. Smith greeted Cyrus warmly, took him into his carpeted, wood-paneled study, and insisted on showing his plans for harnessing waterpower along the Raquette north of Tupper Lake and along the Saranac for electricity. "Cyrus," he said, "we can make Franklin County the wealthiest in the State with electric lighting and railroads. There are a few electric locomotives in Europe and one in Virginia."

"That would be wonderful, Paul," he replied. "I'm sure you'll let me know if I can be of help." Cyrus wondered whether he would be lobbied by Smith to get the Assembly to secure a tax advantage or subsidy to facilitate his schemes. If so, Smith might be inclined to admit the survey error, notify Schuyler, and return the fraction of the sale price to Schuyler for the land that was Phillips' and not his.

Smith rolled up the plans that he had spread on the highly polished mahogany table, tied them, and put them on a shelf. "Can I get you something to drink, Cyrus?"

"No, thank you. I'm fine."

Smith took a bottle and two glasses out of a wall cabinet and set them in front of Cyrus, who had taken a seat at the table. As he poured whiskey into one, Cyrus put his hand over the other. "Really, I'm fine."

"Suit yourself." Smith sat down at the head of the table, savored the first swallow, and finally asked, "Is this a social visit, Cyrus, or do you want to buy land?"

"Neither one, exactly, but some of both."

"Ah Cyrus, you've learned to talk like a politician. Can I trouble you to explain?"

"Well, I always like visiting with you, Paul, and I do have a land matter on my mind, but I'm in no position to purchase."

"What then?"

"Well, to make the story simpler, let me ask if you recently sold land on the western shore of Upper Saranac Lake to J.J. Schuyler?"

The question surprised Smith. He wondered whether a trap was being set, but quickly answered affirmatively.

Cyrus proceeded to tell him of the overlapping land claims of Phillips and Schuyler. "Schuyler hasn't gotten around to registering his deed; the land is still in your name."

"But I sold it to him. It's his problem, isn't it?"

Cyrus detected a hint of doubt in Smith's inflection.

"Well, at the courthouse it's your deed that shows the overlap. Phillips laid claim to the contested land first and your surveyor must have made a mistake."

Smith poured himself another drink. "Could I or Schuyler buy out Phillips?"

"He won't sell. That land is his livelihood."

"What's your interest, Cyrus?"

"George Phillips asked me to look into this. He's my client."

"Why didn't you come out and say so, Cyrus?" Smith asked crossly.

"We've only just gotten into the matter, Paul."

Paul tossed the drink down in one gulp. "What choices do I have?" Cyrus wasn't sure whether Smith was expecting an answer. "I don't like to admit a mistake to a buyer," Smith continued after a brief pause, "and I like refunding money even less." Cyrus remained silent.

"I suppose we could dispute your client's claim." Paul got up and pulled his watch from his vest pocket. "Oh my, I'm late for lunch downstairs. Lydia will execute me." He reflected for a moment, then added, "I hope you'll join us."

Mindful of his potential adversarial relation with Smith on the one hand and of Smith's potential interest in lobbying him on the other, Cyrus quickly said, "I'll be pleased to do so, Paul, on one condition."

Smith instantly grasped that Cyrus would insist on paying. Unlike Lloyd Massing four years earlier, he made no effort to dissuade Cyrus. "As you like, Cyrus; more money for me." Although still poor, Cyrus was not so destitute as when he had to take a second job to pay for his lunch with Massing.

Smith led him out of the study and down a carpeted flight of stairs with round dark-stained banisters on both sides. As they descended side-by-side Smith asked, "What do you think I should do, Cyrus?"

"It's your choice, Paul. Of course, I'll still be representing George Phillips."

"That's not helpful." They reached the landing and Smith led Cyrus to the dining room. Lydia Smith was waiting at the door. Paul introduced her to Cyrus as "our distinguished Assemblyman." She extended her hand while exclaiming, "It must have been weighty business. Paul is seldom late for lunch." Lydia led them to a table near the window where Lower St. Regis Lake was easily visible through the leafless trees of late November.

Cyrus left after lunch. The air was crisp; the sun had passed its zenith and had started its descent to the southwest. Cyrus had taken the more easterly route from Saranac Lake Village early that morning, coming north near Bloomingdale then west through Gabriels. He decided to return on the westerly, less traveled route, going south to Lake Clear, skirting the west side of Upper Saranac Lake, and finally turning east to return to his village.

It was about three o'clock when he stopped at George Phillips' farm. He told George that the land was still registered in Paul Smith's name and ventured a prediction that Smith would refund Schuyler for the contested acres. "If that happens, I'll make sure the boundaries are adjusted in Schuyler's deed so the question will never arise again."

George grasped Carter's hand with both of his. "Thank you, Cyrus. You are an honorable man. "What is your fee?"

On his way in Cyrus had noticed barrels of potatoes on the porch. "I'll settle for one bushel of potatoes, George."

"Are you sure that's enough? I've cost you a whole day, at least."

Cyrus laughed. "I'll just about be able to fit them in my saddle bags. I couldn't carry any more!"

"Well, I owe you, Cyrus. How about another payment when you finish the job?"

"All right. It might turn out more complicated if Smith doesn't do as I predicted." Cyrus loaded the bags with potatoes, mounted his horse, leaned down to shake George's hand, and headed back to the main trail.

The sun cast long shadows to the east and hued the ground golden between the shadows as Cyrus, happy to be near the land, continued his journey. He continued south, past the Wawbeek property, and turned east on the road connecting Tupper Lake to Saranac Lake. He was not immediately conscious that that the land that Mary had sold to the State was on his right. He was taken with the sun penetrating the forest, more in the fall than any other season, and with his own thoughts. When he first saw some smooth stumps a few tiers in, he thought nothing unusual, so used was he to the extensive lumbering in the area. But then, suddenly, it dawned

on him there were no stumps when he and Mary had walked
in this area before she sold the land to the State in order to
protect it from the axe. He dismounted, tied his horse to a
sturdy spruce, and walked further into the forest. He guessed
that the trees had been cut the previous winter and that the
logs had been skidded to Smead's land along the Raquette,
less than a mile away. His mood turned angry as he retraced
his steps and mounted his horse. The land had been poached.
Something had to be done, he realized gloomily as he headed
home into the dusk.

He stopped to rest where the old Indian Carry joined
the east–west road. A few moments later he saw a rider coming toward him from Axton Landing. As he drew nearer he
recognized Peter O'Rourke, his son-in-law and the stationmaster at Axton Landing. They greeted each other warmly
and rode back to Saranac Lake Village together. While the
horses trotted moderately, Cyrus told Peter of his discovery.
Peter said he was not aware of the trespass, which was not
surprising as the purloined logs would have been brought
west to Tupper Lake, either by the river or the railroad, and
not east and upstream to Axton Landing. He had not heard
the jacks talk about it when they came into the tiny station
house in their spare time.

"Well, whoever's doing it is breaking the law. Trees in the
Forest Preserve are protected under Section 8, keeping the
lands forever wild." Peter cast his father-in-law a sideways
glance, amused at Cyrus's legalese.

Back home, Cyrus decided not to upset Mary with the
news but retired to his study after dinner and drafted a letter
to Abner Train, Secretary of the Commission.

Saranac Lake, New York
November 16, 1888

Hon. Abner Train
Secretary
Forest Commission
Albany, New York

Dear Abner,

On my travels around the County I represent, I discovered that land recently sold to
the State for inclusion in the Forest Preserve
had been desecrated. The entire purpose of
the Legislature in creating the Forest Preserve was to keep its contents holy, that is,
forever wild. Indeed the entire purpose of the
seller in this case, was to do exactly that. Nevertheless since the sale, trees have been cut
and removed from the property.

If the Forest Commission cannot uphold
the law with which it was entrusted, the Legislature will have to take further action. I will
see to this in the upcoming session.

Sincerely yours,

Cyrus Carter, Esq.

Assemblyman, Franklin County


Train replied promptly, blaming the failure of the Commission to execute the law on the small amount of funds
appropriated by the Legislature. "The Commission is of the

opinion," he added, "that it is better first to expand the Preserve with the limited funds we have, with the hope that the Legislature will then see fit to give the Commission sufficient funds to make sure that the intentions of the Legislature are enforced."

Cyrus showed the letter to Tommy who wryly commented, "*He's saying half a loaf is better than none. Looks like you've got your work cut out for you.*"

Cyrus had hoped that the coming session in Albany would be a quiet one, but he could see a battle shaping up.

———•———

Before J.J. Schuyler could register the deed for his new property, he received a letter from Paul Smith with a check for one hundred dollars, a refund on the five acres that Smith had mistakenly sold to him. The banker was relieved to have the dispute settled. Quickly, he arranged to have the corrected deed transferred to his name. Phidias Wright reassured him that the five lost acres would have added little to the overall value of the property and what Schuyler intended to do with it. Schuyler, nevertheless, harbored a grudge against George Phillips, which did not get in the way of his subsequently hiring Alan Phillips to build much of the furniture for his camp.

By the end of winter, Wright had completed the plans for the Camp. Schuyler invited him to dinner at his residence on Fifth Avenue. Wright was the only guest, seated at the opposite end of the table from J.J. with the beautiful Ophelia between them. After the plates were cleared, one of the servants brought in candelabra, set them on the table, and lit the candles. Wright spread the plans out, first showing his hosts a map of the camp with an overhead view of the buildings. He named each one in turn, finishing with the boathouse. Pointing to it, Ophelia asked, "Will it have sleeping quarters?"

Wright unrolled the next set of plans, the topmost of which contained detailed views of the boathouse, including a bedroom, fireplace, and galley. "You asked for them, my dear. You have but to walk up a short flight of stairs and there they are. The bedroom opens on to a balcony that circumnavigates the entire structure, almost a widow's watch, but no whalers on this water." Ophelia threw her arms around Wright and kissed him on the cheek. "You are such a darling." Wright turned red, right up to his baldpate.

"When can we start construction?" Schuyler asked.

"As soon as we can hire workers. There's still snow on the ground and that is an advantage for dragging in the lumber. The wood from the trees we cut on site will have to be cured before we can use them. At least a year that would be."

"I don't want you to cut any more than we need," Schuyler commented. "I do want the finest materials and workmanship to go into the Camp. Money is no object."

"Do you mean you won't have the Camp finished until next year?" asked Ophelia.

"Not even then," Wright replied. "But don't despair, my dear. We'll build you better facilities for the coming summer than Mr. Smith's tents provided." He turned to Mr. Schuyler who had resumed his seat at the head of the table.

"About the matter of workers, Sir." We could bring up a crew from the City, but that would cost a fortune and I'm not sure it would be worth it."

"What is the alternative?"

"While visiting you last summer, I met a young man who was heading up a small construction job on the eastern shore of Upper Saranac."

Ophelia interrupted, "Is that the tall handsome man we met when we rowed over to the other side of the lake?"

Wright nodded. "I examined his work carefully. It was of excellent quality."

"That was just a cabin," Ophelia interrupted again. She thought the better of her comment. "But I agree with Phidias, it was very well done."

"This man, John Carter, is a native of Saranac Lake. I've made some inquiries. His father, Cyrus Carter, has been the New York Assemblyman for Franklin County since 1882."

"Carter, Carter. Cyrus Carter—" J.J. turned to Ophelia. "Didn't Paul Smith say Carter represented that fellow Phillips who laid claim to our land?"

Ophelia knew her father could harbor a grudge. "I don't remember, Papa. Besides, Mr. Phillips owned that parcel on the land you purchased from Paul Smith."

Wright intervened. "It's altogether possible that Cyrus Carter was Phillips' attorney, but remember, Mr. Schuyler, it might do well to have a tie to the Assemblyman. You are now one of the biggest landowners in the County."

Ophelia jumped in. "Phidias makes a good point, Papa."

"Very well," muttered Schuyler. "Contact this John Carter. Set a budget for the job and a schedule; whatever you think is reasonable, Phidias. Put in penalties if he doesn't get the job done according to schedule."

"And bonuses if he gets it done ahead of schedule," Ophelia added.

Ignoring her, Schuyler got up reached for a cord to the

servants' quarters. A young man knocked a few minutes later. "Please bring the decanter of brandy and two glasses," Schuyler instructed. Turning to Wright, "An occasion to toast, don't you think, Wright?"

Before Phidias could answer, Ophelia spoke up. "I'm old enough to drank, Daddy. I'd like to be included."

"Very well," he replied, telling the butler to bring a third glass,

"One more thing, Mr. Schuyler," Phidias interjected. "Your Camp needs a name."

"Yes, I'd been thinking about that." Looking at his daughter he continued, "I'd been thinking about 'Camp Ophelia.'"

Ophelia rose and hugged her father. "That's so sweet, but camps are more often named after dead people, and I'm very much alive. I don't think it becoming."

"Have you a better idea?" her father flashed.

She thought for a while. "You know, I've been reading the books by Fenimore Cooper about the noble guide who does everything from protecting women to being a great marksman. How about Camp Natty Bumppo?" Neither man seemed enthralled with it. Disappointed, Ophelia tried again. "He's also called the deerslayer. How about Camp Deerslayer?"

"Well, I do hope to slay a lot of deer in this camp, but that sounds a little too bloodthirsty," J.J. replied.

Phidias countered. "I've heard Cooper's tales named after the deerskin chaps the hero wears to protect his legs. He's also been called after them, 'Leatherstocking.' How about that?"

Father and daughter looked at each other and smiled. "If I'm not mistaken," J.J. said, "Fenimore's pathfinder roamed the woods near here."

The butler returned with a three glasses. He poured the

dark red liquid in the glasses and served them, first to Ophelia, then to the two gentlemen. After setting the tray down on the end table the butler left. J.J. raised his glass and the others followed. "To Camp Leatherstocking," they toasted.

A half-hour later, J.J. ushered Wright into his study where he drew a ledger-size checkbook from the safe. He sat down and wrote a check to Wright. "Well, Phidias, this should keep you going through June." He handed the check to Wright who glanced at it quickly before pocketing it. "I assume you will want to travel to Saranac Lake to hire Carter personally."

"I think it would be a good idea."

Schuyler wrote out another check, payable to John Carter. "If Carter needs persuading, here's a small retainer that might entice him."

On March 31, Wright wrote John Carter, reminding him that he and Miss Schuyler had visited him while he was working on the cabin at Huckleberry Cove. He explained that his employer, Mr. J.J. Schuyler, would like John to head up the construction of the buildings at his great camp on the western shore of Upper Saranac. "If you are interested, I would like to visit with you in the near future at a time and place at your convenience."

*My god!* wrote Tommy after John showed him the letter, *You'll be on the other side now, someday maybe a capitalist.*

"Are you saying I shouldn't do it?"

*It's not for me to say.* Tommy put his pencil down and looked out at the trees just beginning to bud. *Maybe you would be a good boss, like Jared was to us.*

John worried that Tommy would remind him of his plans to become a union organizer. He hadn't come out and said it directly but Tommy made plain that becoming a contractor or a jobber who had to hire workers was "the other side." Tommy had not complained when John hired other men to help with additions to the Carters' house or the Masons' cabin, but those were small, temporary jobs. John knew, and Tommy realized it too, that accepting Schuyler's offer could settle his future.

John had finished work on the Mason cabin in the fall and then spent time hunting with the men who had worked with him. He put more meat on the Carter table than the family had seen since Cyrus had been elected. He spent many evenings with Tommy and Alice, playing cards, he and Alice taking turns reading aloud and each trying to keep the group in good cheer. He had looked for a job at the mill in Tupper Lake but they weren't hiring. He was thinking of going back to Chicago when Wright's letter arrived.

Mary saw nothing wrong with his accepting. She was not thinking of how well he would be paid or how he might compromise his principles but of his being near and doing relatively safe work. She lost patience with John when he tried to explain that he saw himself more a workingman than a foreman or a jobber. "Four men went to the gallows in Chicago fighting for workers' rights, and here I am thinking of going to the other side."

"You did a lot to help the Haymarket men, John. I pray you don't end up like them."

⎯⎯•⎯⎯

One Saturday late in April, John was returning home from the village when, by chance, he met Alice returning from work at Trudeau's. "Do you mind if I walk with you, Alice?" he asked.

"Not at all. It's a lovely day." They walked silently for a while, then Alice commented, "You've been quiet lately, John."

"I don't know what to do, Alice."

"You mean about Mr. Wright's letter?" He nodded.

Alice wanted him to stay but was afraid he might misunderstand if she said so.

They found themselves at Moody pond, not directly on the route home. John picked up some flat stones and skimmed them across the water one at a time. "It's been a week since I received Mr. Wright's letter. I can't put off answering much longer."

Alice had seen Wright's letter. "You don't have to say you'll accept. I don't see how you can; there's a lot to negotiate."

"I suppose I could just say I need to discuss the matter further before I make a commitment." They walked on in silence.

Tommy seemed annoyed when John and Alice arrived home together. He feared Alice was partial to John and he knew John was a better catch for Alice than he was. He began to wonder whether John had more than a friendly interest in her. Tommy had never told John about his kissing Alice, but he thought John would recognize his affection for her and not compete.

John went straight to Cyrus's desk and wrote Wright along the lines Alice had suggested. As he wrote, he thought back to his encounter with Wright the previous summer—and with Ophelia Schuyler. He could not get her out of his mind. If he took the job her father offered, he would see more of her, but, instinctively, he knew nothing good could come of it; she was born to a different class. Even their small encounter on the shore by the Masons' cabin suggested that she looked down on him. Even when walking home with Alice, he was thinking about Ophelia, but again, instinctively, he did not mention her to Alice.

Cyrus Carter returned from Albany in May. As usual, he was relieved to be out of the Capital. He had discouraging news for Mary. Not only was the land she had given to the State being trespassed, but other sections of the Preserve were meeting the same fate; trees of all species and sizes were being chopped. The demand for paper was increasing steadily, making the harvesting of hardwoods, which were used for pulp, highly profitable. The Forest Commission was not helping. At least one Commissioner was in the pocket of the lumber companies. It was not eager to have the Legislature appropriate funds for the purchase of land to add to the Preserve and did not challenge the sale of lands that had come to the State through tax defaults. Cyrus was also surprised that despite the continued logging, jobs were not increasing to keep up. The two-handed saw, other new technologies, and the use of the railroads had reduced the number of jacks needed to get timber out of the forest.

The purchase of large tracts by private parties, including Schuyler's Great Camp, also came to the attention of Cyrus and other legislators. The intention of the new owners was to preserve these lands in their natural state. But one could never be sure that would always be their objective. And even if the private forests were preserved, the owners might not permit others to hunt, fish, hike, or canoe on their property. A new worry was taking hold of Cyrus. He knew that these lands helped sustain his constituents. If they could not hunt and fish on them they would find it hard to survive periods of unemployment.

In the short run, at least, the construction of the Great Camps provided jobs, as Cyrus realized when John told him of Wright's offer. (He harbored doubts about the long run.) Like Mary, Cyrus was pleased that John would contemplate staying. Knowing John's militant labor positions, he worried that John would make demands that Wright, or Schuyler, would not meet. He suggested that John hear what Wright had to say about wages and working conditions before stating his position. Tommy also gave advice: *Get it in writing.*

# 10
# Negotiating

PHIDIAS Wright replied promptly to John's letter, inviting John to meet him at Martin's Hotel at 10 A.M. on the third Monday in May. John walked the mile from the Carter house in unseasonably warm weather, the returning birds filling the air with song. At the hotel, Wright was not in sight. John inquired at the desk and the receptionist sent a bellhop to notify Mr. Wright of John's arrival. Wright came down the stairs a few minutes later, his arms embracing several scrolls of blueprints and other drawings. He led John to the empty dining room where he dropped his parcels on a large table from which the utensils had been cleared. Wright drew aside the curtains over the windows that looked out on the lake. Without so much as a handshake he proceeded. "Let me show you what we are going to do."

John was unsure whether "we" referred to Wright and Schuyler or Wright and John. Wright first unrolled a map of the Schuyler property and showed John where the buildings would be located and what the purpose of each would be. He spoke with animation, obviously proud of his designs. "I propose we start construction of the main lodge first, which will house Mr. Schuyler and his immediate retinue." John thought to ask about Ophelia but decided not to. "I don't expect you and your men to work on the roads into the camp or the paths between the buildings; you can hire others to complete those tasks." John said nothing as Wright hurried on. Next Wright unrolled the blueprints for the main lodge, floor-by-floor and section-by-section. John was amazed at the detail. Not only the exact length of the rooms, but the type of lumber, the specifications for wainscoting, the size of boulders for the fireplaces and of flagstone for the hearths—all neatly written on the diagrams. Finally, Wright looked up. "Well, what do you think?"

John had never worked from blueprints before. He quickly grasped that they were like cooking recipes, making his task a lot easier than starting from scratch. "Very impressive, Mr. Wright."

Wright beamed, "Call me Phidias, please." John was surprised that an aristocrat like Mr. Wright would permit, let alone invite, someone of the working class to speak familiarly in the context of work. But then John also realized that his place in society could be changing; he wasn't sure he was ready. "But I'm not sure I want to do it, Mr. Wright."

The two men had been standing. Now Wright pulled out a dining chair, turned it around and sat down. His legs sprawled in front of him; he looked at John with disbelief. "Why ever not?" He paused, searching his brain to find reasons why any man would refuse. "You'll get paid handsomely." He reached into his coat and felt the envelope that held Schuyler's retainer for John.

"That's part of the problem, Mr. Wright. It's not my salary I worry about but the men's wages. Life is tough up here." Heedless of Cyrus's admonition, he continued. "Neither you nor Mr. Schuyler should think that because jobs are scarce up here you can get workers cheap."

Wright looked genuinely surprised. "That hadn't occurred

to me, and I don't think it had occurred to Mr. Schuyler either." He took his empty hand out of his coat pocket.

John didn't know whether to believe him, but he seized the opportunity. "I don't want you to hand me a pot of money, tell me it's got to last until the first benchmark—for which you will set the date—and leave it up to me to decide how many workers to hire and how much to pay them. Then if we don't succeed you give me less money to reach the next benchmark, or you fire us."

"But if you beat the schedule," Wright replied, thinking of Ophelia's remark, you'll get a bonus."

"I'm not willing to take the chance. What I want, Mr. Wright, is a contract that sets out the work for which my men and I are responsible and pays an hourly wage for an eight-hour workday, with no pay for hours we can't work because of bad weather."

"If the men are getting paid hourly they can string the work out to make their jobs last longer."

John thought for a moment. "Very well. If you set out a timetable for the tasks you want my men to complete, I'll tell you how many men it will take to complete the tasks within the allotted time. I'll tell you how much they want to get paid and how long they're willing to work each day. We can negotiate each of these items."

Slowly, Wright realized he was not dealing with a country bumpkin, but a shrewd negotiator who would not be bought off by a retainer. He began to regret suggesting John Carter. He started to roll up his charts, not answering immediately. "Well, you've made your position clear. I will take your proposal back to Mr. Schuyler. If he has interest in seeing our discussions continue, I'll be in touch."

John did not think this quite fair. "By when might I expect to hear? I will have to make other plans if Mr. Schuyler refuses my conditions."

"We are eager to start work. I'd say two weeks."

"Very well. If I don't hear by then, I'll assume my services are no longer wanted." He held out his hand.

Wright shook it, signifying commitment, but his grip was not firm.

———•———

A week later, Phidias Wright sat in the Schuylers' cavernous Fifth Avenue drawing room. The weather had turned unseasonably cold and Ophelia had ordered a fire. The maids had closed the drapes at sunset and lit the gas light sconces around the periphery and the kerosene lamps on the Phyfe tables. The fire sprang to life, its heat permeating the still somber room by the time the hosts and their guest entered. After the usual pleasantries, Wright described his meeting with John Carter to Schuyler and his daughter, who sat on the deeply cushioned leather sofa. Wright's chair was oblique to the fireplace allowing him to gain warmth without obstructing the Schuylers' view of the crackling flames. As Wright finished, a servant entered, offering sherry to the occupants. No one spoke until he withdrew.

"Let's be done with him," Schuyler announced angrily.

Ophelia twirled the stem of her glass making the wine swirl. She pouted. "That means we have to start all over, looking for someone else."

"I doubt we'll find another crew as able as the one Carter can put together up there," Wright added.

"The man's a labor radical. When I mentioned that I was

thinking of hiring someone from the Adirondacks, one of the men at my Club suggested I have the Pinkertons check into him. I've just received their report. He was involved with the Haymarket conspirators. Let them rot in hell. He'll organize his workers and teach them things they never would learn without him."

"That may be, "Wright replied. "But his father's record in the New York Assembly—I've done my own research-ing—indicates he's one of the few legislators from the Adirondack counties to vote for bills preserving the forests. That's what we want."

"Even though that might hurt his constituents," Ophelia observed keenly.

J.J. turned to look at his daughter. "What do you mean, darling?"

"Preserving the forests means fewer logging jobs."

"Yes that's true," responded her father. J.J. thought for a minute. "But, you know, Carter and his ilk may want to preserve the forests to give the people access to them. That's not what we want." He turned to Wright. "I've also learned that John's brother, Thomas, writes for that radical rag, *The Nation* and his mother is a suffragist."

"There's nothing wrong with that," flashed Ophelia.

"Dammit, girl, I knew I shouldn't have sent you to Smith College."

"Oh Daddy, you know women are at least as smart as men. You didn't want to petrify my brain at age seventeen, did you?" She leaned over and kissed him on the cheek.

"Well if you're so smart tell me what to do about this Mr. John Carter."

Although she had her own opinion, which she believed

coincided with Wright's, Ophelia thought her father would be more responsive if the recommendation came from Wright. "What would you do, Phidias?" she asked.

Wright had sensed with dread that he would have to make a recommendation. Relieved that the question came from Ophelia, he looked at her while answering and played to her desire to spend the summer at the Lake. "If we're going to get a lot of construction in this year, we've got to go with Carter." Turning to J.J., he added, "He's given you some leeway, Mr. Schuyler; he's willing to negotiate the key points.

"I'd be driven out of the Union Club if my friends knew I was hiring a rabble rouser."

———•———

One morning, shortly before the two-week deadline, Alice handed John a telegram that had been delivered to the Carter house as she was leaving for Dr. Trudeau's laboratory and office.

J J SCHUYLER AUTHORIZES ME NEGOTIATE CONTRACT ALONG LINES YOU SUGGESTED STOP WILL ARRIVE VILLAGE JUNE 4 STOP P WRIGHT

Alice stood near John while he read the telegram. "Is it good news?"

"It's from that architect, Phidias Wright." He handed it to her.

She read it quickly, smiled, and threw her arms around his neck, letting go before he had a chance to respond. "I am so happy for you, John. That means you'll be staying a while longer."

"Not so fast, Alice," he grinned. "There's still some negotiating to do. And I've got to hire a crew and get them to agree."

"Oh, John. I'm sure that won't be difficult. You'll get your friends a deal they could never get on their own. They all love you anyway."

It was true. Since John had returned, he had drawn around him a coterie of loyal friends. The nucleus was the men he had recruited to help rebuild the Mason cabin the previous summer. After that was finished, they hunted together in the fall and then fished through the ice in the winter, attracting others who were out of work to join them. His circle expanded further with his visits most Saturday evenings to one of the taverns in the village.

———•———

Two days before Wright's scheduled arrival, John informed his friends at the Blue Moon Tavern that he might have jobs for them over the summer and maybe even longer for those interested. Not often having the prospect of long-term employment, the men were excited. When one of them started to order a round of lager, John grabbed his arm. "Wait," he said. "I can't promise anything yet."

Roger Corn, a robust man about John's age with a thick red beard, asked, "Why not?"

Tommy, who John often brought with him, held up his pad: *You need a contract.* John nodded in agreement.

Roger asked, "What's a contract?"

"We've got to get Mr. Schuyler, who's the owner of the

property on which we'll build, to agree to the conditions under which we'll work and how much he'll pay us."

"I never did that before. If I got an offer of a job, I just took it," Roger replied.

"What if he don't agree to our terms?" another asked.

*Then you won't work,* Tommy wrote.

"That's very well for you to say, Tommy," Roger told him, "but we've got other mouths to feed."

John interceded. "What Tommy means is if Mr. Schuyler refuses what we ask for, we won't accept his terms. Schuyler's eager to get going. He's not gonna find another group like ours so easily up here. If we hold out, he'll come around."

"What are we asking for?" Alan Phillips wanted to know.

"That each man get paid an hourly wage based on the skill needed to perform his job; so, for instance, a carpenter would get paid more than an unskilled laborer."

"Who's going to decide what each job's worth?"

*You will,* Tommy wrote. *We'll meet together to work it out.*

"The hourly wage isn't our only demand," John continued. "We've got to put a limit on the number of hours we'll work each day and when we get time off." The men were incredulous. One said, "If I'm not free to work to the bone, I won't earn enough to make it worthwhile."

"You're wrong there, mate," Roger told him. "We ask for enough money per hour so working eight or ten hours will guarantee us more than if we worked longer, 'to the bone' as you put it."

"It's also safer if we don't work to exhaustion," John pointed out. In Chicago, the workers are fighting for an eight-hour day. I say we demand it here, too, and if Schuyler refuses we back off to ten hours."

Some of the men were wary at first but they came around to John and Tommy's thinking. They agreed to meet the next evening, when others who wanted to work but were absent, could attend, and also to set up a wage scale. Those who were there the first night explained to the newcomers the next evening what they wanted. The Tavern was past its usual closing when they agreed on a proposal, including wage grades that John could bring to Wright on Monday. The men left the Blue Moon a little tipsier than usual.

John Carter and Phidias Wright met again at Martin's Hotel. The intervening days had been full of rain. Though the weather was dry and mild when the two sat down across a small round table on the balcony overlooking the lake, the black flies and mosquitoes, perturbing Wright more than Carter, drove them inside. Wright expressed shock at Carter's conditions, although from their previous conversation he was prepared and authorized by Schuyler to accept the cheapest deal he could get. For his part, and as agreed by the workers, John accepted a fifty-cents-an-hour lower wage at the top pay grade than his original demand and a ten-hour work day, instead of eight hours, five days a week and half-day on Saturday. They shook hands on the agreement. Wright said he had to get it approved by Schuyler and would telegraph him immediately, but, "confidentially," he told John, "you can be sure he will approve. Once I get his approval, I'll open an account for you at the lumber mill in Tupper Lake and start an account at the Bank of the Adirondacks from which you can draw to pay the men's wages and other purchases. You'll give me an accounting at the end of each month." John was so happy and excited that he literally ran home to tell Tommy, who slapped him on the back.

With Schuyler's money, John bought a large flatbed wagon and a team of horses to haul it, heavy beams and boards from the mill at Tupper Lake, and boulders from nearby quarries. He subcontracted with a friend from Tupper Lake to construct a road that would skirt the Wawbeek and George Phillips's farm to reach Schuyler's property. He constructed a primitive dock near the site of the future boathouse so the property could be reached by water as well. His crew, ranging in age from fifteen to fifty, were excited about the prospect of jobs with hours and wages decent enough that they had only dreamed of and that would last at least until the snow fell and likely would resume the following spring.

By the end of July the stone and wood foundations of the main lodge were laid and the men began work on the floor and the first floor walls. News of the project spread quickly; more stone masons, carpenters and other skilled craftsmen applied for jobs than John could hire. It was not easy for him to turn anyone down. If he smelled alcohol on an applicant's breath or if the man spoke disrespectfully of the owner of the property, John apologized and said there were no openings. But so many qualified workingmen applied that he wired Wright that he could start work on the boathouse without delaying completion of the Main Lodge. Wright wired back, "By all means."

Wright, J.J., and Ophelia arrived on August 11, a Saturday. J.J., standing a few yards away from the Main Lodge, was amazed at what had been accomplished. John climbed down from a scaffold at the second floor level, wiped his hands on his Levi denims, and approached the party. Wright beamed as he introduced him to Mr. Schuyler, noting he had already met Miss Schuyler.

Ophelia did not walk past him this time. She offered her hand and said, "I told you last summer you could call me Ophelia."

"I'll try to do that Miss—Ophelia." She laughed. J.J.'s visage turned serious during this exchange. He made a mental note to speak to Ophelia about being so free with her given name.

"I must say, young man, you've made great progress."

"Thank you, Sir. It's the men really. You're paying them well and they're eager to do a good job."

"Is this your entire crew?" J.J. asked.

"No Sir. As long as we're ahead of schedule half the men are off Saturdays."

"And Sunday, of course," Wright piped in.

"Daddy, let's see what they've done about the boathouse." John led them down off the hill on which the Main lodge was situated along a newly built path leading to the Lake. She gasped. The boathouse had been framed and from the landside Ophelia could peer through the open structure to the deck on the lakeside. "It's wonderful," she exclaimed.

"I hope by the time you leave, Miss—Ophelia, that we'll have the structure enclosed, stairs built from about here"—he walked over to the side of the structure—"up to a balcony overlooking the lake. I'm sorry Ophelia, but I don't think we'll have your room and the fireplace finished by then." He turned to Wright. "It's all according to Mr. Wright's plans."

A shadow crossed Ophelia's face when John made his apology, but she brightened quickly. "Well, if you can enclose it soon, I can change here and not have to run up the hill in my wet bathing clothes."

John had built three temporary rooms in the Main Lodge for the Schuylers and Wright. To reduce the risk of fire from cooking, Wright had designed a kitchen and dining quarters a short distance away under open-air tents. In the Main Lodge, one room was set aside for dining when the weather was inclement. The servants and maids were, as previously, housed in tents.

After the Schuylers arrived, construction slackened. John noticed that whenever Ophelia appeared the men stopped work to look at her. When she emerged in her robe from the Main Lodge to walk to the boathouse a lot of necks were craned. There was even greater pause in anticipation of her return when she often carried her wet bathing clothes in her arms. The men waited expectantly to see if her robe might fall open. John reprimanded the men, but it made little difference.

He discussed this one night with Mary, Alice, and Tommy. Mary laughed. "It's just like men. I'm sure they do a lot of daydreaming about her too."

"Is your Miss Schuyler really that attractive?" Alice asked.

She was pained when John replied, "Yes. She's quite beautiful, Alice. I'd say she's a few inches taller than you. Her walk is more like a glide and when she wears her blonde hair loose it comes down below her shoulder. It gets tossed about in a breeze, quite lovely really."

Alice was sorry she asked. She felt very plain in comparison, although a luxuriant sheen had returned to her auburn hair and the streaks of gray were almost invisible.

"Why, John," Mary asked, "you're not smitten with her yourself, by any chance?

"Don't be ridiculous, Mom. She's of another class. She wouldn't be interested in the likes of me."

Alice noticed that John did not answer Mary's question.

Tommy had been writing and now he handed his pad to John who read it out loud. *You're the one who's going to pay for the men's gaping. I think you should talk to her.*

"What would I say?"

"Tell her to stop strutting. That's what I would say," Alice advised with some malice.

"That's a bit blunt," John replied. "And in fairness to Ophelia, I don't think she's even aware of the men's glances."

Mary and Alice spoke in unison. "Oh yes she is."

⎯⎯⎯•⎯⎯⎯

When the problem did not abate, John thought he would punish the first man he caught looking by docking him pay. The next time Ophelia appeared, the five men nearest her all stopped working the same instant. One of them had the effrontery to greet her, "Good morning, Miss."

"It is lovely," she replied with a smile.

"Going for a swim, Miss?" another asked. She walked past him, then turned. "If the water's not too cold." She saw John observing the scene a few yards away. "Good morning, Mr. Carter. Is everything all right?"

"Uh, yes, Miss Schuyler, just fine."

John decided he had to talk to her. Tommy was right; J.J and Wright would blame him for the slowdown. He had to speak to her before they came to him. The next morning he was, as usual, at the work site at 7 A.M., before the men arrived. Often he had encountered Ophelia on her horse at that hour either on the paths around the camp or on the road to the village. He expected a young woman of her breeding to be up late at night and sleeping late in the morning. This morning he was tying up his horse when she trotted up.

She needed no help dismounting; the groom took the reins and walked the horse slowly to the makeshift stable. "You've given him a fine lather this morning, Ma'am."

"Yes, I have, Bill. I've been out since before dawn." She turned to John. "I rode towards Tupper Lake and headed back so I could see the sunrise. You probably had your back to it."

"That's right, Miss—Ophelia. It is a beautiful morning." She looked stunning, her tight jodhpurs tucked into highly polished brown boots, the sleeves of her silk blouse rolled up to her elbows revealing tanned forearms with downy blonde hair, a riding crop in her hands.

She started up the steps of the Main Lodge. John felt his heart pounding; he had just a second to act. "Ma'am, Miss, uhh…If you don't mind I'd like to have a word with you."

She turned back. "I hope it's not much more. Daddy's probably wondering where I am. He doesn't like my riding alone, especially when it's still dark."

"I'll try to be brief." He had trouble starting, especially as she had already showed her impatience. "It's the men, Ma'am." He could not bring himself to say "Ophelia" under the circumstances.

"What about them?"

"When you're about they stop working."

"I hadn't noticed," she lied. "What do you want me to do about it? Stay inside all day? Or return to the City?"

"Oh no, of course not."

"Because you can't fire up your men you expect me to hide when they're about," she accused petulantly.

John thought of retorting, 'it's you who fire them up.' Instead, "It's slowing down the work. We'll fall behind schedule."

Ophelia realized the dilemma. She wanted the work done as quickly as possible, but now it seemed she was responsible for delaying it. Her mood changed and she sat on the second step, her riding crop across her lap. "Here, John." She motioned him to sit next to her. "Let's discuss this. Have you mentioned this to Daddy or Mr. Wright?"

"No, I haven't."

"I'm glad you didn't. Daddy thinks I'm much too forward." She slapped the crop across her hand. "What do you think?"

"Think about what?"

"Am I too forward?"

"I wouldn't say so, it's just that—"

"Just what?"

"It's just that you are beautiful, Ophelia. You attract the men's attention."

She stopped slapping the whip and looked at him, unsurprised by his observation. "What about yours?"

John felt the warmth start from the back of his neck and spread to his face, too late for him to turn away. Her face was immobile, not a trace of emotion. Her eyes were green. Finally, he almost whispered, "Yes, mine too."

She got up suddenly. "I will try to be more circumspect, John. Thanks for telling me directly." She walked into the Main Lodge.

Ophelia did not make an appearance that day. For the next few days several friends of her father visited, and she was kept busy entertaining them. The pace of the men's work increased noticeably.

By the time the Schuylers departed in early September, the Main Lodge was finished, the Boathouse was sheathed

with logs, and the foundations of less important buildings were laid. John told Mr. Wright that unless there was
an early snow he could roof them and get them enclosed
before the full fury of winter. If the roads were passable or
if he could get across the ice, he could do some inside work
during the winter and resume a full building schedule in
the spring. J.J. and Phidias shook hands warmly with John.
When it was Ophelia's turn she grasped his hand in hers
and gently pulled him close so she could whisper, "Have I
behaved better?" The workers were watching. John thought
he heard a whistle. He flushed, answering only with a smile,
which she returned.

"Just one more thing, Mr. Carter," J.J. addressed him. "I
have ordered one hundred 'No Trespassing' signs. I expected
they would have arrived by now. When they come will you
please have them tacked on trees around the periphery of
the property. I've also hired a game warden, Danny Miller, to
patrol the property to make sure there's no poaching."

John was stunned by Schuyler's pronouncement. He and
the men had talked about hunting in the far reaches of the
property. "Does the edict apply to me and my workers, Mr.
Schuyler? We've been hunting and fishing on this land for
many years."

Schuyler was equally taken aback by John's query. This
was, after all, his private park. "You're allowed on the property to do your jobs. Not at other times," Schuyler sternly
replied.

# PART III

# 11
# Taking the Law

THEY carried Tommy up Little Panther Mountain in a crude open sedan chair, John holding the front poles and their friend Alan Phillips the rear ones. Winding up the southwestern side, the trail was less than a mile long, but so steep in places that the chair tilted precariously. They stopped to mop their brows several times during the hot July morning in 1890. With large boulders and exposed roots impeding their progress, more than an hour elapsed before they emerged from the forest of spruce and birch. Little Panther was the first mountain Tommy had been on since his injury ten years earlier.

On the northeastern side, Little Panther fell steeply in ser-ried cliffs. John and Alan carried Tommy close to the edge and set the chair down. Tommy looked over the cliffs to Upper Saranac Lake six hundred feet below. The lake sparkled in the noonday sun. Here and there squalls darted in contrapuntal dissonance as cloud shadows skidded across the surface. On both shores the lake was heavily forested, the cedars at the shoreline clipped neatly by deer who browsed from the ice in winter. Tommy turned to his companions, tears in his eyes. John bent down and hugged him. "Beautiful, isn't it?"

*You can leave me here to die. I couldn't get enough of it,* Tommy smiled as he wrote on his ever-present note pad and showed it to his companions. A breeze fluttered the pages.

John pointed northward, up the western shore about a mile to a steeply roofed boathouse, its walls covered with cedar shingles that interrupted the forest tree line. Two canoes and a guideboat lay across the wooden dock that ran to the water's edge. "What do you think of that, Tommy?"

Craning his neck, Tommy followed John's finger. *You built that? Very impressive.*

Alan said, "John and his crew built the boathouse and the Main Lodge and Dining Hall. I put together the furniture and ornamentation."

"Alan's a master craftsman," John added. He paused for a moment. "Too bad you'll never get to see his work in Camp Leatherstocking."

*Because we've been banished from the property?*

"Yeah! One thousand acres of prime hunting land and ponds and streams for fishing. Those lands provided food for our families over the winter," Alan commented.

"I delayed posting the 'no trespassing' signs Mr. Schuyler requested as long as I could, but Danny Miller said he'd complain to Mr. Schuyler if I didn't put them up."

"Danny Miller?"

"Yeah," John replied. "I guess I never told you that Mr. Schuyler hired him as his game warden."

*That worm. Taking jobs like game warden. He probably did uncouple the caboose that ran me down,* Tommy scribbled furiously.

John motioned to Alan to pick up his poles; they carried Tommy a few yards to the southern side of the summit. Tommy looked out at the new Corey's inn, then turned his head more to the west and jotted a question. *Is that the land Mama gave to the state?* John nodded. It was a peninsula of dense green tall trees surrounded on three sides by saplings and shrubs struggling to emerge among jagged charred stumps in the still blackened earth.

Alan addressed the brothers. "Thank god for people like your folks, trying to protect the land for us by giving it to the state. Left to the railroad companies, the lumber companies, and the Great Camps, there'd be nothing to hunt and fish on."

Tommy reached for his pencil. *Dad says the County can raise taxes on the Great Camps if they don't open up their woods.*

John loved his stepfather, but he laughed when he read Tommy's comment. "Cyrus thinks the law can solve every problem. Schuyler and the other grand landlords will bribe the County Commissioners not to raise taxes. If they don't succeed, they'll pay the tax. It's a pittance for them."

Little was said as John and Alan carried Tommy down the mountain. Over the previous winter, the first in which they couldn't hunt on the land Schuyler had bought, many men in the village, including those who had worked for John in constructing Camp Leatherstocking, had talked about frightening Schuyler so he and the other large landowners would think twice about prohibiting the townspeople from hunting on their land.

John had no great like for J.J. Schuyler, even though he had made John wealthy by local standards when he hired him to build the camp. That was not the reason John did not want to anger him. There was, first of all, his reluctance to initiate an act that could be illegal and might end in violence. Responding to police violence with violence was one thing, but starting it was another. Second was Ophelia. He often thought of the summer day in 1888, two years earlier, when Phidias Wright and Ophelia rowed across the

lake to the cabin John had been building for Eleanor and
Jared Mason. Ophelia lifted her white linen dress above her
knees as she stepped barefoot out of the guideboat. She was
the most beautiful woman John had seen. He remembered
how, one year ago when he told her she was distracting the
men, he blushed as he confessed that she also attracted him
and how she smiled at him when she and her father left
for the season. The completion of Camp Leatherstocking
should have ended any fantasy John had regarding Ophelia.
Still, he did not want to break his good relations with the
Schuyler family.

Coming down Little Panther was more treacherous than
going up; John stumbled over a root and almost dropped his
pole, causing Tommy to list dangerously. When they reached
the base of the mountain, John and Alan lifted Tommy out
of the chair and lashed him and the chair securely on John's
flat bed wagon, returning to the village late in the afternoon.

Early in July, J.J. Schuyler's manager had arrived in Saranac Lake Village to begin recruiting chambermaids, cooks,
and groundskeepers. To those lucky enough to land jobs,
the six-weeks' salary provided a small cushion for getting
through the coming winter, but the special train that carried
the Schuylers to Axton Landing, the closest stop, brought so
many supplies that the camp hardly relied on the shopkeepers of Saranac or Tupper Lakes at all. The Schuylers were not
good for business.

A letter was waiting for John when he and Tommy
returned from Little Panther. He slit the envelope open
and drew out the handwritten letter embossed with the

Schuylers' Manhattan address and tinged with perfume. "Dear John," he read, surprised but pleased by the use of his first name.

> Daddy and I will be arriving on Monday August fourth. There are a few small changes I would like to make in the Boathouse. Daddy is letting me live there rather than in the Main Lodge. He has instructed his warden to permit you to enter Camp Leatherstocking on Tuesday afternoon, August fifth. Come straight to the boathouse.
>
> Yours truly,
> Ophelia Schuyler

Back in his wheelchair, Tommy watched as John read the letter. His heart pounding, John wanted to hide the letter but he had to give some explanation. "It's from Miss Schuyler. She wants me to make some changes in the boathouse." Not interested in pursuing the matter, Tommy did not pull out his notepad.

———•———

John rode out to Camp Leatherstocking at the appointed time. Danny Miller came out of his cabin just inside the wooden gate. "Afternoon, Danny. Miss Schuyler has asked me to come about making some changes."

"Yeah, I've got your name, Carter." He swung back the gate and John rode through, hitching his horse at one of the posts near the Main Lodge. He made his way to the door on the land side of the boathouse. Ophelia, wearing her bath-robe, appeared on the rear balcony, peering down at John, then motioning him to enter. She turned, disappearing into the bedroom.

John climbed the stairs and knocked at the inner door.

"Come, please," Ophelia answered softly. She was sitting at her dressing table, her back to John, her damp blonde hair spilling over her robe. She was trying to fasten a necklace. "John," she said into the mirror in front of her, "come here and help with my necklace. I'm so clumsy at these things."

"I'm afraid I won't be much better, Miss Schuyler," but he walked toward her.

His face disappeared from the mirror as he approached and she saw only his torso. She turned and looked at him directly for the first time, smiling winsomely. "Well, give it a try." As he reached her she turned back toward the mirror. John took an end of the necklace in each hand, examining the clasp analytically. He had little trouble connecting the strands. Ophelia reached up to test the necklace and then grasped John's hands in hers, holding them quietly for a moment. Then she pulled them forward over her shoulders to her breasts. Her eyes closed, she spoke softly. "I've dreamed of you all winter, John." Ophelia stood, turned to face John, letting her robe fall to the floor. She started to unbutton his shirt.

Heart pounding, all John could say was, "I thought you wanted some changes in the Boathouse, Ophelia."

She led him to the bed. "This is the change I was talk-ing about. Everything you did was perfect. I'm sure you can keep it that way."

A half-hour later a bell rang from the dining hall. "Oh

dear, time flies when you're having fun. I must dress for dinner. You'd best be off."

Gathering his clothes, John asked, "Can I see you again?"

"Daddy doesn't want you or your men on the grounds now that the work is completed." Struggling into his pants, John said nothing, wondering whether he had satisfied her lust for all time. "That seems unjust to me," Ophelia continued. "Come by the lake after dark on Thursday. You know the narrow beach just below the boathouse. Land your boat and come up if my lamp is on. The Guards make their last rounds about ten o'clock. Maybe we can think of some small projects to allow you to keep coming."

Walking back to his horse, John played out the scenarios. He would wait until everyone was asleep, then ride to the Indian Carry—almost an hour from the Village—launch the boat and row up the lake to the Schuyler camp—another half hour. And what if her lamp was off? Retrace his steps, get home well after midnight, and not even a pleasant memory to show for it.

What if her lamp was on? That raised even greater problems. Yes, it was a new and exciting experience to him, but what would come of it? He was a bastard himself. In his parent's case, he was sure—having been told by Cyrus and his mother—that she and Jean loved each other and would have married had Jean not been killed helping Cyrus break the logjam. John did not want to sire a bastard. He hoped he hadn't already.

John was surprised when one of the few women from the village who worked at Camp Leatherstocking as a maid brought him a letter from Ophelia the next day. She had gone to school with John and waited as he opened and read it.

> Dear John,
>
>    Daddy learned of our tryst. He insists that I sleep in the Main Lodge and has given our warden orders that you are forbidden on the property. He discards you as an old shoe once he has gotten what he wants. He told me I would not be happy with you. That is for me to decide. I am a grown woman.
>
>    I fear what my father would do if you were caught. We will have to make some other arrangement.
>
>    Fondly,
>    Ophelia

For the moment, Ophelia had solved John's dilemma, at the same time declaring her concern for his safety. Maybe she really did love him. He looked up, surprised to see the woman waiting. "Did she tell you to wait for a reply?"

"No, John. I thought—"

John did not want to be curt. He confided, "It's not the kind of letter that can be answered right away."

———•———

Thursday night, when Ophelia might have been waiting for him, John was at the Watering Hole, one of the Village's taverns, with five of the men who had worked with him at Schuyler's and Tommy in his wheelchair.

A few of the men had tried to hunt on the property after

the Schuylers had left and had been run off by Danny Miller and his dogs. They did not know how their families would make it through another winter. Tommy passed around a note. *Tar and feather Miller.* Silence prevailed until everyone had read it.

John looked at his brother in disbelief. "How can you think of doing such a thing?"

Roger Corn, who had used pine tar to waterproof the window frames and doors at Leatherstocking, laughed, "Why not? It's more humane than killing. You can get the tar warm enough to pour and still not burn. I've stuck my hand in warm pitch and I'm fine." He held his hand up to show it was unscarred.

Alan Phillips, still annoyed that Paul Smith and Schuyler had tried to steal his father's land, said, "I've just read *Huckleberry Finn* in which Mr. Twain has the Duke and Dauphin, who committed one fraud after another, tarred and feathered by the townspeople. What Schuyler and his accomplice Miller are doing is a lot worse than fraud; they'll kill people by starvation."

Tommy had been writing as he listened. *If we tar and feather Miller, no one will risk taking his place. Schuyler might not change his mind but no one will enforce his 'no trespassing.'*

One of the others said, "We can do it in the dead of night; drag Miller out of his cabin near the entrance of Camp Leatherstocking and pour the tar and feathers over him before he realizes what's happening." The others nodded in approval.

John felt uncomfortable. He had seen what violence was like. Shooting to kill was worse than tar and feathering. He was bothered that the men would do it surreptitiously, but he realized if they were to do it openly they'd go to jail and their families would be worse off. It was the first time that he and Tommy had disagreed openly. He turned to his brother, "You're not seeking retribution for Miller's uncoupling the caboose?"

Tommy glared at his brother. Thinking for a moment, he wrote, *There's no evidence he did.* Most of the men knew what the brothers were talking about. They turned angrily against John. John regretted that he questioned Tommy's motives.

With another round of beers the men raised questions about the actual plan: How could they rouse Miller from his cabin? How could they escape unseen? A lot of debate concerned the feathers, which they would dump on Miller after the tar was poured. Pulling the feathers off tore the skin under the tar unless it was done gently while the man soaked in hot water that would soften the tar. They concluded that one of the men would shoot two ducks—enough to yield the feathers while at the same time providing a good meal for his family.

John sat glumly as the men, including Tommy, ironed out the details. *Am I beginning to think like a landowner? Am I letting my feelings for Ophelia get in the way?* He concluded those were not his concerns. He told himself that the tarring would be unlikely to scare off either Miller or Schuyler and would end badly for the men involved. Still, as he listened to the men he was uncertain. The plan had an appealing bravado. In a lull in the conversation, the men turned to him. "Are you with us, John?" Roger asked.

He answered slowly. "I don't know better than any of you whether this plan will work, but—" he hesitated, "I think Schuyler's policy needs to change and changing the law will take too long." Again he paused, then smiled wryly, "I'll provide the cauldron to warm the tar and the wagon and horses to get us to Camp Leatherstocking." The men applauded and slapped John on the back. Tommy sat quietly. It was past midnight when they broke up, agreeing to meet at the Blue Moon Tavern a few days later to make the final preparations and select the date, a night when the moon would be down.

John wheeled Tommy home, saying nothing. He was angry with Tommy for suggesting the plan. *Tommy won't even be there*, he thought. *What right does he have to suggest it?*

Everyone was asleep when they got home. Instead of going to bed, Tommy wheeled himself into the parlor, wrote a note, and handed it to John. *You need me along John. I can be your decoy.*

"You're crazy, Tommy. What if something goes wrong? How are we gonna get you out of there?" John noticed that the fire Cyrus had built after supper had not died out completely and threw another log on to dissipate the chill of the August night. Tommy wrote for a few minutes before he handed his pad to John.

*You can drop me at the foot of Indian Carry, and I'll row up the lake in Dad's guideboat, beaching it near Leatherstocking's boathouse. Sitting in the boat, I'll draw attention away from you by firing three shots, using Dad's old musket. Schuyler's guards will come to investigate. By the time they get there, I'll be rowing down the lake in darkness. The shots might awaken Miller—he's only a half-mile away—and he'll come out of his cabin and you can grab him. I'll wait for you at the foot of the Indian Carry. I may not be able to move my legs, but my arms are as strong as yours for row-ing.* He flexed his biceps to emphasize his point. He wrote some more. *You didn't think I meant to allow others to expose themselves to danger without exposing myself?*

John realized he should have known that Tommy would want to be part of the action. He hugged him and took his notes and threw them into the fire.

Over the next few days, Tommy worked on another article for *The Nation.* He showed it to John, but no one else, before the next meeting at the Blue Moon.

> More than one hundred years ago, large landowners in England began to merge strips of common land and enclose them, making it impossible for small farmers to earn a living from planting in the commons. The practice forced many people from rural areas into cities where they became grist in the mill of the industrial revolution. Parliament passed laws ensuring that the lands remained enclosed. Today we are witnessing a kind of enclosure much closer to home.
>
> The Adirondacks, a region of high mountains, pleasant valleys, and crystal clear streams and lakes, were almost laid waste by lumbering companies who denuded softwood forests and then refused to pay their taxes, moving elsewhere to continue the process of ravaging the woodlands. The naked lands fell to the New York State government, which did little to improve or restore them. The iron mines and foundries in the area cut the hardwoods to make charcoal for their furnaces. The hardwoods were further excised in the eighteen seventies, when railroads replaced the rivers as the principal pathway by which timber was brought to market.

Slowly, it dawned on downstate citizens that if the process continued it could interfere with New York City's water supply while increasing the chance of flooding upstate, as well as fire in periods of drought when sparks from railroad engines were particularly likely to ignite the detritus left by the loggers. Some railroad magnates recognized they would be left without a growing source of revenue if the burgeoning tourist trade in the Adirondacks, which was built on the appeal of unspoiled mountains, lakes, and streams, were cut dead in its tracks at the hands of the logger's axe. In 1885, the New York legislature recognized the problem and declared that Adirondack land owned by the State should be "forever wild," prohibiting further logging on it. The State has, however, been slow to buy land that has not yet been logged. Wealthy bankers and businessmen from downstate stepped into the breach, buying large tracts of unspoiled land from local farmers and entrepreneurs. Herein lies the new form of enclosure. For several years New York has had a law that allows landowners to establish private parks from which they can forbid anyone from hunting and fishing without the consent of the owner and can also forbid trespassing. Penalties can be exacted.

Although not in the public domain, the forests, lakes, and streams have been used by the local population for hunting and fishing. The wildlife—moose and deer on the land, trout and bass in the streams and lakes, birds in the air—are an important source of food for the families who live in the region year round. Now the downstate capitalists are building "Great Camps" and *enclosing* the surrounding forests for their private hunting and fishing preserves, using the Private Parks law to do so, not because they need the food but for their own recreation. They have forbidden trespassing.

The logging that once sustained the local population has now gone, either because the woods have been lumbered out or because the remaining forests have been enclosed. With little livelihood, the people who live in the Adirondacks the year round face privation if their food supply is cut off. This desperate situation has led some to take direct action, having received no help from a legislature in the hands of vested interests, including wealthy landowners. A game warden working for one of these landowners was recently tarred and feathered by an unknown group, presumably locals, for strictly enforcing his lord's "no trespassing" edict. The people cannot tolerate a legislature that places nature's bounty outside honest people's domain.

> Thomas Carter
> Saranac Lake, NY
> September __, 1890

———•———

As planned, the men met at the Blue Moon a few days after their last meeting. One of them carried a sack full of feathers that he handed to John. "A great plan so far," he said. "My family sure appreciated those ducks." John reported that he had procured the pine tar and could load the cauldron on to his wagon. He told the men that Tommy had volunteered to serve as a decoy, rowing to Schuyler's beach and firing three shots to divert attention from the gate to the camp, near Miller's cabin. The men slapped Tommy on the back, thanking him for his bravery.

"Tommy's written another article for *The Nation*," John told the men. He pulled it out of his jacket pocket. "It's too long to read now, but here's the last paragraph." In a low voice, he read it to them. When he finished he told them, "Of course, he's not going to send it until after we carry out our plan."

They agreed on the early morning of August 23, a Saturday, when there would be a waning moon that would set early. The best time, they decided, would be before dawn. If Miller heard Tommy's shots he would run out and they could nab him before the dogs were aroused. If he didn't, one of the men would fire his gun. They concluded only three men were needed, one to serve as lookout and shoot the dogs if necessary and two to capture Miller and carry out the punishment. John said he was definitely one of them. Everybody else wanted to go. Alan Phillips got six straws from the bar. He cut two of them short and then gave the bunch to Tommy who wrapped his fist around them so they all seemed the same length. Roger and Alan both drew short straws. All of the men vowed secrecy.

At three-thirty of the appointed morning, John arrived at the Indian Carry with his flatbed wagon loaded with Tommy, the cauldron filled with warm pine tar, Cyrus's rifle, gunpowder and balls, and the pair of oars. In darkness except for the star speckled sky, he carried Tommy down the Carry and sat him on the narrow beach. Walking a few steps, he turned the guideboat over and hauled it out of the bushes to the shore. He sat Tommy in the boat, handed him the oars, the rifle and ammunition, and pushed him afloat.

Having hitched their horses to trees a short distance from the Carry, Alan and Roger met John as he returned from the lake. They climbed on to the wagon and headed west and then north, stopping fifty yards short of the gate to Camp Leatherstocking. From the lake they heard a loon wail, but no other sound.

When Tommy started rowing the shore looked impenetrable. By the time he approached the boathouse his eyes had accommodated to the darkness; he had no trouble recognizing the structure, though the lake was shrouded in mist. No breeze ruffled the water. Across the lake the eastern horizon glowed faintly. Quietly, Tommy nudged the stern of the boat onto the beach, so it just stuck. He heard the loon wail and also the mate's answer farther up the lake. By this time, he thought, John and the other two would have reached the gate to the Camp. He had loaded and cocked his rifle, preparing to fire the first shot, when he heard hoof beats coming toward him. *Who could be out at this hour?* he wondered. John had told him the guards stopped patrolling around ten o'clock. *Could someone have revealed our plot to Schuyler, or was John wrong about the guards?'* At a slow canter, horse and rider emerged on the beach not five feet away, barely visible against the black forest. The horse slowed to a walk, continuing off the beach on to a thin path along the water's edge. As he raised his rifle to fire into the air another

rider emerged on to the beach, trailing the first by twenty-
five yards. Tommy doubted either rider had seen him, but
he was sure they were on to the plan. *The point of my being
here is to distract Schuyler's guards. If I fire into the air, one of these
men will surely shoot me. Better I disable one of them.* With the
time it took to reload, he knew he could not shoot both of
them. The first rider was now to Tommy's left and would
soon be out of sight. He lowered his rifle and fired. Startled,
the horse leaped ahead, running into the lake. The rider fell
with a splash. The second rider halted abruptly. Seeing the
flash from Tommy's rifle, he fired twice in rapid succession.

Tommy did not realize he had been hit until he felt
warm liquid on his chest. He was desperate to give John and
the others a warning. "AAAAaaaagh," he screamed, emitting
the sound with a torrent of bloody foam. "I've got my voice
back," he said happily as he took his last breath.

The second rider dismounted and ran to the lake. Sobbing, J.J. Schuyler lifted his daughter from the water, laying
her on the narrow beach. In the faint light he could see the
crimson stain on her tunic and the ghostly white of her face.
Schuyler ran to the boat, expecting to find John in it. As he
rolled Tommy over, he heard the dogs wailing near the gate.
Putting one foot on the transom, he shoved the boat adrift
in blind fury.

John and his companions quietly entered Camp Leatherstocking through a narrow gap in the shrubs just to the
right of the gate. They waited outside Miller's cabin until
they heard three shots. They did not hear Tommy's scream.
The shots awakened Miller. As he emerged, the men threw

a hood over his head, ripped off his nightshirt, and silently dragged him through the gap where they poured the liquid pine tar over him followed by the feathers. They jumped on the wagon, and John whipped the horses as Miller's dogs barked from their compound. Reaching the Indian Carry, Alan and Roger jumped off and mounted their horses, heading back to the village.

John doubted Tommy would have yet reached the southern shore and took his time walking down the carry. The glow on the eastern horizon had expanded and John could see wisps of mist rising from the lake. The morning was unusually warm for late August. Pleased to have carried off their escapade, he stretched out on the beach, leaning on his elbow and plucked a few blades of grass, chewing them slowly as he looked over the lake, waiting for Tommy to appear.

# 12

# First Burial

JOHN waited until the sun was just high enough for him to see past Birch Island almost up to The Narrows. Fortunately, the mist shrouding the lake at dawn had lifted. Because the lake bulged to the west he could not see any of Camp Leatherstocking or the water immediately to its east from his vantage point. If Tommy had stuck to the western shore when he rowed south to the foot of Indian Carry he would have been visible by now. The lake was perfectly calm, offering no resistance even to a weak rower, and completely empty; the fishermen were not yet out. If Tommy had beaten him back, he would have to wait for John to lift him out of the boat. John walked along the shore to satisfy himself that Tommy was not there. Reluctantly, he left the lake and headed up the Carry to where he had left the wagon. He made sure the cauldron was securely fastened; the remaining tar in it was cold and barely malleable to his touch. He drove back to the village, not encountering any wagon or riders in either direction. As quietly as he could, he unhitched the horses, led them to graze in back of the house, pulled the wagon into the shed, covering the cauldron with a tarpaulin—he'd get rid of the scab of tar later—and walked to the front of the house. Alice was just coming out of the door and greeted John cheerily. "My, you're up early this morning."

"Yes I wanted to see the sunrise," he replied flatly.

Alice looked at him closely. "John, you look like you've been up all night." She surveyed him from head to foot. His clothes were rumpled. She wondered if he had been with that woman from the Great Camp.

"No, I—"

"Look at your boots," she interrupted. "What is that black stuff? What have you been doing?"

He looked at his feet, then at her. "It's a long story, you'll be late to work if I start now."

"Very well, maybe this evening?" She turned to the street.

"Maybe," he replied.

Mary and Cyrus were having breakfast when John entered, having set the horses to graze after meeting Alice. "Were you out for a swim in Moody Pond? It's hot for this hour." Mary asked. She looked him over carefully, as she was wont to do, and answered her own question. "Doesn't look like it. But it does look like you've been up for hours."

John struggled with what to say. Neither Mary nor Cyrus knew anything about the planning for the previous night's escapade. Wishfully, he asked, "Is Tommy up yet?"

"Haven't seen him," Cyrus answered unconcernedly.

John cut himself a slice of bread and put it on the stove iron to toast. He wasn't very hungry. The three of them were sitting at the kitchen table when Eleanor Mason rode up.

---

The morning of Saturday August 23 was exceptionally warm, one of those rare late summer days when the trees and leaves stood motionless in the early morning and the reflection of the sun in the lake was as bright as the sun itself. As usual, Jared had slept soundly, undisturbed by the gunshots or the barking of the dogs on the west side of the lake. Next to him Eleanor still slept. During the mild night she had thrown off the covers; nightgown gathered around her hips revealed her thighs and legs. Jared resisted the urge to stroke them and decided instead to get up. He joined Henry at the small table in the kitchen. Up with the sunrise two hours earlier, Henry had made coffee on the new pot-bellied stove. When he heard Jared stirring, he came in from the small porch, where he had been reading, to pour Jared a cup. Neither spoke for a few moments.

Draining his cup, Jared broke the silence. "Such a rare morning, Henry, I feel like a swim."

"When's the last time you swam here, Jared?"

"Not since the summer before Eleanor and I were married."

"Not that my advice is worth much, Jared, but I think you need to be sure you're close to a cure before you plunge in. The air may be warm, but the water's cold."

Resigned, Jared knew Henry was right. Yet he wanted to be on the water. "I'll take out the dinghy and just enjoy the water from the surface."

"That's better. But if you tire, take a rest and turn around."

John and his crew had built the Masons a small dock on wooden stilts, which were sunk deep into the muddy bottom. Jared loosened the painter from the cleat on the dock, coiled the rope neatly in the bow of the boat, then set out toward the mouth of the cove, coming close to a loon that dived as he approached, surfacing much farther away. As he turned west into the main channel of Bartlett's Bay a family of river otters broke the water and swam alongside playfully before disappearing in the dark waters. Silence prevailed. A gentle breeze came up from the west, quietly ruffling the water.

Still feeling strong when he reached the mouth of the bay, Jared turned south towards the Indian Carry. Glancing up the lake, he spotted another boat in front of Birch Island, not far from him. He did not see anyone in the boat. *Must have not been moored securely,* he thought. He pivoted his dinghy around and rowed toward the boat, his back to it. Turning his head when he got closer, he recognized Cyrus's guideboat. He remembered back to the day after Cyrus and Mary's wedding in 1860 when Cyrus and Mitchell Sabattis had found the same boat adrift on the lake, which led them to the realization that Peter O'Rourke's father and the Reverend Loguen had been kidnapped.

The boat was perpendicular to Jared's, one oar dipped unattended into the water. He brought his boat around parallel to the guideboat and rowed alongside. So unprepared was Jared to see the supine body lying on the boat's ribbed bottom, a clotted mass of blood around it that a few seconds passed before he recognized Tommy, his eyes staring at the blue sky unseeingly, the traces of what might have been a smile on his lifeless lips.

Jared's first thought was not what had happened to Tommy but how he was going to tell Mary. *Why me, again?* he asked. Thirty years before when Mary's lover, Jean, had been killed in the logjam that also broke Cyrus's leg, it was Jared who broke the news to Mary.

Moving forward, Jared untied the painter from the bow, carried it to the stern. From there he pushed the guideboat aft of his dinghy, tying the two together, stern to bow.

Suddenly he was exhausted. Hauling the extra boat

more than doubled his load, but it was the discovery that weighed him down. With a rifle on the floor of the boat, Jared fleetingly wondered whether Tommy, discouraged by his condition, had taken his own life. But Tommy would have needed help getting into the boat, and his arms were not long enough to pull the trigger with the muzzle close to his chest.

Long awake, Eleanor was out on the large rock in front of their cabin, worrying what had happened to her husband, when she saw him entering the cove, another boat in tow. As he approached, she stepped on the dock, grabbing the bow of the dinghy as Jared pulled alongside. He pointed to the guideboat and started to cry. Eleanor gasped as she recognized Tommy's corpse. She inspected it for a moment then untied the painter from the stern of Jared's dinghy and used it to drag the bow of the guideboat on to the shore. Then she untied the painter, placed it back on the bow of the dinghy, which she secured to the dock. She helped Jared on to the dock and the two of them dragged the guideboat farther up the sloping bank. Jared leaned on her for the short walk up to the cabin.

"Jared found Tommy Carter in Cyrus's guideboat," she told her father.

"Is he all right?"

"He's dead. Looks like a gunshot wound in the chest."

Jared sank down in one of the chairs at the kitchen table and buried his head between his arms. Henry sat down next to him put his arm around Jared's shoulder. "Who would have done a thing like that?" he asked, pausing reflectively. "You don't suppose he—"

Jared raised his head. "He'd have a hard time shooting

himself in the chest with his rifle." He sunk his head back on the table.

Eleanor stood beside him, putting her hands on the back of his neck. "I will saddle the horse and drive to the village to tell the Carters."

"No, dear, I'll go." When he told Mary thirty years ago that Jean was missing and presumably drowned she became hysterical. He worried she would receive news of her son's death the same way.

Eleanor looked at his face, more haggard than it had been for weeks.

"You've done more than enough for one day, darling. It will be almost as hard on you as it will be on Mary and Cyrus. I'll go."

"Eleanor is right, Jared. Let her go." Henry said softly.

Before she left, Eleanor helped Jared and Henry lift Tommy from the boat and lay him on the hearth of the fireplace. She removed his shirt and immediately saw the bullet wound. Turning him over, she saw no exit of the bullet. "I'm sure Mary and Cyrus will come out to view him and collect the body. The two of you can clean the blood away. Jared, maybe you can put one of your clean shirts on him."

———•———

"Eleanor!" Mary called out as she let the doctor in. "You're here so early. Is someone in the village sick? Or having a baby? I hadn't heard of anyone who was—" She stopped as Eleanor, grief on her face, came forward and hugged Mary tightly. Realizing something terrible had happened, Cyrus got up. John remained seated, closing his eyes tightly. "It's Tommy," Eleanor said softly.

"What do you mean? Tommy's asleep in his room." Slowly, uncertainly, Mary released herself from Eleanor's hug and walked to Tommy's room, knocked and opened the door. She returned to the table, took her seat. "Where is he?"

"He's at our cabin. He's been shot." As if receiving a blow, Cyrus staggered to the table and sat down. "Is he OK?" Eleanor did not answer. "How badly hurt?" Cyrus continued. John lifted his head inquiringly.

Eleanor bade Mary sit down. "Jared went out for a row—I guess it must have been around seven o'clock. He found your guideboat just outside of Bartlett Bay, Tommy lying in the bottom, his chest covered with clotted blood, a rifle on the bottom of the boat. He was shot in the chest."

"Dead?" Mary asked.

Eleanor nodded. "Jared pulled the dinghy back to our dock. I'd say Tommy had been dead for several hours. He's at our place now."

Cyrus placed his hand on the table to steady himself as he rose and walked into the parlor, returning a moment later. "My rifle is missing." He turned to John. "Tommy couldn't have gotten it down without someone's help." John got up, tears streaming down his face, and threw his arms around Cyrus, something he had not done since infancy. Cyrus pried his arms away. "You didn't—?" Mary looked at John numbly.

Shaking his head, still sobbing, John sat at the table. "I loved him. I never should have let him come. I wish I had his strength. We wanted to teach Schuyler a lesson."

"Schuyler?" Mary asked. "That man you worked for? What has he got to do with this?" Trembling, she got up and ladled a glass of water from the bucket, placing it on the table in front of John, spilling part of it. He took a few swallows and soon was able to talk calmly.

"Schuyler's forbidden us from hunting and fishing on the property. It means starvation for people up here unless we put a stop to it." He paused to glance at Cyrus who stared back unmoving. "Last night I took Tommy to the foot of the Indian Carry, set him in the—" again he glanced at Cyrus, "in your guideboat, with your rifle, and pushed him off to row to Schuyler's beach. The idea of Tommy's getting involved was his own."

"Yes, Tommy would want to be involved." Mary inserted.

"What were you going to do?" Cyrus asked.

John continued, apparently ignoring Cyrus's question. "Then I met two of my friends where the Carry crosses the road, and we drove my wagon to the gate of the Schuyler camp. Tommy was going to give us time to get there and then fire three shots to divert attention from what we were about to do. Then he was going to row back down to the Carry. We heard the shots." As he spoke and recalled the sound of the shots it occurred to him that they had come too rapidly. Despite Tommy's expertise with Cyrus's muzzle-loader, John doubted he could have reloaded quickly enough to fire them that fast.

Impatiently, Cyrus repeated his question. "What were you about to do?"

Putting the puzzle of the shots out of his mind, John continued. "We were going to tar and feather Danny Miller, Schuyler's game warden." He stopped again. No one spoke. "The shots that Tommy fired from lakeside awakened Miller. We grabbed him as he ran out of the cabin near the main gate, poured pine tar over him and then threw the feathers on the tar. The three of us took off in the wagon before the dogs could get out. I waited past sun-up for Tommy at the Carry. There was no sign of him on the lake when I headed back home."

Cyrus got up and began to pace back and forth. "How could you, John? Taking the law in your hands," he sputtered. "Violence begets violence! You've proved it yourself now." Calming down a bit, he said, "Now is not the time to discuss this, John. Go and hitch the horses to the wagon. We've got to get Tommy."

"Do you want me to come?"

"That's for you to decide," Cyrus replied curtly.

"Yes, we do want you to come, dear," Mary said to her son, trying to feel more sympathy for him than her husband did.

Eleanor hugged Mary. "I'll meet you at our cabin," she whispered and departed.

Mary did not cry until she saw Tommy's body, but even then her tears were more subdued than John's outburst when he learned that his brother had been killed. "We were lucky to have Tommy with us so long," she said. "But I didn't expect him to die this way." Cyrus hugged her tightly.

"What are you going to do with his body?" Jared asked.

"Bury him," Mary immediately replied. "The sooner the better."

"But there's a killer loose," Cyrus said. "If we can't produce the body, who ever did it goes scot-free."

"I don't want an eye for an eye, Cyrus," Mary replied. "We've had enough pain. It took years to get a conviction on Frank Miller." She paused to wipe her eyes. "Let's say Tommy died of natural causes. God knows he had enough reason."

The Carters brought Tommy and the rifle back to the

village. Cyrus hung the musket back on the parlor wall. John walked over to Lisa's house and told her what had happened. She returned home with him, and she and Mary, with much crying and tenderness, laid Tommy on his bed and prepared his body for burial.

---

An unusual number of new patients kept Alice for more than her half day's work that Saturday so the Carters had already brought Tommy's body home when Alice returned from Dr. Trudeau's. She gasped to learn that he had been killed. "Tommy was such a sweet boy," she cried. "Who would want to kill him? We took such good care of him. He could have lived for a long time."

John had enough lumber in the shed to start working on a coffin. In the evening, Alice came out to watch him. Neither of them spoke for a while. "Tommy once told me he loved me," she said softly."

John looked at her. She had washed away her tears and her face was calm. He hammered another nail in the coffin. He wanted to ask, "Did you love him?" but saw no purpose in the question. Instead, he said, "He never told me."

She continued to reminisce. "It was on a bitter cold day before I had gone to work for Dr. Trudeau. I lifted him out of bed and slipped. I fell on top of him and we kissed—" Quickly, she corrected herself, "and he kissed me."

John stopped hammering and looked at her. Now she looked wistful. She was pretty, he thought. "You were much older than Tommy."

She shook off her reverie. "Nine years. He was only fourteen years older than my son, Donald." She replied so

quickly that John knew she had memorized the age differences. "I knew nothing could come of it. It was then that I
decided to get a job and spend less time with him, hoping
his infatuation would pass."

"Did it?"

"You know as much as I do, John." She watched John
work a little longer, then quietly returned to the house. She
had meant to ask him about the black stuff on his shoes, but
had forgotten.

———•———

On Sunday, they buried Tommy in the cemetery on the
Bartlett's property where John's father and Mary's uncle
were also at rest. John, Cyrus, Jared, and Peter O'Rourke, Jr.
were the pallbearers. Mary, Alice, Eleanor, Lisa O'Rourke,
and Henry Weinberg followed them.

Eleanor went to the Town Clerk's office on Monday and
filed the death certificate. They had agreed to list the date of
death as August 22, a day before the shooting and four days
before Tommy's funeral. "Pulmonary congestion," Eleanor
wrote as the cause of death. At the same time, John went
to the office of *The Daily Enterprise* to file Tommy's obituary, saying he had died on August 21 after a long illness. He
said to the man behind the desk, "I've been absorbed by my
brother's death. Anything newsworthy happening?"

"Nothing newsworthy ever happens around here," he
replied.

# 13

# Second Burial

AFTER Schuyler set the guideboat adrift, he walked quickly back to Ophelia. When he heard the dogs barking at the main gate on the other side of his camp it occurred to him that the man he had just killed might have been part of a plot. Yet he was so laden with the death of his daughter that he could not think clearly. He laid Ophelia in front of the pommel of his saddle, mounted his horse and returned to the main lodge at a stately walk. A few of Schuyler's servants having heard the shots met him on the path. In the dim light, they saw Ophelia's body lying across the horse's withers. Schuyler motioned them away. Quietly, they followed the horse and its rider to the lodge.

When they heard the dogs bark, two other servants ran in the opposite direction to the gate to investigate. They arrived back at the lodge within moments of Schuyler. "Sir," one of them started to say, but Schuyler, dismounting, motioned him away.

As Schuyler started to lift his daughter off, the horse took a step forward and Ophelia's body slipped to the ground. One of the maids and Schuyler's steward stepped forward and with Schuyler they carried Ophelia into the lodge, laying her on a sofa. J.J. Schuyler knelt beside her body, laid his head on her breast and wept quietly. The maid and steward retreated to the far end of the room. After a few minutes,

Schuyler roused himself and addressed the steward. Have the maids clean my daughter and prepare her for burial."

"Yes Sir. Do you want me to call the sheriff?"

Schuyler looked at him blankly. "Why?" he asked.

"Sir, your daughter's been murdered. There's a killer loose."

*No there isn't,* he said to himself. Out loud, he said absently, "Yes, notify the sheriff."

"Besides, Sir," the steward continued, "your game warden, Mr. Miller, has been tarred and feathered."

"Tarred and feathered? What in the world for?"

"I have no idea," the steward replied.

"Who did it?"

"No one here, Sir. We found him outside the gate."

"Is that why the dogs were barking?"

"I suppose so, Sir."

"Is Miller all right?"

"Two of your men who went to investigate found him trying to rip the feathers off. It was not pleasant, Sir. Every time he did, he pulled away his skin and screamed. The men brought him back to the main kitchen. One of the housekeepers had set large pots of water to heat. The men sat Mr. Miller in a tub and poured the hot water over him. The water softened the tar and let the men scrape it loose without tearing off the skin beneath."

"Did he see who did it?" Schuyler asked.

"Mr. Miller said they tied a hood over his face, never said a word, and left by horseback before he could pull the hood off. He thinks there were two men at least."

Schuyler thanked his steward and went upstairs to his room. Fully clothed, with his boots still on, he lay on his four-poster, staring up at the canopy, playing over in his mind the early morning's events. He had gotten up early to follow Ophelia. He knew she sometimes liked to go for long rides before dawn but after discovering her affair with John Carter, he became suspicious that she was meeting him. *John might have thought,* Schuyler concluded, *that if he could not have Ophelia, nobody would.* But the man in the boat, the man he had killed, was not John. *Who else might have wanted Ophelia dead? Maybe the man in the boat was John's agent, paid to carry out an act that the young builder was too cowardly to perform himself.* But he knew that didn't ring true.

The dogs' barking brought his thoughts back to Danny Miller. *Could Ophelia's killer have been part of the plot to tar and feather Miller? Maybe the killer didn't know it was Ophelia he killed; it was still dark. Perhaps he had beached the boat on Schuyler's property to serve as a getaway for the tar and featherers, or, more likely, to use his rifle to signal them.* Yes, this seemed more likely. Now, thinking more clearly, he realized he had made a terrible mistake. *I shouldn't have shoved the boat off. Then I could prove he was trespassing, probably in conjunction with the tar and feathering, and I would have been justified in shooting him.* He sighed. *Why did I set the boat adrift?* The reason was immediately apparent: *I did it in blind fury.* The question Schuyler asked himself was, *Should I admit to killing Ophelia's killer and face a charge of murder? Who was the man, anyway?* Schuyler knew that if he was going to confess, he had to do it soon, even before the body of the man he shot had been found. He did not need a lawyer to tell him that once he denied killing the man in the boat, or professed not to know anything about a boat and a dead man in it, things would go a lot harder for him once the body was found. *Maybe they won't find the body,* he thought irrationally.

His thoughts turned back to Ophelia and John Carter. He could not get it out of his mind that John was somehow responsible for her death. *Why not?* he thought suddenly. *I could claim that John Carter shot Ophelia.* The idea comforted him. Having had nothing to eat since the previous evening, Schuyler felt momentarily queasy as he rose. Beckoning his steward, he asked if someone had been sent to notify the sheriff. The steward assured him he had. Only then did Schuyler have a light breakfast.

———•———

Warren Scott had been elected sheriff for lower Franklin County in 1882 and again in 1886. He lived in Saranac Lake Village, had an excellent record of maintaining law and order, was generally liked, and so was not opposed for reelection for the next term. The coming of the great camps, and their owners' insistence under the Private Parks Act that trespassing for any purpose on their property be prosecuted, had put him in a difficult position. The majority of his constituents were opposed to the law because it greatly restricted their access to hunting and fishing, which was a necessity for their families' survival over the harsh Adirondack winters. He tried to discourage trespassing, but he refused to use his deputies to patrol private lands, leaving it to the landowners to apprehend violators and file criminal complaints. He tried to extract promises from the accused that they would not repeat their offense and then tried to get the owners to drop charges. He feared that the owners of the Great Camps would use their wealth to run an opponent for sheriff who would enforce the law more strictly.

Schuyler's messenger—one of the few locals he had hired—found Sheriff Scott in his office in the Saranac Lake Town Hall. On the way out to Camp Leatherstocking the two rode side by side and conversed part of the way. "When did this happen?" Scott asked.

"Early this morning. Mr. Schuyler brought her back from the lake about six o'clock."

"Was she dead?"

"I would say so. Her dress was covered with blood and from the look on her father's face, I was pretty sure she was dead. I never saw Mr. Schuyler get angry or show his emotions, but his grief was unmistakable."

"Do you think the killer is still on the property?"

"We've done a search, Sheriff, and haven't turned up anybody. Most likely he came and left by boat."

*That would have been at least six hours ago. He'd be off the lake by now,* the sheriff thought. They rode on silently, but as they approached the gate to the Camp, Scott asked, "Anything else unusual happen last night?"

He was stunned when Schuyler's man answered, "Yes, Sir. Mr. Schuyler's game warden was tarred and feathered in front of the gate. Must've been close to the time Miss Schuyler was shot.

"Danny Miller?"

"Yes, Sir."

A few minutes later they arrived at the gate. Scott did not need a guide to show him where the attack took place. The ground was covered with shards of tar, some with feathers attached. Some fine drops of tar led to the path that came off the Saranac-Tupper road and stopped abruptly. He noticed some wagon wheel tracks close by. The two men proceeded on to the main lodge, where Sheriff Scott dismounted and tied his horse to the rail.

Schuyler got up from the rocker on the porch and walked down the steps as Scott approached. "I'm sorry to hear of your loss, Mr. Schuyler. A real tragedy." He put one hand on Schuyler's shoulder and shook his hand with the other.

"Thank you, Sheriff. Would you like to see my daughter?"

"Yes, that's one way to begin."

Schuyler led him into one of the smaller rooms off the great hall. The maids had placed her on a divan under a tall window that looked out toward the lake. She was covered with chenille spread. Schuyler drew it down revealing her head and trunk.

Even in death she was one of the most beautiful women Scott had ever seen. The maids had dressed her in a short-sleeved pale blue silk dress that obscured the bullet hole. "Do you mind if I examine her," Scott asked.

"That's your job," Schuyler replied.

"Perhaps you'd like to step outside." Schuyler started to say that he would stay and then realized the sheriff was telling him to leave. Once he did, Scott unbuttoned Ophelia's dress far enough to see the bullet wound. It looked like an exit wound. He unbuttoned the dress further to remove the sleeves and expose her shoulders and exquisitely formed breasts. Gently he rolled her over. Just to the left of the spine at about the level of the fourth rib he saw the bullet's small entry hole. Sliding the dress down further, he saw no other bullet holes or any signs of violence. He re-did her dress and returned Ophelia to the supine position, covering her with the spread.

Schuyler was waiting in the great hall. "I believe," said the sheriff, "your daughter was shot once from behind. The bullet pierced her heart or aorta and emerged through her chest. I'd like to see the dress she was wearing to confirm that the bullet passed out. Schuyler sat down and started to sob. He thought he had gotten over the shock, but he hadn't. Scott sat down next to him, placing his hand on Schuyler's knee. "If it's any consolation, Mr. Schuyler, your daughter died instantly. She felt no pain."

"Thank god," whispered her father.

The steward who was standing quietly by the entrance to the room came forward and whispered into Schuyler's ear. Schuyler turned to the sheriff. "Is it all right if we bury her?"

"Are you planning the funeral here, or in New York City?" Scott asked.

Schuyler had not thought about it and stood quietly for a moment, trying to decide.

"There won't be much of a funeral. Just me, really. All our guests have gone. I think she would want to be buried here. She loved Camp Leatherstocking."

"Then here?" the sheriff asked. Schuyler nodded. "Yes, you can go ahead. There are several ministers in the village if you need one to officiate."

"Yes, yes," Schuyler said absently, glancing at his steward who immediately got the message that he was to take care of this and turned to leave.

"I know this has been a hard day for you, Mr. Schuyler, but I'd like to see the place where you found your daughter. I doubt I'll be lucky enough to find the bullet but I'll give it a try. If I don't succeed, my men will do a thorough search tomorrow."

Schuyler momentarily panicked. *What if he finds the bullets I shot at Ophelia's killer?* But quickly he recalled that he had fired toward the water and that if both bullets hadn't lodged in the man's body they would be at the bottom of the lake.

On the way to the lake, Scott continued his questioning gently. "Do you know of anyone who would want to kill your daughter?" Schuyler did not answer right away. "A few weeks ago, I discovered Ophelia was seeing John Carter, the young man who built most of this place."

"John Carter? His father's the Assemblyman from Franklin County."

"Yes, I know," Schuyler said absently. "Ophelia was staying in the new boathouse, up the lake a bit, and he visited her there." He paused as they stepped over a protuberant root. "She rejected him. After that, she slept in her room at the Main Lodge."

*Not good enough for her,* the sheriff thought to himself.

"Last week I learned she was waking before dawn, taking her horse from the stable and riding for several hours."

"So yesterday, you decided to follow her," the sheriff came to the logical conclusion.

"I had asked my steward to awaken me if Ophelia called for her horse. My horse was waiting in front of the lodge. One of the grooms told me Ophelia had headed for the lake. I was twenty-five yards in back of her, just entering the beach, when I heard the shot." Schuyler realized he was sweating.

"What did you do?" Sheriff Scott asked.

Understandably, Scott thought, Schuyler was wrapped in grief and did not answer. He rephrased the question. "Did you go to your daughter?"

Schuyler nodded and started to sob. Scott wanted to know if he had seen the killer, but considering Schuyler's grief he decided to defer the question. They walked on toward the lake in silence.

The sheriff broke the quiet. "Did your men search the boathouse?"

"They searched all of Camp Leatherstocking!"

"In your daughter's room in the boathouse, was there, uh, any sign that the bed had been recently used?"

Schuyler flushed. "I'm not sure. We'll have to have a look."

They reached the lake. Schuyler showed the sheriff where he had found Ophelia, her face and upper body lying prone in the water just at the point where the path turned away from the lake.

The sheriff calculated the trajectory of the bullet from Schuyler's description of where Ophelia's horse was when the shot was fired. He got down on his hands and knees and searched the ground near where the bullet should have exited her body. He found one in a patch of grass just off the path. "I've got a bullet," he announced to Schuyler. "I'm not sure it's the one we're looking for. It's for one of those old muzzle-loading muskets, and I doubt they're still around."

They walked on along the path around a bend to the boathouse, a gorgeous two-story structure of cedar shingle with ramps and a dock protruding into the water from the lower level that housed several canoes. They climbed to the upper level on which a balcony looked over the water straight into Ampersand Mountain across the lake. On the top of the low balcony wall, evenly spaced flowerpots filled with geraniums, petunias, and other flowers added festive color to the building. Inside, the bed was made up; it had not been slept in.

As they returned to the Main Lodge, Scott said, "I understand another crime was committed at your Camp last night…" Schuyler froze but kept walking. *How did the sheriff know?* He was relieved when Scott continued. "I understand your game warden was tarred and feathered. I'd like to interview him."

Schuyler slowly exhaled. "I think he's in the Main Kitchen. I'll arrange to have him brought to the Main Lodge, but if you'll excuse me I'm rather tired."

"I can understand. Your presence won't be needed."

"Oh, one question, Sheriff." Scott looked at him. "Are you going to question John Carter?"

"Let's wait until Monday before we question him. Knowing his family, I don't think he'll be going anywhere."

———•———

Miller was sitting in a small room in the Main Lodge, streaks of tar on his arms. "How are you feeling, Danny?" the sheriff asked

"Could be better," he replied gruffly.

"Any ideas?"

"About who did it?" He paused, picking gingerly at a strip of tar on his arm. "I've been thinking about it. My only possible enemy is Tommy Carter. I've heard that he suspects me of uncoupling a caboose so it rolled down a trestle on which he was working. That was ten years ago. The accident paralyzed Tommy and he's been confined to a wheelchair ever since." Scott made a mental note to look for wheelchair tracks near the gate to Camp Leatherstocking as Miller continued. "No. It wasn't Tommy. Many in these parts resent the Great Camp owners forbidding hunting and fishing on their property after they've left for the year. Some of them may have taken it out on me as Mr. Schuyler's game warden. They should have tarred and feathered him. I'm just doing my job. Still, I'm not sure I want to risk being killed next time."

"You going to quit?"

"I don't know yet."

The sheriff went on to another line of questioning. "What made you come out of your cabin early this morning?"

"The shots."

"Shots?"

"At least two, maybe three. I was sleeping pretty hard. I was awake to hear two. I'm not sure about another, but something woke me up with a start."

"Where did they come from?"

Miller thought for a moment. "Not close by. Probably down by the lake."

"Three shots?

"At least two, for sure."

"So you ran out—"

"And whoever it was dropped the sack over my head and tied it. They tore off my night shirt—"

"You were naked?"

"Except for that hood." Miller paused, felt his crotch. "I don't know how I'm gonna get all the tar off down there."

The sheriff stood. "I'm truly sorry, Danny. We'll do our best to find out who did it." He started to go out, then turned back to Danny, who was slowly getting up. "You do know about Mr. Schuyler's daughter?"

"That she was killed? Yeah, they were talking about it in the kitchen when they were pulling the tar off me. I'd rather be in my condition than hers." He trailed the sheriff to the door. "Some coincidence to happen on the same night, ain't it?"

"Sure is," the sheriff mumbled as he unhitched his horse. At the main gate he dismounted and took a careful look at the ground. There were no wheelchair tracks.

In the village, Scott stopped at Reverend Lindy's rectory. He told him that J.J. Schuyler's daughter had been murdered and that her father wanted to bury her "up here," as the sheriff put it. The Reverend was immediately out of his chair, ready to go. "I'll see if I can help comfort the poor man."

On Sunday, about the same time that Tommy was laid to rest, Ophelia Schuyler was buried in a grave at Camp Leatherstocking, the Reverend Lindy officiating.

# 14

# Arraignment

SHERIFF Scott had to ride up to Malone on Monday August 26 to meet with the County Prosecutor about pending cases. While there, he mentioned that he had a murder and a tarring in the southern part of Franklin County and would need to involve the prosecutor once he had apprehended suspects. Dusk had fallen by the time he returned to the village.

It was the sheriff's custom to pick up *The Daily Enterprise* on his way to his office and read it over coffee. When he did so on Tuesday he was pleased that the paper did not carry stories of either Miller's being tarred and feathered or of Ophelia Schuyler's murder. *If the tarring was not publicized*, Scott thought, *the men who planned and executed it might get careless and hint at it to others, especially if they wanted publicity.* He'd have to alert his deputies to be on the lookout. *And if Ophelia's death were publicized, suspects in her murder would be on guard when I come to question them. The killer might even leave town.*

When he turned to the Obituaries he was astonished to read of Tommy Carter's death:

Carter, Thomas, on August 21. Beloved son of Mary and Cyrus Carter, passed away after a long illness. In addition to his parents, his sister, Mrs. Lisa

O'Rourke, and his half-brother, John Carter, survive him. Funeral private.

Even without Danny Miller's reminding him, the sheriff
knew that Tommy was paraplegic and mute. He often mar-
veled that Mary had been able to keep him alive and well for
almost ten years after his accident.

The coincidence of deaths stunned him.

The sheriff decided that he would pay his condolences to
the Carters and ask to question John. Although he doubted
that John Carter was the killer—especially with the murder
taking place two days after his brother's death, he knew he
was obliged to question him. If he didn't, J.J. Schuyler would
make his life and his reelection difficult.

The weather had cooled off over the weekend and the
trees were tinged yellow and red. The sheriff enjoyed the
brief walk from the Town Hall on Main Street to the Carter's home on Helen Street. Mary met him at the door.

"Good morning, Warren," she said.

"Mary, I saw the notice in this morning's *Enterprise*.
I'm terribly sorry. Tommy made the most of life despite his
handicaps since the uh, accident."

"Thank you, Sheriff. Thank you for coming over. Would
you like to come in for a moment?"

He stepped inside. "Must have come as a terrible blow,"
he said.

"It certainly did," said Mary suppressing a tear with
a sniffle. "Would you like something to drink, coffee,
perhaps?"

"No, thank you, Ma'am. I'd best be going." He turned,
preparing to leave when Cyrus came in from his study, hav-

ing heard Mary conversing with Scott. "Ah Sheriff, thanks for coming over."

Scott shook Cyrus's hand, putting his other hand on Cyrus's arm. "I know how difficult this must be."

"We'll get by," Cyrus replied.

The sheriff turned to leave. "Oh, I'd like to express my condolences to John, if you don't mind."

Cyrus and Mary stole a glance at each other. "Now that he's not working, Mary said, "he sleeps late, but he's up now having his breakfast." She led the sheriff into the kitchen. Cyrus followed. John got up from the table. "Hello, Sheriff, what brings you here?"

"Well, I wanted to express my sympathy about your brother's death."

"Yes, it came as a shock to all of us."

I'd also like to ask you a few questions, if that's all right?" John nodded. The sheriff turned to Mary and Cyrus. "Alone if you don't mind."

"He won't need a lawyer?" Cyrus asked jokingly.

Scott thought the better of answering, *not at this stage.* Instead he laughed and said, "Of course not." Before she left, Mary again offered Scott a cup of coffee. This time he accepted.

The two men sat facing each other across the kitchen table. John was just finishing his coffee. Scott's first question put John at ease. "Do you know Ophelia Schuyler, John?"

"Yes, of course I know her. She was often around when we were working on Camp Leatherstocking."

"Is that all?"

"What do you mean?" John started to feel uncomfortable.

"I mean, did you have, uh, uh, an intimate relationship

with her?" The sheriff took a swallow of coffee and put his cup down.

All that John could think of was that she was pregnant, although not a month had passed since they had made love in the boathouse. Instead of answering, John asked, "Why do you want to know?"

The sheriff stared hard at John for a few moments. John stared back. The sheriff took another swallow of coffee. "Ophelia Schuyler was shot in the back last Saturday morning. On the beach at Camp Leatherstocking."

Stunned, John half rose out of his chair. His eyes opened wide and he gasped. "Is she all right?"

"No. She was killed instantly." John sank down in his chair. Scott reached into his pocket and put the bullet on the table. "I found this bullet near the scene."

John recognized the bullet. *Tommy?* he asked himself.

Scott had to repeat his next question before John heard him. "Do you own a rifle, John?"

"No. When I hunt, I borrow my father's."

"Do you mind if I have a look at it?"

Looking back at this moment, John thought it must have taken an eternity for him to answer; such a delay would have increased the sheriff's suspicion. In reality, John realized his dilemma very quickly. *If I ask the sheriff to produce a search warrant, I will arouse his suspicion. If I bring him the gun, the bullet will almost certainly match.* He got up, Scott following him into the parlor where Cyrus's rifle hung on the wall. Cyrus came in behind them. "The sheriff wants to look at your rifle, Dad." Now it was in his father's hands.

"By rights, Sheriff, you need a search warrant." Scott nodded. "But seeing how we're good law abiding citizens."

Cyrus said, "and you'll get one eventually if you really need it, go ahead and have a look."

John took the old musket down and handed it to the sheriff. John followed him back into the kitchen, signaling his father with a glance not to join them. The sheriff examined the weapon. "Springfield 1855 rifled musket," he stated. "Can be a darn accurate weapon in the right hands." He dropped the bullet down the barrel. It fit perfectly. He looked at John. "John, I've known you for many years. You went off and got mixed up with those labor radicals in Chicago, but since you've come back you've been a model citizen. I don't want to believe that you killed Miss Schuyler, but I have to caution that the bullet makes you a prime suspect." He paused. John looked at him blankly. "It could help matters if you told me where you were in the early morning of Saturday August 23rd?"

John did immediately reply. "Am I required to answer, Sheriff?"

"No. This is not a court of law."

"Then I'd rather not."

Scott realized he was sweating. He seemed to be more fazed than John. He sat down at the table and wiped his brow with his shirtsleeve. He looked down at his hands and thought for a while and finished his coffee. Then he got up. "All right, John. Think about it. Go seek counsel if you have to. I am taking a big chance, but I don't think you're going to leave town—"

"I give you my word on that," John said.

"And don't get rid of that rifle." He picked up the bullet and slipped it back in his pocket. He passed Cyrus and Mary on the way out and smiled at them. "Again, I'm sorry for your loss." He took Mary's hand. "Good bye."

Cyrus and Mary rushed into the kitchen where John sat quietly. "What was that all about?"

"Ophelia Schuyler's been murdered."

"What does that have to do with you?" Mary asked.

"It happened early Saturday morning. The bullet was fired from your musket, Dad."

"I thought the only violence was the tarring and Tommy getting shot."

"That's what I thought." Cyrus and Mary sank into their chairs, waiting for John to continue. "I told you Tommy was supposed to fire three shots—in the air—to signal that we should go ahead, and to wake Miller." John paused, thinking again about the spacing of the shots. Then he blurted out, "Now I understand."

"Understand what?" Cyrus asked.

"The shots were fired too close together. Tommy could not have reloaded your musket that quickly. The second and third shots had to be fired by someone else. One of them killed Tommy." He stopped, visualizing the scene in his mind. "Tommy must have seen Ophelia; she sometimes rides before dawn. He would not have recognized her in the dark—she rides astride—and must have thought a guard was making the rounds." He paused again. "Tommy must have shot Ophelia."

Mary gasped. "Oh my boys," she cried, "what have you done?" Cyrus put his hand on hers. Soon she stopped sobbing.

"Would Ophelia have been armed?" Cyrus asked.

"No. Never," John replied.

"Then there has to be someone else who shot Tommy." They were all quiet for a minute, each trying to fathom what had happened. "Did the sheriff mention Tommy?"

"No. He thought he had died peacefully two days before."

"Then why would he come to question you?" Cyrus asked.

Another silence before John answered. "Ophelia and I were, uh, seeing each other. Last week, her father forbade her from seeing me ever again."

"Did you?"

"No, Sir."

"So her father has reason to suspect you might have killed her," Cyrus continued.

"Why?" Mary asked. "If John loved her, why should he kill her? More likely he'd kill her father."

They all were quiet for a while. Finally, Cyrus said, "It looks pretty bad for you, John. The only alibi you have is to admit you were tarring Danny Miller at the time Ophelia was killed."

John raised his head, looked straight at Cyrus, started to speak, but stopped. Behind his calm exterior his mind was racing. What his mother had said triggered his thinking. *Yes, I'd like to kill her father, not because he stood between Ophelia and me but because he's keeping the people off land that should be theirs to hunt and fish. That's why we tarred and feathered Miller.* "If I admit to the tarring and feathering, I will exonerate myself of Ophelia's murder but I will incriminate Tommy. And I will be his accomplice; he couldn't have gotten the rifle or gotten into the boat without my help." He paused, his thinking catching up to his speech. "And Tommy's murderer will still be at large."

"Yes, John," Cyrus said quietly, "but your motivation for assisting Tommy was not to have him kill Ophelia, but to sound warning shots. He looked at Mary. "The sheriff will want to—"

Mary interrupted bitterly "Warren Scott knows where Tommy is; he read the obituary."

"Sheriff Scott is too thorough to accept that. He will want to see the body."

"We won't let him. Let Tommy have some peace," Mary said and wept.

"*Corpus delicti*," Cyrus said. Mary and John looked at him. "If we want to find Tommy's killer, then we have to prove that he's been murdered."

"What good will it do finding his killer? It won't bring Tommy back," Mary sobbed.

"Even so, if John claims that Tommy was in the boat when he was shot, the sheriff or the prosecutor will get a writ to exhume Tommy." Mary shuddered but said nothing.

"If John refuses to say where he was on Saturday morning, then he will be found guilty of Ophelia's murder. I've little doubt of that."

John ended the silence that followed. "I'm pretty sure I know who killed Tommy." They looked at him incredulously. "Ophelia wrote me a few weeks ago that the grounds are not patrolled after ten o'clock. I think her father was trailing Ophelia, and when Tommy shot her, he shot Tommy, probably thinking it was me who had killed her."

Finally, Cyrus said. "The sheriff will want to see the bullet hole in Tommy's body before he goes after Schuyler or anyone else."

"Oh, Cyrus, what should we do?"

"That's up to John."

———— • ————

About the time that Sheriff Scott was visiting the Carters, J.J. Schuyler inquired of his staff whether they had heard of any new developments in his daughter's murder. None had.

*Maybe the body of the man I shot won't be found,* he thought optimistically. *Surely it would have turned up by now. The longer it goes undiscovered the greater the chance it will decompose and the less chance it will be associated with Ophelia's death.* He was in a brighter mood than he had been since his daughter's death and decided to ride into the village.

When Sheriff Scott returned to his office in the Town Hall, J.J. Schuyler was waiting for him. "Any progress?" Schuyler asked. The sheriff sat behind his desk and Schuyler took a seat in front of it.

"I've just questioned John Carter." Schuyler looked at him inquiringly. "It's likely the bullet I found on Saturday came from his father's musket rifle."

"Well that proves it, doesn't it?"

"Not necessarily. Somebody else could have used the musket." The sheriff looked directly at Schuyler. "John seemed surprised to hear that your daughter was dead."

Schuyler laughed. "You mean he didn't jump up and admit his guilt? Surely that doesn't surprise you, sheriff."

"No, but I'd like to gather more evidence before I have him arraigned. John is not going to flee our jurisdiction. He and his family are going through a rough time; his brother Thomas died last week."

"I'm sorry to hear that." Schuyler stood, ready to go. "You're right, sheriff. It seems reasonable to make the case airtight."

"Oh Mr. Schuyler, I meant to ask you on Saturday—he looked innocently at Schuyler—how many shots did you hear right before you found your daughter?"

"Why just one," he hesitated as if thinking. "No. Just one."

Scott stood. "I'll keep you posted. I understand your

eagerness to bring your daughter's killer to justice. Thanks for stopping by."

As Schuyler was walking out the door of his office, Scott called him back. "Before you go, I'd like to have a word with you about Danny Miller's tarring." Impatiently, Schuyler came back and sat down. "Have your guards found any men hunting or fishing on your property?"

"They haven't reported any. Neither has Mr. Miller."

"Are you planning to leave the 'No Trespassing' signs on your property after you leave?"

"Of course I am," Schuyler replied indignantly. "It would cost a pretty penny to take them down. Besides, I don't want anyone on my property; the buildings and their contents are too valuable. And I don't want my herds of deer and the fish in my streams and ponds depleted when we—" a look of grief crossed his face, "when I return next summer."

"They aren't exactly your herds and your fish, Mr. Schuyler."

Schuyler's voice rose angrily. "When they're on my property, they're mine."

"The waterways belong to the State, as I'm sure you know."

"If any man, woman, or child steps on my land to get to the waterways, Mr. Scott, they're trespassing and will be ejected and prosecuted. The courts have convicted those who've been caught, my lawyer tells me."

"Winters are pretty rough up here, Mr. Schuyler," the sheriff said quietly. "Families here depend on the land for their food over the winter, game and fish especially."

"My land is not the only land around here. They can hunt and fish on the public lands."

"You do know the people up here resent the Great Camps?"

"That's too bad. I've spent my hard-earned money buying property up here and nobody's going to tell me how to manage it." He was considerably worked up by now, but reflected for a moment. "You don't think Miller's tarring was because of the 'no trespassing,' do you?"

"I don't know, Sir," the sheriff replied, "but I'd be careful if I were you."

Schuyler got up and walked out quickly.

————•————

Schuyler came back on Wednesday demanding why the sheriff had not yet arrested John Carter. "You've got the bullet. You've got the motive. What more do you want?"

At the moment, the sheriff could think of no other leads that he could follow to prove John's guilt, or innocence. Still, he had his doubts of John's guilt. Nevertheless, shortly after Schuyler's visit, Sheriff Scott sent a message to the Prosecutor in Malone, advising that he was about to arrest John Carter, stepson of State Assemblyman Cyrus Carter, for the premeditated murder of Ophelia Schuyler. He asked the Prosecutor to let the County Judges' office know so a judge would come down for the formal arraignment.

Something bothered Scott. *How could John go to Camp Leatherstocking two days after his brother had died? Was he madly in love with Ophelia? I didn't get that impression.* The sheriff was perplexed. He walked down the hall to the Town Clerk's office. "Any death certificates filed lately, Sam?"

"Two patients of Dr. Trudeau's, consumption, I'm afraid, and this one on poor Thomas Carter came in Monday. Pity about him. I imagine he must have been in some pain. At least he's free of that now."

"Do you mind if I take it back to my office, Sam?"

"I've transcribed it already. Just as long as you bring it back."

"Have no fear, Sam."

Scott brought the certificate back to his office. "Date of death: August 22, 1890. Cause of death: Pulmonary congestion." The certificate was signed, "Eleanor Mason, M.D." He had never met Eleanor. He knew her father, Henry Weinberg. Everybody in the towns of Altamont and Harrietstown knew him. Eleanor had taken over the old man's practice recently. Scott knew her husband Jared, who was the Health Officer for lower Franklin County. He took down his hat and put on his sheriff's badge and told the receptionist he was going over to Tupper Lake.

Several patients were in Dr. Mason's waiting room when he entered. There was no secretary. He saw a sign-in book on a drop-leaf table, put his name down, and sat on a hard-backed chair. The doctor came out, looked at the book, and called the person whose turn it was. Scott waited patiently for about forty-five minutes. Surprisingly, no one had come in after him.

Finally, Eleanor called, "Warren Scott." The sheriff got up and approached Eleanor. She saw the badge on his shirt. "Ah, Sheriff Scott, I'm glad to meet you finally." She ushered him into her combination office and examining room and closed the door. "What's bothering you?"

"Actually, Dr. Mason, I'm fine. It's not me I've come to see you about." Neither of them had taken their eyes off each other. Scott took the death certificate out of his pocket and handed it to her. Eleanor's heart started to pound and she wondered whether her face had changed color.

"Have you been caring for Mr. Carter, Dr. Mason?"

"Yes, since I took over from my father. He didn't need much care. His parents and sister and his older brother did a remarkable job."

"Were you there when he, uh, died?"

"No, I wasn't."

"When did you last see him alive?"

Eleanor knew she was weaving a mesh of lies around her. "The previous Sunday." She didn't wait for the next question. "He was having trouble breathing."

"Did you examine his lungs?"

"Yes. He had pneumonia or heart failure. There was nothing I could do for him except tell him to rest."

Scott turned the death certificate so he could read it. "Is that why you wrote the cause of death was—" he looked down at the box on the certificate, "'pulmonary congestion'?"

The room had become unbearably warm, Eleanor thought. "Yes," she answered quietly.

"What exactly does that mean, doctor?"

"It means that there's fluid in the lungs, which could be either from pneumonia or heart failure."

"Any other type of fluid?" Looking puzzled, Eleanor did not answer. "Blood, for instance?"

"That would be unusual unless—"

"Unless he was shot?"

"Speaking in general, yes, if someone was shot in the chest."

Scott stood, picked up the death certificate, and offered his hand to Eleanor. "Thank you for your time, doctor. I appreciate it." At the door, he turned, looked once more at the death certificate, and asked, "It says you signed it on Saturday August 23rd."

"That's correct," she said. The Carters didn't notify me until Friday, when I had patients all day."

Eleanor's demeanor puzzled Scott. She was almost too matter of fact about it. He thanked her for her time and returned to Saranac Lake where he went directly to the village's only mortuary. "Jake," he asked the owner, "Did you fix up Tommy Carter for burial?"

"No, sheriff, I didn't. First I heard of his death was when I read it in the paper yesterday. The family must have laid the lad out themselves. I don't know why. They can afford my price."

"Thanks, Jake. Sorry to trouble you." *Maybe I shouldn't have notified the Prosecutor. Still, what choice did I have?*

———•———

Then the sheriff went to the Carter house on Helen Street. In front of John's parents, he pronounced, "John Carter, by the powers vested in me by Franklin County in the State of New York, you are under arrest for the premeditated murder of Ophelia Schuyler in the early hours of August twenty-third at Camp Leatherstocking."

John held out his hands.

"I don't think I need to handcuff you. Unfortunately, I don't have the authority to set bail; you'll have to wait for the judge for that."

Mary hugged John, quickly put together some of his personal belongings and sent him off with the sheriff with tears in her eyes and Cyrus's arm around her shoulder.

# 15

# The Trial

ON Thursday August 28th, Alice bought *The Daily Enterprise* on her way to work, as she usually did. Even though she knew of the murder, she was shocked to see the banner headline:

## MURDER AND MAYHEM
## AT CAMP LEATHERSTOCKING

Standing in front of the newsstand, she read both stories as others bought the paper and passed her in the street. Underneath the headline, two stories appeared, one in the first column, the other in the last. Alice read the one in the last column, which began: "Ophelia Schuyler, twenty-four-year-old daughter of J.J. Schuyler, New York banker and owner of one-thousand-acre Camp Leatherstocking, was shot dead early Saturday morning, August 23. Her father found her lifeless body. John Carter, son of Mary and Cyrus Carter, has been charged with the murder and arrested by Sheriff Warren Scott. He is being held without bail in the County Jail in Saranac Lake. Cyrus Carter is the New York State Assemblyman for Franklin County."

She turned to the first column: "Unknown assailants tarred and feathered Danny Miller, game warden of Camp Leatherstocking, outside the entrance to the Camp early on Saturday morning, August 23. Mr. Miller survived and is expected to recover. It is unknown whether the murder of Miss Ophelia Schuyler was related to the tarring. The two events took place at approximately the same time but at opposite ends of the thousand-acre Camp."

Alice had been at work when Sheriff Scott questioned John on Tuesday. When she returned from Dr. Trudeau's that evening, John told her that he might be arrested on suspicion that he had killed Ophelia Schuyler. That was the first she had heard of the woman's death. Alice threw her arms around him, stroking his hair and crying. "You are not a murderer, John, I know it." For over a year, Alice had resented Ophelia, but she took no satisfaction in her death. She let go of John, tears streaming down her face. She loved John even if her love was unrequited.

John took her hands and smiled. "Don't worry, Alice, I didn't kill Miss Schuyler. The tar on my shoes will prove that."

She looked at him quizzically. "The tar? What do you mean?"

"The black stuff you noticed on my shoes last Saturday. It will exonerate me. You'll see," he answered cryptically.

The story in the first column of *The Enterprise* two days later told Alice what he meant.

---

Reluctantly, Cyrus agreed to represent his stepson. Lawrence Venable was now confined to a wheelchair, and he occasionally forgot events that had occurred in the recent past. Cyrus was not confident that other attorneys in Franklin County were up to the task. One or two of them coveted his seat in the Assembly and could not be trusted to pull out all the stops. Cyrus realized that if he lost and his son was convicted as a murderer, his career as an Assemblyman would almost certainly end. He confided to Mary, "a murder trial got me into the law and a murder trial might get me out." Still feeling guilty that John did not regard him as his father, Cyrus felt he owed it to his stepson to defend him. He did not exonerate John for the tarring but he was not defending him for that offense.

Ten days after his arrest, John was formally arraigned before the judge, who asked how he pleaded.

"Not guilty, your honor."

"Counsel has advised you of your options?" the judge asked.

"Yes, Sir," John replied. The judge set bail at $500, advised John not to leave the county, and set the date for the trial to begin on Monday October 6, 1890.

Alan Phillips was among John's visitors over the next few weeks. "Look, John, Roger and I know where you were that night and that you couldn't have killed Miss Schuyler. We've talked it over and we are willing to testify."

"That won't be necessary, Alan. Don't say anything and you'll see. There's no need for you to admit what we did, and I will never mention your and Roger's involvement. I can't say more now, but please, trust me."

"Of course we will, John."

———•———

Sheriff Scott was in the courtroom when John pleaded "not guilty." Although he had charged him and made the arrest, he still had doubts. He returned to the scene of the crime and concluded that the shot that killed Ophelia might have been fired from a boat very close to the shore, possibly beached on it. If anything, that pointed more to John. Scott had also made inquiries in the village stores about purchases of bullets of the type he had found when first examining the scene with J.J. Schuyler. The response to those inquiries also pointed to John. But two things bothered him. First was the close coincidence of Tommy's death with that of Ophelia Schuyler. Dr. Mason had given a plausible explanation for Tommy's death and she was not the sort of person who would lie, although she seemed a trifle over confident when he questioned her in her office. Maybe that was like doctors. *Still,* he thought, *you'd think they'd have brought Tommy to Jake's mortuary to prepare the body for burial.* The private funeral also puzzled him.

Second was the discrepancy between Mr. Schuyler's insistence that he had heard only one shot and Danny Miller's claim that he had heard at least two shots. Could the killer have fired twice or three times? If the murder weapon was Cyrus's musket, reloading would have taken considerable time, making three shots implausible.

A week before the trial, Scott went back to Camp Leatherstocking to question Danny Miller, who was still working there. Miller showed him the few scars he had from the tarring but told the sheriff, "I got off lucky. Mr. Schuyler's maids did good by preparing that hot bath to get the tar off."

"Danny, tell me again, what woke you on the morning of the tarring?"

"Like I said, sheriff, I heard shots, at least two, coming from the lake side."

"Could there have been more?"

"Well," Danny replied, "I might have slept through the first one or two; the ones I heard came close together."

"Close enough to be fired from the same gun?"

Miller thought for a few moments. "Not a muzzle-loading rifle. Maybe one of them new revolvers, though."

"Well, Danny, stay well. Keep out of trouble. Maybe I'll see you in the courtroom next week."

When he returned to his office he summoned his chief deputy. "Get a few reliable men," he told him, "and go to the beach at Camp Leatherstocking, just where the path comes closest to the lake before it turns back to the Main Lodge. Take your waders and sift the lake bottom for bullets or shells. Also search around the beach. I know it's been over a month since the shooting but if there are bullets they won't go anywhere, except deeper in the muddy bottom."

The posse found one bullet under the muck in shallow water. It came from a thirty-eight caliber Smith and Wesson. Sheriff Scott didn't know what to make of this finding, but he notified both the prosecution and the defense.

⸻

The trial began on a crisp autumn day in the Saranac Lake Town Hall. On the hills surrounding town, the hardwood trees were dressed in their gaudy shades of red and yellow, a startling contrast to the evergreens. Cyrus limped into courthouse, Mary on his arm. Cyrus, his hair and beard totally white, the latter hiding deep lines on his face but not the furrows on his brow. His old leg injury acted up as he had grown old; often he walked with a cane, though not when in court or on the floor of the Assembly in Albany. Mary had aged almost overnight. Her hair was more gray than brown, wisps escaping from the bun she used to tie so neatly. She was stooped as she clung to Cyrus's arm and her face, like her husband's, was lined. She let go of Cyrus as they reached the front row, taking a seat next to Alice Massing who had been given time off from work by Dr. Trudeau. Lawrence Venable was wheeled in by his wife, who placed his chair just behind the defense's table, near Mary and Alice. These people had all been at Frank Miller's trial, twenty-four years before; Alice had been only twelve when she attended with her father. In back of the prosecution, J.J. Schuyler, who had returned from New York City, sat stiffly erect. John's friends were scattered throughout the audience.

At the start of the trial, Cyrus did not move for dismissal and the two lawyers went straight to *voir dire* to select the jury. The Prosecutor challenged most of the prospective jurors from Harrietstown because they admitted knowing the defendant. Finally, twelve men and two alternates were selected.

The courtroom was packed when the prosecution called its first witness, Sheriff Warren Scott, who told the court how he had been summoned by J.J. Schuyler to Camp Leatherstocking, had examined Ophelia's body, discovering that the bullet entered her back and exited through her chest, and that he had found a bullet near the scene of the crime.

"Do you have the bullet?" the Prosecutor asked.

Reaching into his pocket, the sheriff said, "I do." Under questioning, the sheriff described the bullet as of the Minié Ball type that was used in muzzle loading rifled muskets in use until the eighteen seventies when breech loading rifles replaced them." The Prosecutor turned to the Judge. "Your Honor, I would like to enter this bullet in evidence as Exhibit One."

Cyrus objected. "How does my worthy opponent know that this particular bullet was the one that killed Ophelia Schuyler?"

"I was about to show that, your Honor, and if my worthy opponent wants the court to wait until I do so before entering the bullet in evidence, I will defer." Cyrus said he preferred to wait.

The Prosecutor returned to the Sheriff. "Sheriff Scott, what makes you think this bullet killed Ophelia Schuyler?"

"Three reasons, Sir. First, from the horses' footprints and the impression of the deceased's body resulting from her fall from her horse at the edge of the beach, I calculated the path the bullet would have traveled through her body while she was sitting astride her horse, taking into account its deceleration after passing through said body. I found the bullet very close to where my calculations predicted.

"Second, "I have inquired of the proprietors of the stores in the village that sell ammunition whether they have recently sold Minié balls similar to the one that I found near the beach." Cyrus looked at John; they had not discussed this. "Only Tobias Brown's hardware store still carries this old-fashioned type of ammunition and it had made only one sale in the month prior to August twenty-third. It was to John Carter." A murmur surged through the courtroom like a wave. Cyrus and John bent their heads close together. The Judge banged for order.

"Third, I have located a rifled musket into whose barrel this bullet"—he held up the bullet again—"fits snugly."

"And whose weapon is it?" The prosecution asked.

The sheriff pointed at Cyrus. "Mr. Cyrus Carter." The courtroom broke into commotion.

The judge had to bang his gavel many times before order was restored. He motioned both attorneys to approach his bench where he conferred with them privately. "Mr. Carter, this is highly unusual. As it seems you are implicated, perhaps as an accessory to the crime, do you not wish to recuse yourself?"

"No, your Honor, I do not. Although the rifle is mine, I give you my word that I did not condone its use by anyone on the day in question. Nor did I use it."

The judge turned to the Prosecutor. "Do you intend to call Mr. Carter to testify?"

"I do not, your Honor."

"Very well, you may proceed." In open court the Judge turned to Cyrus. "Do you withdraw your objection to entering the bullet in evidence?" Cyrus nodded.

"Where did you find the rifle, sheriff?" the Prosecutor asked.

"Hanging on the parlor wall of, uh, Mr. Carter's home." The sheriff produced the musket rifle and it was introduced as Exhibit Two.

"Had it been used recently?" The Prosecutor looked at Cyrus, expecting him to object.

"It wasn't covered with dust and there were traces of powder at the end of the barrel."

"I have no further questions for the witness, your Honor." The sheriff did not move, certain that Cyrus would cross-examine.

"Mr. Scott," Cyrus began as he approached the witness. "You said that only Tobias Brown's store in our village still carries this old-fashioned type of ammunition and it had made only one sale in the month prior to August twenty-third. Is that correct?"

"Yes, Sir," the sheriff replied.

"Did you ask the proprietor about sales before that?"

"No, Sir, I did not, but—" he paused.

"'But' what?

"Mr. Brown told me he stocked them because one customer bought them periodically."

"And who might that customer be?"

"John Carter." People turned to look at each other, puzzled about this new bit of information.

Cyrus paused to drink from a glass of water on the defense's table. Slowly, he walked back to the dock. "Mr. Scott, you told the court that you found the musket into which your bullet—Exhibit One—fit hanging on the wall of the parlor in my house. Is that right?"

"Yes, Sir."

"Did you go to my house to look for that rifle?"

"Not really, Sir."

"Then why did you visit my house on Tuesday morning, August twenty-sixth?"

"Because, Sir, I read in the newspaper that morning that your younger son, Thomas Carter had died on August twenty-first. I went to pay my respects. While there, I questioned your stepson, John."

"Why did you want to question John?"

Scott turned momentarily to look at J.J. Schuyler sitting in the front row behind the Prosecutor. "Because Mr. J.J. Schuyler suspected that John had murdered his daughter, Ophelia." Cyrus waited for the sheriff to continue. "Mr. Schuyler had forbidden his daughter from seeing John. He said John was, uh, pressing his affections on Ophelia."

"Were those his exact words?"

"I don't recall."

The Prosecutor smiled as he heard this exchange. *Carter is presenting part of my case.*

"Did you tell John that Ophelia had been killed?"

"I did, Sir."

"Did he seem surprised?"

"Quite, Sir. I showed him the bullet and asked if he owned a rifle. He said he used his father's, uh, yours, Sir."

"Then what?"

"He told me it was all right for me to examine the rifle, which I did, finding the bullet—Exhibit One—fit. Then I asked John where he had been early Saturday morning, August twenty-third, the time of the shooting."

"What did he say?"

"He refused to answer."

Cyrus turned to the judge. "I have no further questions, your Honor."

Sheriff Scott sat in the witness chair for a few moments, surprised that the cross examination ended abruptly on a note incriminating Cyrus's son.

The Prosecutor could not believe that Cyrus was making his case. *What could be more an admission of guilt than refusing to answer? What is Cyrus up to?* he wondered.

The prosecution's next witness was J.J. Schuyler. The Prosecutor began by saying, "I know how painful it is to speak of the death of your daughter, but we must establish the facts of her leaving us." Somberly, Schuyler nodded. "Can you tell us how you learned of her death?"

"She often rides before dawn. I followed her on horseback coming out of the path to our beach on Upper Saranac Lake about twenty-five yards behind her, At that point, I saw the flash of a gun—it seemed to be at the water's edge, maybe from a boat—followed immediately by the shot. The shot must have startled Ophelia's horse; he whinnied, must have leaped in fright, and then galloped off. I heard a splash, dismounted, and crawled toward the sound, fearful that the gunman might shoot me." Schuyler started to cry and wiped his eyes with his handkerchief before continuing. "She was lying face down, the upper part of her body in the water. I lifted her out and turned her over. Peering closely, I realized her chest was covered with blood. She was lifeless." Again he sobbed and a sigh of grief echoed through the courtroom.

"Did you see the killer?"

"No, I did not. Only the splash led me to Ophelia. It was too dark."

The Prosecutor paused momentarily to let emotions subside. "Why were you following your daughter at such an ungodly hour?"

Schuyler looked at John Carter sitting at the defense table. "It's like Sheriff Scott told the defense counsel: John Carter was pressing his affections on my daughter. I feared he might kill her."

"Did you have any evidence of this?"

"Yes, I did. John Carter had helped in the construction of Camp Leatherstocking. He had on several occasions spoken with Ophelia and two weeks before her death, he was seen by one of my guards entering the boathouse in which Ophelia—my daughter—lived. It was late in the day, just before dinner. I became suspicious that he was pressing his affection on my daughter."

"What did you do about it?"

"The next day I questioned her. She burst into tears and told me that he had come to tell her he loved her and wanted to marry her. She told him that she did not love him and did not want to see him again. She said she was frightened he might do something to her and begged me to allow her to move out of the boathouse and back to her room in the Main Lodge. Of course, I arranged it instantly."

"No further questions, your Honor." Schuyler started to step down when he saw Cyrus approach. He sat back in the witness chair.

"Mr. Schuyler, I sympathize with your loss because I, too, have recently lost a child, my son Tommy, as you have heard from Sheriff Scott." Schuyler nodded his recognition. "Have you ever met Tommy, Mr. Schuyler?

The question was so unexpected that the Prosecutor never thought to object.

"I have not had that pleasure. I am sorry for your loss."

"Thank you." Cyrus paused, before returning to the matter at hand.

"Isn't it possible, Mr. Schuyler, that your daughter loved John Carter, a mere working man," *Cyrus could not resist mentioning that,* "that she had invited him to see her, and that you wanted to stop *her* from pursuing him?"

"That's ridiculous," Schuyler said angrily. "She had the wealthiest, handsomest men in New York groveling at her feet. Why would she want a man like Carter?" A wave of grumbling went through the courtroom and a few laughs.

When order was restored, Cyrus changed direction. "Mr. Schuyler, do you own any firearms?"

"Certainly, I am an avid hunter."

"Oh yes, of course." Cyrus paused, walked up very close to Schuyler, looked him directly in the eyes, as if daring him to lie, and asked, "Did you have a weapon with you when you trailed your daughter on August twenty-third?"

"I did."

"What type of weapon was it?"

"I'm not certain. I think it was my Smith and Wesson."

"Revolver or rifle?"

"Revolver, I think."

"Repeat action? It could fire more than one bullet without reloading?"

"Yes, that's right."

"Mr. Schuyler, what would you have done if it was light enough on the beach that morning for you to recognize John Carter, the defendant, with a rifle in his hands?"

"I would have—"

"Objection, your Honor?" the Prosecutor shouted before Schuyler could complete his answer.

"Sustained. Mr. Carter, I must warn you against hypothetical lines of questioning."

Cyrus meekly bowed his head. "No further questions. The witness may step down." Grasping the railing for support, a shaken J.J. Schuyler stepped down and returned to his seat.

"The prosecution rests, your Honor."

"This looks like a good time to recess for lunch," the Judge announced. "The court will re-convene at two P.M." The bang of his gavel ended the session.

———•———

Shortly before two o'clock, Eleanor Mason hitched her horse in front of the Saranac Lake Town Hall and entered the courtroom. She found a seat on the second row, behind Mary. Cyrus walked in soon after and reached over Mary's head to shake her hand. "You got my message! Thanks so much for coming Dr. Mason. I know it won't be easy." Eleanor smiled and gave his hand a tight grasp. Schuyler took his seat behind the prosecution's table. The Judge entered and all stood.

"You may call your first witness, Mr. Carter."

"John Carter." John walked from the defense table to the dock, took the pledge, and sat down.

"John, let's dispose of the matter of the Minié Ball ammunition first. Sheriff Scott says you bought those balls periodically. Is that true?"

"Yes, Sir, it's true."

"For what purpose?"

"My brother Tommy could not use his legs, but he wanted to become a good shot so he could hunt from his wheelchair. He practiced often, using our father's musket. After I returned from Chicago, I bought him the ammunition from Brown's Hardware since it was difficult for him to get into town by himself."

"Thank you." Cyrus paused to drink from the glass of water on the defense table. He returned to the witness.

"John, where were you in the early morning of August twenty-third?"

"At Camp Leatherstocking." A collective gasp went through the courtroom.

"What were you doing there?" The room was deathly silent.

"Tarring and feathering Danny Miller." Another gasp.

"Can you tell the court why?"

"Yes. Mr. Schuyler and other wealthy landowners have forbidden trespassing on their great camps under the Private Parks Act. This means that I and many others who live near these woods all year round will have to travel far to find public lands where we can hunt and fish legally in the winter when these private parks are uninhabited by their owners. Hunting and fishing on their lands is how we've been putting food on our families' tables over the winter months. We tarred and feathered Danny Miller, Mr. Schuyler's Game Warden, as a warning that the people here are angry with the selfish behavior of the owners of the Great Camps." A smattering of applause started in the back of the courtroom and spread quickly until it was clear that most present were clapping. J.J. Schuyler sat in stony silence. The Judge banged his gavel to restore silence.

"Did anyone help you?" Cyrus asked.

"My brother Tommy, now deceased."

"Your brother Tommy," Cyrus choked up at this point, stifling a tear, "my son, was paraplegic and mute. How could he help you?"

"I carried him to the southern shore of Upper Saranac Lake where our family—you—keep a guideboat. I put him in the boat with a pair of oars and, uh, your rifle, and pushed him off. Tommy cannot use his legs but his arms are—were—extremely powerful and he is—was—an excellent marksman. Then I took my wagon with a cauldron, in which I had just melted tar, and a bag of feathers and drove to the entrance to Mr. Schuyler's camp. I had arranged with Tommy to fire three shots after he thought I had enough time to get to the entrance. The shots were intended as a diversion and also to awaken Danny Miller. Tommy was supposed to row back to the foot of the lake as soon as he fired the shots. Just before dawn I heard three shots. A minute later Danny Miller ran out of his cabin. I put a sack over his head and then poured the tar and then the feathers over him and left to get Tommy." It seemed as if everyone was holding their breath while John gave his testimony, for when he finished they sighed all at once.

"How long did you wait for your brother?"

"A long time. Until the sun cast enough light so I could see up the lake. There was no sign of Tommy, so I continued on home with the wagon and the cauldron."

"You said you heard three shots. Mr. Schuyler said he heard only one."

"There were definitely three shots."

"Were they evenly spaced?"

"Pretty much. They were in rapid succession."

"'In rapid succession.' Could Tommy have fired all of them?"

"Objection your Honor. The witness will be speculating; he is not an authority."

The Judge thought for a moment. "As the witness is familiar with the weapon, and with his brother's capabilities, I'm going to overrule."

John answered. "No. Even Tommy was not fast enough to reload that quickly."

Cyrus turned to the Judge. "No further questions, your Honor."

J.J. Schuyler felt a bead of sweat roll down his side.

The Prosecutor cross-examined. "Can you prove, John Carter, that you are the one who tarred Danny Miller?

"You have my word, Sir. I am under oath."

"Did you have accomplices?"

John expected the question and was prepared to answer. "With all due respect, I refuse to answer."

"On what grounds?"

"On the grounds that it might incriminate them."

"You realize, don't you, John, that they are in the best

position to exonerate you of the charge of murder for which you are currently on trial?"

"I do, Sir, but if there were such accomplices, my naming them would incriminate them in the crime of tarring and feathering."

"I can request that the court order you to answer or have you held in contempt if you do not."

John shrugged. The Prosecutor hesitated, saying finally, "No further questions."

Cyrus next called Alice Massing to the stand. He established that she was a boarder in the Carter house and worked for Dr. E.L. Trudeau. Then he asked her, "Did you encounter the defendant on the morning of Saturday, August twenty-third?"

"I did, just as I was leaving for work."

"Was there anything unusual in his appearance?"

"Yes, there was. He had black stuff on his shoes and his trousers."

Cyrus walked over to the defense table and opened a box from which he withdrew a pair of shoes. They were covered with tar. "Are these the shoes?" Alice said that was what John's shoes looked like and Cyrus entered them as exhibits.

"Did the defendant tell you how his shoes got that way?"

"No, Sir. He never did."

Eleanor Mason was Cyrus's next witness. Although she usually wore trousers, Eleanor walked to the witness stand wearing a long tweed skirt, which had required her to ride sidesaddle to the village, and a beige blouse. Her dark brown lustrous hair was not parted but ran with a slight curl down to her shoulders.

Cyrus began by establishing her credentials as a medical doctor. Then he asked, "Dr. Mason can you tell us where you were early on the morning of Saturday August twenty-third?"

"I was at our cabin on Upper Saranac Lake with my husband Jared and my father, Henry Weinberg." In response to Cyrus's questions she then told how her husband, who had gone out for a row, had found Cyrus's old guideboat adrift in the lake near Birch Island with Tommy's body in it and towed the boat back to the Mason's dock.

"Tell us what you found when you examined the body?"

"Blood covered his chest. It came from a small circular wound, slightly to the left of the midline, bullet wound most likely."

Cyrus walked back to the defense table, picked up a sheet of paper, and showed it to Eleanor. She identified it as Tommy Carter's death certificate. "It says," Cyrus said, reading the death certificate, "that the decedent died on August 22$^{nd}$ and that the cause of death was pulmonary congestion. How can you reconcile that with your testimony?"

Eleanor hesitated before answering, summoning all her courage. Not a sound could be heard. "I falsified the death certificate." The courtroom erupted with one collective gasp.

"Can you tell the court why?" Cyrus asked after order was restored.

Quietly, Eleanor explained. "When we found Tommy's body, I rode into Saranac Lake Village to inform his parents. His brother John Carter was there too. When I told them what had happened, John cried and hugged Cyrus. He told us about the plot, hearing three shots, and waiting for Tommy at the foot of Indian Carry until sunrise. He suggested that one of Schuyler's men had shot Tommy twice after Tommy fired his shot. Mary, Tommy's mother, said she didn't want to go through a trial to convict her son's murderer. I love Mary and respected her wish that the death certificate say that her son died of natural causes." She paused and then told Cyrus, "I intend to file a modification of the death certificate."

On cross-examination, the Prosecutor approached Eleanor. "Miss—"

Eleanor interrupted. "It's Doctor."

The Prosecutor began again. "Doctor Mason, did you happen to turn Thomas Carter's body over?"

"Yes, of course I did. There was no sign of a bullet hole in his back."

"What would you conclude from your examination?"

"That the bullet is still in his body."

"Thank you. I have no further questions."

The Prosecutor asked the judge's permission for both he and the defense to approach the bench. "Permission granted," the judge said. Cyrus trailed the Prosecutor to stand before the judge.

"Your Honor," the Prosecutor began, "this afternoon, we have been confronted with two claims regarding the role played in this drama by the late Thomas Carter: that he served as a decoy in the plot to tar and feather Mr. J.J. Schuyler's game warden and that he did not die a natural death but was, presumably, shot in the chest. His true role can be established only by exhuming his body. That will tell us if he died peacefully or from a bullet. And if the court requests an autopsy, the type of bullet can be ascertained. The Judge addressed Cyrus. "Mr. Carter?"

"Much as it pains me, your Honor, I have no objection."

———•———

The trial was halted until Tommy's body could be exhumed and autopsied. When it reconvened, the Pros-

ecutor asked for permission to reopen his case. Cyrus did
not object. The Prosecutor called Sheriff Scott to the stand.
"Sheriff, let's take things in chronological order. You notified
defense counsel and me that you returned to the beach at
Camp Leatherstocking to look for additional bullets or bullet casings. Can you tell us why you did that?"

"Well, I went back and questioned Danny Miller, Mr.
Schuyler's game warden, about the number of shots that
roused him out of his cabin. He insisted there were at least
two, maybe more. So I had my men search the beach and the
lake bottom off shore for bullets or casings." They found one
bullet, a thirty-eight caliber, in shallow water off the beach."
He produced the bullet, which was made an exhibit.

"Thank you, Sheriff. Can you tell us the finding from
the exhumation of Thomas Carter's body?"

Sheriff Scott told the court that a bullet was found lodged
against Tommy's thoracic spine. "It matched the one my men
found on the lake bottom. Both were of the caliber that fit
the revolver that J.J. Schuyler admitted he carried when he
discovered his daughter's body." Pandemonium erupted and
several villagers in the courtroom made menacing gestures
at Mr. Schuyler who sat immobile in the front row.

While order was being restored, the Prosecutor conferred with Cyrus and then with the judge. When the
courtroom was quiet, the Prosecutor addressed the judge.
"Your Honor, in view of the evidence Sheriff Scott has just
introduced, I move to dismiss the case against John Carter in
the murder of Ophelia Schuyler. The evidence, your Honor,
suggests that Miss Schuyler was killed by Thomas Carter, but
not with malice aforethought. In any event, Mr. Carter has
already paid the supreme penalty, most likely at the hand of

Mr. J.J. Schuyler on whom I will press charges of murder in the first degree. As for the defendant in this trial, Mr. John Carter—he must stand trial for the tarring and feathering of Mr. Danny Miller, game warden for Mr. Schuyler. "

The Judge asked defense attorney Cyrus Carter if he had anything to say. He stepped before the packed courtroom. Half facing the judge and half the audience, he began by thanking Sheriff Scott for the thoroughness with which he did his job. "So far as the accusation of murder against John Carter," Cyrus continued, "justice has been done by the Prosecutor's motion." He turned to judge. "I would beg the court's indulgence to consider some related matters here."

The Judge looked at the prosecutor who shrugged. "You may proceed, Mr. Carter," the Judge said.

"First is the matter of justice in the killing of Tommy Carter, my son." A somber J.J. Schuyler, who did not know the results of the autopsy until the sheriff announced them, sat stiffly, staring straight ahead as Cyrus spoke. The shots presumably fired by Mr. Schuyler were in response to the shooting of his daughter and occurred so rapidly, that they were not premeditated. Many of us seeing our child shot might respond the same way. In the dark, Mr. Schuyler had no other way of identifying the killer, other than by shooting at him. Mr. Schuyler might also have thought his own life was threatened by his daughter's killer. If the shot that killed Ophelia was fired from a boat floating in the water, Mr. Schuyler may not have had any other means of apprehending the killer. Mr. Schuyler has not admitted to firing any shots. Lying is not a capital offense, however; my wife Mary and I are guilty of lying about the circumstances of Tommy Carter's death." He paused. "In any event, Mrs. Carter and I are not seeking an eye for an eye." A murmur ran through the courtroom and Schuyler's taut posture relaxed a little.

Cyrus continued after a brief pause. "I would like to turn to the tarring and feathering of Danny Miller, Mr. Schuyler's game warden. I had hoped I had raised my children to turn to the law to correct injustices for which there are legal remedies, but young people are often impatient and cannot wait for the law to take its course, especially when more people are hurt by the delay, and when neither the legislative nor the judicial branch can be counted on to administer justice. Even so, I will not defend John Carter in his commission of an illegal act, one that inflicted bodily harm on a person who had not committed any crime and who was enforcing the law.

"That brings me to a final matter, an injustice that cannot be remedied by law because it is the law. The Private Parks Act that Danny Miller was enforcing forbids trespassing in private parks. As you have heard, this provision threatens the survival of year-round residents up here. Its repeal would not come close to depleting herds and fishes for landowners' pleasure when they visit.

"The New York State legislature, of which I am a member, has been two-faced in the matter of protecting forest land for the benefit of the people. In 1885, we created a Forest Preserve in the counties containing the Adirondack and Catskill Mountains and declared that State lands in the Preserve shall be forever kept as wild forest lands. The intent was to protect them from decimation by lumber companies and to preserve them for the people. At the same time the Private Parks Act allowed those with enough money to buy up large tracts of private land and enclose them, preventing the people from hunting and fishing on them. Since 1885, the State has not bought much additional land for the Preserve, but wealthy men, like J.J. Schuyler, have purchased large tracts that they have turned into their exclusive playgrounds."

Cyrus noticed the audience getting restless. He paused and limped to the rail that separates the audience from the Court, just in front of where J.J. Schuyler sat. "I would like to remind Mr. Schuyler that his daughter would not have died if he had allowed the citizens of Harrietstown, Altamont, and other townships to hunt and fish on his property for the eleven months of the year when he and his family and friends were absent." He turned his back to Schuyler and returned to his seat at the defense table. When the applause subsided the judge banged his gavel. "The prisoner is free to go. This court is adjourned." He banged his gavel again.

# 16
# Reprise: Forever Wild

J.J. Schuyler was never tried for the murder of Tommy Carter. He did not return to Camp Leatherstocking in the summer of 1891, nor did he do so in succeeding summers. On the anniversary of his daughter's death, he arranged to have flowers placed on her grave on a grassy knoll near the Main Lodge. In 1895, he donated the forests of Camp Leatherstocking to New York State for inclusion in the Forest Preserve.

With time off for good behavior, John finished his eight-year sentence for the tarring and feathering of Danny Miller in 1895. His accomplices were never identified. John started his own construction company, which prospered as many residents of Saranac Lake Village decided to modify their homes or build new "cure cottages" to house the tuberculosis patients that flocked to Dr. E.L. Trudeau.

Alice Massing continued to work for Dr. Trudeau, becoming his Manager. Her son, Donald, wrote to her for the first time in 1894 when, at eighteen, he finally emerged from the grip of his paternal grandparents. The school he and his sister attended was obliged to hand over the letters that their mother had written to them over the years. The letters had been withheld at the instruction of their paternal grandparents, the children's legal guardians. In his letter, Donald expressed the hope that he could see his mother in the not too distant future. Donald's sister Elizabeth was still in boarding school. Donald wrote that their grandparents had withheld all information about their mother from them, and they could not write to her without her address. Alice shared Donald's letter with John, to whom she had grown very close, visiting him in jail every day after work. The news that her children had not forgotten her buoyed her and she grew more animated and seemed younger. Gradually, John fell in love with her. They were married soon after he completed his prison sentence. From their combined earnings, they purchased a lot on Helen Street and John started construction of a modest home for them.

Among the patients who had flocked to Dr. Trudeau was Jared Mason, whose tuberculosis had progressed slowly but steadily since he had returned to the Adirondacks in 1884, much as Dr. Trudeau's own disease was progressing. Jared died in a "cure" cottage in Saranac Lake in 1892. After his death, Eleanor continued to live with her father in Tupper Lake, providing him company and care and continuing to practice medicine out of his former office.

The Harrietstown School Board appointed Mary Carter headmistress of the village school, which had grown as Saranac Lake expanded, with a classroom for every two grades. Reverend Jones and Lawrence Venable were gone and the new, younger school board insisted on proper credentials from teacher applicants who also had to pass Mary's close scrutiny before being hired. All were women who had graduated from teachers' colleges. With Mary, many of them became active in the newly formed National American Woman Suffrage Association.

Cyrus and Mary moved into a new more comfortable

house that John built for them high up on Main Street, overlooking the Saranac River and farther from the growing downtown area and Mary's school. But they had a more spacious, beautiful lot, with the river roaring on the bottom of the cliffs beside their house. The O'Rourkes, with the addition of Rachel, born in 1891, moved into the old Carter house at Helen and Shepard streets. Lisa taught at Mary's school, and Peter, Jr., continued as stationmaster at Axton Landing.

Cyrus Carter was sixty-four when he completed his fourth term as New York State Assemblyman from Franklin County in 1890. In every session of the legislature, he had introduced legislation for a workman's compensation act that would bring some relief to workers injured on the job, as Tommy had been in 1880. No compensation law was enacted in New York until 1913, two years following the Triangle Shirtwaist Fire.

Distressed over the continued logging in the state-owned land that comprised the Forest Preserve, a result of the duplicitous enforcement of the law by the Forest Commission that was supposed to protect the preserve, Cyrus was not ready to give up the fight for forever wild. He recognized that without further protection of the forests, the tourism that was providing a livelihood for an increasing number of year-round residents in Franklin and surrounding counties would decline. He was pleased that in 1890 he and his fellow legislators had, for the first time, appropriated twenty-five thousand dollars for the State to purchase land that would be added to the Forest Preserve. Cyrus hoped that by expanding the Preserve, the State would reduce the availability of prime land for Great Camps, thereby protecting the land for the people of the State and visitors. The legislature's creation in 1892 of an Adirondack Park, consisting of almost three million acres containing all or part of five counties, including Franklin, within its boundaries was controversial; Cyrus abstained in the roll call vote creating it. Although the new law said the lands within the Park's boundaries "shall, subject to the provisions of this act, be forever reserved…for the free use of all the people for their health and pleasure," it did not stipulate they should be "forever wild." "Subject to the provisions of this act" left room for amendments that would allow lumber companies to expand their activities in the Park. John Carter and some of his friends pointed out to Cyrus that nothing in the Act prevented the robber barons from continuing to keep their Great Camps and surrounding forests and streams for their exclusive use and maybe increasing them. Cyrus realized that the Act left undefined just what "private" meant. Presumably, the people who lived there all year round would not be dispossessed, but many among them worried that their livelihoods might be destroyed.

Cyrus had promised Mary when he ran for a fifth term in 1890 that he would not run in 1892. As the election approached he regretted his decision; the protection of the Adirondacks was far from certain. His regret was offset by his realization of the enormity of the task of protecting not only the forests of the Adirondacks but its people. *I've done enough,* he thought. *There are a few younger assemblymen from the Adirondack counties who share my view. It should be up to them.* He was angered, but not surprised in 1893 when the legislature further corrupted the "forever wild" provision of the 1885 law by giving the Forest Commission the authority to sell standing timber in the Forest Preserve.

Cyrus was helped out of his frustration when prominent conservationists decided to introduce an amendment at the New York State Constitutional Convention of 1894 that with one important addition incorporated verbatim the language of the "forever wild" section 8 of the 1885 law that Cyrus helped pass. The addition, tagged on to the end, said, "nor shall the timber therein [the Forest Preserve] be sold, removed, or destroyed." If the Convention adopted it, and the people ratified, it would be very difficult to repeal.

Mary did not object when Cyrus stood for delegate to the Constitutional Convention and was elected despite opposition from the logging, lumber, paper, and railroad companies. On September 13, 1894, the Convention unanimously adopted the amendment. In November of the same year, the voters of New York overwhelmingly ratified it, and the Amendment went into effect on January 1, 1895, not before a vain last minute attempt to build a railroad through part of the preserve. Large tracts of private land remained in the hands of wealthy landowners who continued to restrict access to them, occasionally leading to violent reprisals by the people who had used them to hunt and fish to feed their families.

Cyrus hoped passage of the "forever wild" Amendment would end the struggle to protect the Adirondacks without compromising the welfare of its citizens. Its passage was only the beginning.